Spring Tide

A novel by

KI STEPHENS

Cover Design: Ki Stephens
Editor: Sandra Dee, One Love Editing

ISBN (paperback): 978-1-915593-05-4

This book is intended for an 18+ audience.
For content warnings, please visit www.kistephens.com.

For my little toucan. My miracle girl.

Playlist

MAINE | NOAH KAHAN	♥	3:53
RIPTIDE | VANCE JOY	♥	3:24
SUNFLOWER, VOL. 6 | HARRY STYLES	♥	3:42
MOONLIGHT | DHRUV	♥	2:39
BLOOM | PAPER KITES	♥	3:30
DANDELIONS | RUTH B.	♥	3:54
HIGHER GROUND | ODESZA	♥	3:35
LOVERBOY | A-WALL	♥	3:45
ALWAYS THERE WHEN I NEED YOU | SALT CATHEDRAL	♥	4:04
LATE NIGHT TALKING | HARRY STYLES	♥	2:58
ALL THAT AND MORE | RAINBOW KITTEN SURPRISE	♥	2:51
NIGHTS LIKE THESE | BENSON BOONE	♥	2:53
YOU AND I | LÉON	♥	3:44
I NEED U | YAEOW	♥	2:23
NEON STARS | WILD RIVERS	♥	2:41
WE'LL BE ALRIGHT | JOSH SAHUNTA	♥	2:29
FALL IN LOVE WITH YOU | MONTELL FISH	♥	2:12
THINKING 'BOUT LOVE | WILD RIVERS	♥	3:19
NO RIGHT TO LOVE YOU| RHYS LEWIS	♥	3:58

HARPER

THE BEACH never used to be my favorite place. The coarse scratching of sand on my thighs. The grainy, unnerving squish between my toes. The ice-cold salt water splashing in my eyes.

It was pure torture. Until one day, it wasn't.

I remember it so vividly, that summer day when I turned sixteen. It was the day I decided that the beach was my salvation.

It all started with a boy, of course. A much older boy who gave me my first kiss. An innocent game of truth or dare in the basement of his parents' house. But then that dreamy college freshman, the one who spouted empty promises, would end up sleeping with someone else.

And I would end up crying on the beach alone, wondering where I went wrong.

Until the moment I saw them—the electric-blue waves that lit up Cape Casserat. It was natural bioluminescence, a rare sea sparkle caused by microscopic plankton. But for me, in that silent crestfallen moment, it was pure fucking magic.

I'll never forget the way I felt that night, staring out at the bright blue shore. The truth, *my* undeniable truth, hit me like a tidal wave. This life is too damn good, too beautiful, to cry over greasy boys with sloppy tongues.

I didn't grow bitter that night. I didn't lose my faith in relationships or decide that boys simply aren't worth my time. Rather, I learned that it's okay to like something and then lose it. To love and then let go. Because something beautiful, something brilliant, is waiting just around the corner.

Now, six years later, I still carry that little piece of wisdom with me. Instead of tucking her away in a spare corner of my heart, I wear her proudly.

"Heads up, Harper!"

My gaze cuts to the left, arms raised to catch a wayward volleyball. It sits heavy in my hands as I turn it over. My heart sputters, fingers drumming in time against the patchwork leather, a quick repetition of three soft beats.

So I guess he *does* know my name. Nate Gunderson, Coastal U's star baseball player and sunshine in human form. The curly-haired senior who spent his summer hanging out at Amber Isle: playing volleyball, drinking beers, and tanning those glorious abs.

My bare, sand-covered toes tap against my lifeguard stand. Nearly giddy with anticipation, I straighten my posture as he approaches, his lips turning up in a genuine smile.

"Nice catch, Harps," he says, charming me with a casual nod of his head.

Oh wait, was that a *nickname?*

"Thanks for the warning," I chirp back, gazing down at him. "I probably wouldn't have caught it, but I was watching you play. I mean, not *you* specifically—your friends." My fingers nervously twitch against the ball. "You guys come here a lot."

His grin widens. "Aren't you supposed to be watching the water?"

"Oh!" My knee is bouncing now, cheeks tightening with an unabashed smile. "I can watch both. I'm a great multitasker."

"I bet you are." His palms raise, fingers slightly curled as I toss him the ball. "You think you could take a break, though? Join us on the court?"

"My shifts are only four hours," I confess, one palm flattened against my shaking knee. "I'm not allowed to take breaks, really. But thank you for the invite."

"Sure thing, Harper," he says with a wink.

An actual *wink*. Nate Gunderson, my junior summer crush, has just winked at me. Or, at least, I think it was a wink. Maybe he was blinking away a piece of sand. Either way, he clearly knows who I am now.

I'm pretty sure that's the first step to any great love story.

These days, I find myself falling for a new boy for breakfast and then forgetting his name by dinner. I'm not afraid to lean into a fleeting infatuation. But when it comes to Nate, there's something about him that draws me deeper.

In public, he's always smiling, always joking, always radiating positivity. But I think, behind closed doors, there might be something hidden there. Something in his spirit that resonates with mine.

This term, I'm determined to prove myself right. To find out, once and for all, if Nate Gunderson is worth pining for.

It's dusk by the time my shift is over. Although it's only seven o'clock, a tiny sliver of moonlight peeks through the gray-blue sky. The waves are quiet tonight. Slow, steady, a sweet, lulling swoosh at low tide.

I soak it all in before padding over to the Surfbreak Grill, the one and only restaurant on Amber Isle. It may be kind of a dive, but it's located right beside the Boyer Inlet Pier. I suppose convenience, and good-ass burgers, are their only keys to success.

Oh, and I may be biased, but their staff is pretty top-notch.

"Hey, Stell," I call, scooching my way onto the outdoor patio.

Stella Reilly, my roommate and my best friend, has been a waitress here as long as I've been a lifeguard—three whole summers and counting. I'll never forget that fateful June night when we first met. Stella indulged in a little too much gin after her first double shift and I held her hair back as she retched into the ocean.

It was a tumultuous start to a beautiful friendship.

"Hey, babes, I brought you an outfit from home." She beams at me, swiping a rag over the six-top between us. "It's in my bag behind the bar."

"I have a change of clothes in the beach hut."

"Yeah, but these are *party* clothes, Harper." Her lips lift in a teasing grin. "You know, something tight and sexy."

"It's a beach bonfire. Cool and comfy seems more up to speed."

"You're right. Why don't you just throw on a new bikini and call it a day?"

I glance down at my uniform, a tight red one-piece and tiny drawstring shorts. "It gets a little cold out there," I say, an unwelcome shiver dotting up my spine.

"Yeah, that's when you get some lucky guy or girl to warm you up." Her eyebrows wiggle. "Speaking of, we really should've invited Nate to this."

"Stella!" I chide.

My gaze darts around the empty patio, scanning for any stragglers who may have overheard. Fortunately, everyone seems to have cleared out for the night. The Surfbreak Grill is closing early, for once, a welcome reprieve as they host their annual End-of-Summer Bash.

"What?" Her brow crinkles. "Is it some big secret now? That's not the Harper I know."

"Yeah, but I think this might be an actual crush," I quietly explain. "Like, the kind where I get to know the real person and not just the one I created in my head."

She laughs, tucking her dirty rag into the front of her apron. "Oh wow, you mean Nate gets to be a *real boy*?"

My lips crack with a smile. "Only if he proves himself to be brave, truthful, and unselfish."

"Alright, Blue Fairy. Let's—"

A loud boom cuts her short, the unexpected sound ricocheting off the pier. The two of us turn our heads, gazes snapping to the source. Ah, there's Luca Reynolds, tossing hundred-pound crates around like they're nothing.

Luca's a fellow Coastal U student and well-renowned football player. He's also worked at Amber Isle for years now, but our paths have barely intersected. On weekend nights, when we all stick around to celebrate, Luca slips silently into the night.

He never stays back, never lingers. It's like the idea doesn't even cross his mind.

"Stell, do you think Reynolds was invited tonight?"

She snorts, gathering trash from the bin. "He'd have to talk to someone to be invited."

"Okay," I say, cautiously stepping over the patio divider. "I'm gonna see if he wants to come, then."

She gives me a wide-eyed glance, amusement dancing in her eyes. "Good luck."

My feet quickly carry me across the worn and weathered slats of the pier. There's a gentle pep in my step as I approach Luca, a tiny buzz of excitement bubbling in my stomach.

"Hey, Reynolds!"

His head tilts in response, a barely perceptible nod. I pause for a beat, unsure of what I'm waiting for.

"The staff at Surfbreak are hosting a bonfire tonight," I continue, breaking through the stilted silence. "Us lifeguards will be there, too. Would you like to join?"

His features instantly pull tight, almost as if he's holding back a wince. Unprompted, he schools his expression, a careful retreat back to a blank canvas. "I have some other plans."

"Oh, alright," I murmur. "Something with the football team?"

"Nope."

He carries on stacking his gear, pulling some twisted line from a fishing rod. It takes him a few quiet seconds to wrangle them into the correct place. With a displeased grunt and no further acknowledgment, he tosses the fixed rods into a separate pile.

"You don't really spend much time with them, do you?"

"The team?" he clarifies, finally meeting my gaze. "We have practice almost every day."

"Right, practice," I echo. "I meant, outside of practice. You know, on the weekends and stuff?"

He shuffles some more gear around before he says, "I have work to do."

"Oh, okay." I press my palms together, offering a smile. "I'll leave you to it, then."

With a tiny sigh, he shakes his head. "I meant, I have work whenever I'm not at practice."

"I guess I didn't realize you worked that much," I say, genuine surprise coloring my tone. "That's pretty admirable, actually. I've been working a lot this past summer, but I'll cut back to weekends once the term starts. Then, come November, lifeguarding won't really be an option anymore."

"Hm," he grunts out a nonresponse.

I pause, waiting for something more. But nope, that's it. That's all he has to say.

I try again, hopelessly attempting to elicit a small sliver of information. "Do you plan on working during the school term?"

He bends forward, brows pinched together as he lifts the crate. "Yep."

Okay, now *that* was definitely a wince.

"Alright." I give him a gentle smile, finally picking up on his not-so-subtle hints. "Well, for what it's worth, I'm really sorry you can't make it tonight. I'll see you around, Reynolds."

I take one step back before he stops me in my tracks. "Hold up a second."

"What's up?"

He brushes his palms down the front of his jeans and says, "It's Luca."

"What?"

"The name," he clarifies, tipping his chin. "Call me Luca."

"Oh, definitely." I take a careful step forward, right arm jutting out as I reach for his hand. Once the initial shock wears off, his fingers wrap around mine for two quick shakes. "I'm Harper, by the way. Harper St. James. I'm glad we've finally met, although I feel like I've known you for a while now."

He stares back, eyes locked on mine. There's no instant spark of recognition in his gaze. No subtle upward curving of his lips. It's just him, plain and bold, leveling me with an open stare.

"Well, see ya, Luca."

He nods. I slowly pull back. My brain threatens to betray

me, so I pinch my lips together, fighting to keep my wandering thoughts at bay.

I'm dying to ask him what he's really doing tonight, why he never seems to hang out with anyone, how he manages to juggle football practice and work and school. All of it. But he seems so *shy*, so hesitant to meet new people and break free from his shell.

So I don't ask him anything. Instead, I leave it at that, filing away the endless stream of questions for another day.

By the time I've wandered back to the patio, Stella's already finished stacking the chairs. She's sweeping now, carelessly swiping at the floor as she jams out to King Princess.

"How'd it go?" she asks, tossing her broom behind the bar.

"Good," I say earnestly. "It went good, I think."

Her brows shoot up. "So, he's coming?"

"Um, no." I nibble at my lower lip. "He's busy tonight, but he did talk to me. You know, just a little bit."

"Shocking," she snickers.

"I think he's just shy, honestly."

"I doubt he's shy, babe. Reynolds is a D1 football player." She moves behind the bar, scrubbing her hands in the sink before tossing a beach tote over one shoulder. "He probably thinks he's above it all."

I glance back toward the pier, squinting in the darkness until I can make out the shape of him. "I think you might be wrong."

She moves closer, slinging an arm around me. "I think *you* just like to be right."

"Okay, now that part might be true."

"It's all part of your charm, Blue Fairy." She laughs, the soft sound warming me from the inside out. "Come on now. Let's go get pretty."

Chapter Two

LUCA

I'M UNBELIEVABLY TIRED.

No, it's more than that. I'm fucking exhausted. Strung out. Spread thin. Not sure how much longer I can withstand this torture.

Every morning, I wake up at 5:15 a.m. and head to the Intramural Training Building. There, I spend an hour in the weight room, followed by a grueling forty-five minutes of outdoor conditioning. Then I sit through a few boring lectures until it's time for afternoon drills.

Once I'm finally finished, nearly twelve hours after my morning alarm, I drag myself down to the Boyer Inlet Pier. I was unfortunate enough to grow up just outside this tiny town with a population even smaller than my bank account.

Boyer is three square miles of beach and bullshit. Sand and scum. Ocean and pure lack of opportunity. The fishing pier is this town's only redeeming quality, and it's been my job to keep it running for the past four years.

It's hard work, honest work, and it pays the goddamn bills, which is the only part I care about. That, and the fact that my boss, Pawel Nowak, has become like a second father to me.

"I need you to scrub the benches before you close up," Pawel orders, slapping a wet rag onto my shoulder. "There's gull shit everywhere."

Oh, did I say second father? What I meant to say is—this crotchety old man is a huge pain in my ass.

"You got it, sir," I mutter.

"I'm heading out in a minute," he tells me after he's rung up the last round of customers. "You stickin' around for the kids' bonfire?"

I slide a hand across my forehead, pushing back my sweat-damp hair. "You already know the answer to that."

His brow furrows. "Thought that pretty little lifeguard might've convinced you otherwise."

"Harper?" I suppress a scoff. "No, she's . . . I'm not interested in any of that."

"Any of what, son? Beautiful women?"

"No. I mean, *that*," I clarify, gesturing toward the cramped beachfront. "The crowds of people I don't care to know. It's all fake. And God knows, I'm just too tired for it."

Pawel sighs, slipping a faded Carhartt jacket over his frail shoulders. "It's 'cause you work too damn hard."

"I do what's necessary."

"That you do, son." He claps a firm hand against my back. "Just don't forget to live every once in a while, will ya?"

My lip twitches, a smile threatening to break free. "Sure thing, old man."

By the time the last fishermen have cleared off the pier, the sky has shifted from nautical twilight to the deepest dusk. On the shoreline, flames from a distant bonfire illuminate the crowd of strangers.

All those unknown people out there, drinking and laughing and celebrating another summer's end. Faces I've repeatedly seen but don't bother to recognize. Names I've heard for years but don't care to remember.

And then there's Harper, bouncing and giggling under the

dim coastal lights. She's tripping over her own feet now, dangling onto the arm of a Surfbreak waitress. They may be all sorts of tipsy, but at least they're fucking happy together. Joyful. Giddy. There's a closeness there that's easy to spot, even from my safe distance at the pierhead.

Although I've only just met Harper tonight, I've seen her around for the past three summers. It's not like I'm oblivious. And Harper's not exactly an inconspicuous girl. She's all sorts of shiny, bright like the blazing sun, and sugary sweet.

Of course, she seemed to know me just as well. Hell, every student at Coastal U pretends to know me. Luca "Ötzi" Reynolds, MIKE linebacker, total loner, and cold as fucking ice. My teammates, and the rest of the student body, seem to enjoy inventing stories about me.

People tend to do that—fill in all the blanks the way they see fit. But I suppose I can't complain. Otherwise, I might actually have to fill them in myself.

With one last lingering glance, I shut down Boyer Pier for the night. The heavy chains wrap around my fist as I drag them across the gate. The padlock clicks into place. Now, after five draining hours, it's time for me to get the hell out of here.

By the time I make it back home, my left leg is shaking. A dull, seething ache radiates from the inner portion of my knee, settling in the form of a splitting headache.

I undoubtedly fucked up today.

It was a careless, arrogant move tossing those crates around, mostly because my knee injury is only getting worse. During our first preseason game, Jaquan Thomas tackled the shit out of me, popping my knee inward with the force of two hundred and sixty-five pounds. Over the past week and a half, I've been icing and bandaging and resting as much as physically possible.

But I have to keep faking happy at practice. If Coach finds

out I'm injured, let alone with a possible MCL tear, I could be benched for nearly half the season.

As I hobble up the front steps to my house, a fuzzy ball of energy bounds into me, licking and nipping at my ankles. It always boosts my mood when I see my sister's golden retriever, Bentley. His eager greeting nearly knocks me off my feet, but I manage to brace myself against the doorway.

"Hey, buddy," I coo, carefully bending down to pat his head.

My sister's panicked voice calls out from the other room, "Luc, that you?"

"Yes, Tay," I shout back. "Of course, it's me."

My older sister and I have lived together for two terms now. Taylor's a graduate student here at Coastal and happens to be three years my senior. Thankfully, with the help of her favorite professor, she's conned us into this low-budget housing arrangement.

During my first two years of undergrad, I made the careless mistake of living with my fellow teammates. There were nearly twenty of us sharing a house near Greek row, and as one might expect, the whole thing quickly devolved into a shitshow.

I couldn't fucking handle it, from the wild parties to the fake friendships to the forced proximity. Not to mention all those random expenses that kept cropping up. Luckily, before I completely lost it, Taylor swooped in and saved my sorry ass.

"Luca!" Taylor shouts again. "Come in here, please."

I ruffle the fur under Bentley's neck, holding back a weary sigh. Taylor's a fantastic sister—a great friend and an even better confidante—but she's also way too fucking protective of me. I know what she's about to ask, and I definitely don't have the answer she's looking for.

Regardless, I square my shoulders, rubbing against the

inside of my knee with a tight wince. With only a slightly guilty conscience, I plaster on a blank expression and wander into our living room.

"How's it going, Tay?" I ask, tight-lipped and sure-footed.

She peers over at me, her gaze carefully sliding from my forehead down to the soles of my work boots. "Did you make that doctor's appointment?"

"Not quite," I grit out. "Everything's fine, Taylor. The knee's feeling pretty solid."

A heavy puff of air escapes her lips. "That seems like a lie."

"It's not, and you have enough to worry about already," I murmur. "So stop fussing over me."

"Fine. If your coach says that you're good to go, then I guess I have to trust that." She tips her head forward, gathering her loose curls into a tight bun. "Could you let Bentley out one more time before bed?"

"Of course."

"Thanks, hon." She pats her thigh, ushering the dog to her side. With a soft smile, she coos her goodbyes in his ear, gently petting him before heading to another graveyard shift.

Outside of her graduate courses, Taylor bartends at a night-club in the city. She's a true Reynolds, through and through. What can I say? The two of us were born into a hardworking family. With six siblings total and two blue-collar parents, it's simply in our bones.

As soon as I hear the heavy slam of the front door, a deep breath escapes my lungs. I nearly collapse onto the couch, but one last thread of restraint stops me in my tracks. I need to ice this shit, pronto.

After retrieving a gel pack from our freezer, I carefully hobble back into the living room. With shaking hands, I shimmy out of my jeans until I'm limping along in my boxers.

Then I brace myself into a sitting position, hoist my leg onto a pillow, and cautiously unwrap the ACE bandages holding me together.

Oh, fuck.

My left knee is purple, swollen, and stiff as hell. This shit looks bad, but maybe I overworked myself today. Maybe, if I can manage to take it easy for the next week, then everything will be just fine.

Yeah, I can take care of this shit on my own. And nothing, not even a busted knee, can keep me from playing the field. I don't have that luxury anymore, not as a senior. I need to keep this momentum going if I want a fair chance at the draft.

This is my last collegiate football season—my last shot at proving my worth—and I'm not gonna give it all up over a little bruising.

Chapter Three

It's the first day of term, and I'm officially running late. Or late for me anyway.

Typically, I prefer to be at least fifteen minutes early for each lecture. Prompt and punctual. This way, I can mingle with my classmates, prep my supplies, and potentially catch my professor's attention. I'm not a teacher's pet, per se, but recognition is important in any major.

At a large school like Coastal, much like in real life, you have to make an effort to stand out. Otherwise, you may as well be lost in the crowd, swept up in an endless sea of faces without a name.

With three minutes to spare, I hastily stumble into the lecture hall and scan the room for my friend, Eden Levine. She's sitting front and center, as per usual, only three rows back from the professor's main podium. Her dark hair is tucked neatly behind her ears, two large clips holding back the thick strands.

I shuffle into my seat beside her, grinning as our eyes meet.

"Hey, girly," I quietly murmur. "Thanks for saving my seat."

"Of course," she whispers back, eyes wide. "I almost thought you weren't gonna make it."

"I wouldn't miss out on our first day with Professor Gill."

She presses a flat hand across her lips, barely suppressing a giggle. "You're obsessed."

Eden's accusation is spot-on.

Professor Ainsley Gill is my official teacher crush—strictly in a professional sort of way. For the most part. She's highly intelligent, well respected, and she's also one of the most approachable faculty members at Coastal U.

Last year, she came to Biology 270 with a fully dislocated shoulder. Apparently, in a rush to head out the front door that morning, she popped it out of place. Instead of canceling class, Professor Gill called in a guest lecturer to assist with a readjustment. According to her, it was the perfect opportunity for a "live demonstration."

The woman is my actual hero.

"Hello, everyone," Professor Gill greets, her assertive tone cutting through the hushed murmurs. "Welcome to SPME 495: Fieldwork in Sports Medicine."

Her introduction is met with reverential silence. It's not necessarily the norm here at Coastal, but we all know how lucky we are to be sitting here today.

"Class will be short and to the point," she continues. "Please refer to the roster posted on our course website. You'll find your assignments listed, as well as the contact information for your team supervisors. I'd like for you to reach out to them at some point today."

Following her announcement, I boot up my laptop and sign in to Canvas. There's a loud shuffling as my classmates eagerly search our assignment roster. Once I've loaded it myself, my gaze trails across the page in search of my placement.

Please be baseball. Please be baseball.

And there I am: *Harper St. James—Men's Sports, Football*

under the supervision of Senior Associate Athletic Trainer, Jaqui Nerrie (jaqui.nerrie@coastal.edu)

Well, screw me sideways. That's certainly not what I was hoping for.

Of course, the odds of a baseball placement were about one in twenty. But still, I'm usually a fortunate girl. And Harper plus baseball, *man*, that would've been the perfect catalyst in operation Date Nate™.

Oh well.

At least I've heard that Jaqui Nerrie is an absolute goddess. She graduated from Coastal U four years ago, yet she's already worked her way up to senior associate. Anyone would be lucky to work with her.

"Eden," I whisper-hiss, gently nudging her with my elbow. "What'd you get?"

"Baseball," she mutters, dejected. "I'm so annoyed. I mean, why would they assign us spring sports? I'm not even gonna get to stand on the sidelines for their games."

"Wait, seriously?" I choke out. "Would you rather have football?"

"Um, hell yeah, I would. Is that what you were assigned?"

"Mhm." I frantically nod. "Would you maybe want to swap?"

"Yes!" she instantly replies, then reconsiders a moment later. "Wait, no, I couldn't ask you to do that."

I lean closer, whispering conspiratorially, "Let's just say it'd be mutually beneficial."

"But why would you want baseball?"

I quickly glance around, ensuring our privacy. "I may have a little thing for the starting pitcher."

"Gunderson?"

"Mhm," I confirm, barely concealing my grin.

"Oh my God." She's giddy now. "Okay, yes. Do you think Professor Gill will actually let us swap, though?"

"Only one way to find out."

"You're right," she agrees. "Let's ask her before we leave today. The worst she could say is no."

"Exactly," I whisper back.

The two of us spend the rest of the Q and A session in hopeful anticipation. I'm absentmindedly chewing my nails, attempting to listen as my peers recite their endless stream of questions.

It's sweet. I can tell that everyone's excited, anxious but eager to begin their internships, to finally have a taste of the real-world experience.

By the time Professor Gill ends the short lecture, I'm practically shaking.

"Please remember to contact your supervisors by the end of the day," she announces. "I'll see you all on Friday."

I bolt out of my seat, rushing to her podium with Eden in tow.

"Excuse us, Professor," I say, summoning my most professional tone.

"Yes, ladies." She grants us both a warm smile. "How may I help you?"

"We were wondering if we could swap assignments for the internship," Eden says, cutting straight to the chase.

"Sorry, ladies." Her smile fades, replaced by tight-lipped sympathy. "I've already stated that all assignments are final."

"Right, we heard you say that," Eden cuts in, clearly lying through her teeth. "But, um, we were wondering if you might consider a swap due to extenuating circumstances?"

"Of course." Professor Gill knits her brows. "If there's a legitimate concern with your assignment, please tell me."

And that's when it hits me—the perfect little white lie.

"It would be a conflict of interest for me," I blurt.

Eden's head snaps in my direction; eyes widening for a fraction of a second.

Professor Gill purses her lips. "How so?"

Well, fuckity fuck. "Because I'm, uh, I'm dating someone on the football team."

"Oh, very well." She nods her agreement, scribbling a quick note into her folder. "I can see how a relationship of that nature may be considered inappropriate."

A wave of relief washes over me. "Right, exactly."

"Thank you for informing me, Miss St. James." She gathers her materials, tucking some loose files under one arm. "I suppose, due to the circumstances, I could allow you to switch with Miss Levine here."

"Thank you, Professor," I counter, equal parts uneasy and delighted. "I just wanted to keep things professional."

"Of course. Please send me a reminder email, and I'll change the official roster."

"We appreciate that," Eden chimes in. "Thank you."

"Have a nice week, ladies." She perches her glasses back into place, signaling our dismissal. "I'll keep an eye out for your email."

I duck my chin, carefully concealing an ear-splitting grin. As Eden and I exit the lecture hall, we're tripping over our own feet, bursting at the seams by the time we reach the quad.

"Oh my God," Eden whisper-shouts. "That was kinda badass. I can't believe we pulled it off."

"Please, I was practically pissing myself the whole time." My hands are shaking, nervously twisting into the ends of my now-tangled hair. "I really hate lying."

"But it's for the greater good."

"True, and now—"

"St. James, hold up a second!"

We stop in our tracks, heads turning toward the sound of a male voice. I carefully glance over at Eden's shocked face. She's staring, open-mouthed, spine stiffening as our classmate approaches.

Grant Fletcher's now flanked by a group of unfamiliar friends. He's a large guy, with broad shoulders and an even broader personality. He's also nearly impossible to miss in a crowd, no matter how much Eden wishes she could.

"Hey, Fletcher." I awkwardly clear my throat. "What's going on?"

"I saw your name on the roster." He's speaking directly to me, but his attention is clearly elsewhere. "It looks like we'll be working together this term."

"Oh, um, Eden's actually gonna be working with you." I wince, gently nudging her forward. "I'm officially on baseball now."

"What?" His jaw drops, gaze darting between the two of us. "Gill said our assignments were final."

"Yeah, but she's already swapped us."

"Why would she do that?" His eyes narrow. "Matter of fact, why the hell would you be up for a swap? Baseball's in the off-season right now."

"Oh, it's, um . . . there was just a conflict of interest on my end." One shoulder lifts in a noncommittal shrug. "That's all."

"A conflict of interest?" he scoffs. "What, Coach your dad or somethin'?"

"Um, no," I stutter. "You know he's not."

"What is it, then?"

"It's none of your business, Grant," Eden bites out. "That's what it is."

"It's fine, Eden." I nervously tug at my hair. "Uh, we told Professor Gill that I'm dating a player. That's the reason she allowed it."

"That true, St. James?" His brows skyrocket. "Or did you lie so *Princess* Eden could have what she wanted?"

"I, uh—"

My friend steps forward, leveling him with her stony gaze. "She's not lying, asshole."

"No?" One corner of his mouth tugs up in a smirk. "Then tell us who the lucky guy is."

"More like *imaginary guy*," his buddy cuts in, coughing under his breath.

"Come on, Fletch," another pipes up. "You know we've never seen her at their parties."

"No." I fold my arms across my chest, going in for the kill. "They're right."

"They are? You actually lied to Gill?" His grin is full-blown now. "I thought you were, like, in love with her or something."

"No, it's just, Luca's not really into the whole party scene," I blurt, nearly flinching as his name rolls off my tongue.

Oh God. Now I'm spiraling.

"Luca?" Fletcher raises one dubious brow. "Luca Reynolds?"

"Mhm," I murmur my agreement, willing my lips to stay closed. The bigger the explanation, the bigger the lie. And I can't afford to keep weaving this web.

"You're dating Ötzi?"

"Ötzi?" I echo, confused.

"You know, the Iceman?" his buddy clarifies. "'Cause that kid's cold as ice. Never fucking talks to anybody."

"Oh, right." I square my shoulders, indignant. "Well, he talks to me."

"Right." Fletcher's lip curls. "So how'd you guys meet, then?"

"What is this?" Eden demands, voice dripping with irritation. "Are you testing her or something?"

"If I were, she probably wouldn't be passing."

"Actually, we met at Amber Isle," I cut in, another half-truth slipping from my lips. "Luca works down at the pier, and I lifeguard. But you already knew that."

"Huh, for real?"

"Yep."

"You know, you probably should've kept that to yourself, then," he finally concedes. "If you stayed with football, you and Ötzi could've spent a ton more time together."

"Yeah, well, I was worried about keeping things appropriate."

His gaze slowly drags across my frame. "I bet you were, Sunshine."

"Grow up, Fletch," Eden grumbles, visibly annoyed.

"Make me," he shoots back, his words vaguely reminiscent of a toddler.

Eden snorts, clearly fuming and unafraid to show it. In fact, her anger's practically dripping onto the tops of my sandals at this point. But I can't fault her, not when her ex-boyfriend is purposefully baiting her.

"We have to get going, Fletch," I murmur, looping one arm around my friend. "See ya later."

"See ya, Sunshine." His gaze cuts to Eden, then, "See ya, *Princess*."

Chapter Four

LUCA

I WAS WRONG. So dreadfully wrong.

My knee didn't magically heal itself over the course of a week. In fact, the pain is now excruciating. Intolerable. By the end of each day, I'm so stiff that I can barely flex the joint even a fraction of an inch. Yet somehow, my knee also feels . . . loose. Disjointed. As if one misstep might result in complete dislocation.

I need a skilled eye to take a closer look. But I still can't allow this shit to appear on my medical record, not if I want to keep it from Coach.

I pinch the bridge of my nose, rereading through this email for the third time.

> **From:** *jaqui.nerrie@coastal.edu*
> **To:** *Undisclosed Recipients*
> **Subject:** *Student Interns*
> *Ospreys,*
> *Please welcome your new team interns, Eden Levine (eden.levine@coastal.edu) and Grant Fletcher (grant.fletcher@coastal.edu). Eden and Grant are seniors in the sports medicine program, working under my close supervision. You may notice them on the sidelines at today's practice. Please feel free to intro-*

duce yourselves. For the duration of this term, consider
them your first official line of contact for athletic
training.
Jaqui Nerrie
Senior Associate Athletic Trainer
Coastal University

My eyes trail over her correspondence, a dark thought
manifesting inside my brain. Perhaps I could convince one of
them to secretly evaluate me. Maybe they'd take a vow of
silence, some sort of bribe to keep their fucking mouths shut.

But I suppose that would be far-fetched, wouldn't it? I'd be
asking them to jeopardize their academic status—their future
careers—just to save my skin. Besides, I have virtually nothing
to offer them in return. It wouldn't be a fair exchange.

I'll need to continue wrapping the joint myself, icing after
practice, and taking it day by day. I could always research some
exercises to help the healing process. Isn't that what sports
medicine is, anyway? Just a bunch of shit you can google in a
few minutes?

I'm not trying to discredit the profession as a whole, but
WebMD exists for a reason. And I've already properly diag-
nosed myself. I'm sure of it. I've finally come to the conclusion
that it's not just a bruise. Actually, I'm fairly certain I've torn
my medial collateral ligament.

But it's likely a minor tear. A Grade I or maybe even II, at
the most. Something totally treatable without surgical intervention.

Definitely.

I know we're technically supposed to warm up our joints
and muscles prior to training, but I'm on my second ice bath of
the day. It's the only thing I've found that effectively numbs the

pain, just enough for me to make it through two hours of practice drills. They're effective, but they still fucking suck.

It's mostly the shriveled dick part that bothers me.

A displeased groan escapes from the back of my throat as I settle into the tub. Like clockwork, the ice-cold water constricts my veins, blood slowly draining from my shaft. It's a mild form of self-inflicted torture, but I guess it's worth it in the long run. It's not as though I even have time to beat off anyway. Instead, my dick is constantly deflated and neglected these days.

That's just the way it is.

After nine minutes of full submersion, my hand reaches for the grab bar as I hoist myself out of the tub. My body's shivering but sated. My injured knee's completely numb.

Well, *goddamn*, that must mean it's officially go time.

THE FIELD IS PACKED TODAY. First and second stringers are gathered together, running warm-ups and taking turns introducing themselves to the sports med students. The male intern seems pretty tight with a few of my teammates already. His female counterpart, however, has devolved into a blushing, fumbling mess.

Unfortunately, it's only spurring my teammates on. They're floundering over a pretty new face, and it's starting to piss me off. She's not here to flirt—she's here to work. And this is all a needless distraction, considering our first away game is this Saturday.

As defensive captain, it's my job to take control of the situation. So I march up to the group of safeties, determined to wipe the smirks off their arrogant faces.

"Defense," I bite out, "focus on your shit, and stop flirting with the interns."

I fold my arms across my chest, impatiently waiting while they turn on their heels. As they retreat, I hear one of them mutter, "You're in charge, Ötzi."

And there it is, that fucking nickname again. Iceman Ötzi. Yeah, my teammates nicknamed me after a fucking glacier mummy. I wouldn't normally give two shits, but that's the kind of lighthearted joke you'd make between friends. And we're not fucking friends.

A puff of heated air slips from between my pursed lips. My fists clench, unclench, and eventually relax against my thighs. I turn to face the female intern. "I'd appreciate you keeping professional boundaries with my team," I mutter in lieu of a greeting.

The dark-haired girl parts her lips on a gasp. Her cheeks flush pink, thick eyelashes fluttering as she blinks.

"Wow." A stunned silence precedes her next words. "*They* approached me, just so you know. And that's no way to greet a new member of your team staff."

I reel back for a moment, contemplating the truth behind her words. "You're right. I'm Luca Reynolds, MIKE linebacker." My hand is outstretched now. "Defensive captain."

She grasps my palm, delicate fingers curling around mine. We shake twice while she presses tightly in what I assume is her version of a vise grip.

"Eden Levine, student intern. Highly professional member of the sports medicine program." She rolls her eyes, nudging the male intern with her elbow. "This is Fletcher. Same deal or whatever."

Fletcher takes an even step forward, a wicked grin twisting his features. "I've heard a lot about you, man. Although"—his harsh gaze cuts back to Eden—"I'm surprised this is the first time you've met my girl here."

"I'm not his girl, just to clarify," Eden cuts in, eyes narrowed. "Please ignore him."

My brow lifts. "Okay."

"It's just," Fletcher continues, arrogance seeping from his tone, "Eden's great friends with Harper. Figured you all would have spent some time together by now."

Harper? As in, Amber Isle Harper? The same Harper who introduced herself to me at the pier last week after three silent years of working just a stone's throw away.

"Harper St. James?" I clarify.

Eden's nod is practically frantic. "Yes, your girlfriend," she spits out. "We've been friends since freshman year, remember? She probably mentioned me a time or two. You know, the quirky, overly talkative girl from her major." She gives me a pleading look. "Well, that's me."

I ponder her nonsensical words for a long moment. Harper St. James—my *girlfriend?* Since when do I have a fucking girlfriend? And I had no clue Harper's major was sports medicine, nor would I ever have a reason to.

"Harper," I repeat, bewildered. "Sports medicine."

"That's right," Eden prompts, a sense of relief washing over her expression. "She's such a star student, our girl Harper. Ratted herself out to Professor Gill immediately."

"She told you what happened, didn't she?" Fletcher cuts in, his amused gaze darting between the two of us. "Harper had our professor switch her placement from football to baseball. She wanted to ensure professionalism since you two are together now. Don't worry, man. I stuck up for you. I told her it was a pretty careless move."

"It's not *careless*, Fletch," Eden bites out, shaking her head. "Apparently, Luca's all about professionalism too. Isn't that right?"

"I, uh." What in the fuck is happening? "Yes?"

"Right answer." Eden smiles, reaching up to pat me on the shoulder. "That's part of what makes you and Harper such a perfect match."

My mind is scrambling, searching for some hidden secret message behind her words. These two dipshits seem to be speaking a foreign language now. "We . . . I don't—"

"Harper wants you to message her after practice today." Eden gives me a reassuring nod, brows waggling. "She has some important news to share with you if you catch my drift."

I give both of them one last disparaging look, the tips of my ears burning with a mixture of confusion and embarrassment. "Okay, this conversation is officially a waste of valuable practice time. Just leave me out of . . . whatever this is."

Fletcher's smile is smug. "You got it, Ötzi."

I stifle a flinch, eyes pinched shut for a quick moment. "Reynolds is fine." I toss the heated words over my shoulder, pacing away from the odd pair.

What. The. Fuck?

Is this some sort of weird, twisted game they have going on between them? Some kind of impractical joke they decided to play on the team loner? Or did Harper truly insinuate that the two of us are dating?

There's no fucking way. Harper St. James is definitely not, nor will she ever be, my girlfriend. The two of us make no sense together. And it's not only because we're opposites, like oil and water or fire and ice. No, it's more than that.

Harper and I, *shit*, the spaces between us are like the ocean at spring tide. The highest highs and the lowest lows; that's what separates the two of us.

I'm fairly certain that girl's spirit is filled with sunshine and rainbows and fucking butterflies. And then there's . . . well, there's me. I am who I am. And she's just—

No, you know what? I barely know one real thing about her, other than the fact that we'd probably find each other insufferable. If she's actually spreading some ridiculous rumor that we're together, then she must be desperate, even more so than I am.

Fortunately for me, desperate people are willing to do desperate things.

If this girl is truly using me—for some unknown, confusing, and undoubtedly nefarious reason—then hell, she owes me a thing or two. An eye for an eye. Her secret for mine. Now *that* would be a fair exchange.

Chapter Five
HARPER

As Eden rambles on beside me, a thin line of sweat breaks out across my brow. My fingers mindlessly drum against the side of my thigh. Tap, tap, tap. Every few beats, the nail on my index finger lightly pierces the skin. It's not painful, but it's there. A casual reminder to think positive thoughts.

Fletcher, *that arrogant asshole*, spilled the beans at practice. Eden's words, not mine. He brought me up in front of Luca, and she attempted to save face. A shoddy attempt, based on Eden's version of events, but it worked.

Luca probably thinks I'm ridiculous and irrational, lying about dating him to all my friends. Like I'm some schoolgirl with an unrequited crush and he's the sexy, brooding football player who barely has a clue who I am. He must think I'm desperate.

Unfortunately, I am. Or, I *was*. Desperate enough to incidentally spread this silly rumor, an untruth that involves a completely innocent party. Oh God, I've dragged Luca into my own personal melodrama, haven't I?

It's equal parts selfish and unfair.

It's okay, though, because I can apologize the next time I see him. Luca's bound to understand; he seems like a reasonable man. Practical. Logical. Perhaps he's not even giving this a second thought. In fact, he still hasn't reached out to me after two long days.

Maybe the whole thing has slipped his mind. Maybe everything will be just fine. And maybe, just maybe, this will all be swept away with the tide, caught in the undertow of Luca's busy life.

THERE'S something about the ocean at high tide, when it hits directly following the sunrise. The sky glows a soft orange, waves creep up the shore, and the current crests against the rickety posts of my lifeguard stand.

It's bliss. The sky is alive, and the ocean is full. The beach-front is empty, save a few early risers. It's a time when I have complete and utter peace, both inside my head and out. My hands are calm. My mind is still. And my heart, it beats slowly and surely inside my chest.

Today, however, my eyes are drawn to the Boyer Inlet Pier. I can spot him from over a hundred yards away. Luca Reynolds, the boy who's occupied my mind for days. He's bending over, dipping at the knees, tossing rope off the edge of the pier and tying it down.

And I'm helplessly staring—stalking, really—when his gaze darts up to meet mine. *Oh shit.* I know he's seen me now, but I can't make out his expression from this distance. Is he confused? Angry? Surprised?

Maybe he's indifferent to the situation. For me, it would be ideal. For him, it would be on brand.

With a phony spring in my step, I hop off my stand and stroll in his direction. I summon years' worth of false confidence as I approach the pier. My eyes squeeze shut for a quick moment, shoulders retracted and grin perfectly placed.

"Luca, hey!" I call, a few feet from the edge now. "How's it going?"

"Just fine," he retorts impassively.

He's still leaning over, tying off rope after rope as he grits his teeth. Tiny droplets of sweat have pooled on his forehead. Smudges of dirt and sand and grime cover his hands. He's wearing his signature outfit, a black tee with a faded Boyer Pier logo and a pair of worn Levi's.

It's nearing eighty degrees on a Sunday morning. And Luca, hell, he looks completely strung out.

"Why are you here so early?" I murmur, confused. "Didn't your team have an away game in Pittsburgh, like, fifteen hours ago?"

"We did. Then I drove home." He ties off one last knot, wiping his damp palms along the front of his jeans.

"Wow, that must have sucked." My cheeks tighten with an encouraging smile. "Congratulations, by the way. I heard the Ospreys killed it."

"Thanks," he mutters.

"You must be exhausted."

"I am." He's full-on standing now—in all his six-foot-something glory—gaze undeniably boring into mine. "I'm also very confused."

"About . . . ?"

"You know, Harper." His voice is toneless. "Tell me why you lied."

"Oh, *that*. Right." I worry my teeth over my bottom lip. "Eden said you spoke with her and Fletcher. Listen, that, well . . . it's not so much a lie, just more of a misunderstanding."

"Seems like a bald-faced lie to me." His stare is open, blatant, unwavering as our eyes meet. "You've somehow convinced your friends that we're dating, yet you barely know a thing about me."

"I know you," I argue, fighting a hopeless grin. "You're Luca Reynolds: linebacker, defensive captain, Boyer Pier employee. We've worked at Amber Isle together for years now. We go way back, pal."

"Pal," he mirrors, unamused. "Is that what you'd call your boyfriend?"

"I, um—"

"See, I really can't figure this all out." He's shaking his head, palm meeting knuckles as he cracks one fist against the other. "I've spent the last few days drawing up my own hypotheses, but none of them seem to ring true. Tell me, Harper—what makes you so desperate?"

Panic rises in my throat. My mind starts to spin with useless untruths and half-baked apologies. But I'm not a seasoned liar, and I'm not the greatest at avoiding confrontation. So, in the end, I settle on unfiltered honesty.

"Well, see, the thing is . . . I have a crush."

"You—I mean, *fuck*, I'm flattered." His lips press together, eyes wide. "Really. I just—we aren't—and I . . . we hardly know each other, Harper."

"Oh my God. No, I'm so sorry. Not on *you*, Luca," I hastily add. "I have a crush on this baseball player at our school. I just, I needed an excuse to swap teams, and it all spiraled out of control."

For several long moments, he makes no sound at all. He's silent, unmoving, astounded as his gaze drops. "So you *are* using me?"

"I am," I confirm, hoping he can sense my regret. "And I'm so, so sorry that I dragged you into this."

He immediately waves off my concern, brows pressed into a hard line. "No, it's fine."

"It is?"

"Sure it is," he repeats. "You use me, then it's only fair that I use you."

"What do you mean?"

Our eyes lock again, and I'm nearly squirming. His chest slowly rises and falls with two deep breaths.

"I need you, Harper."

"You—"

"I have a secret, a lie of my own," he clarifies. "If you want me to keep yours, then I'm gonna need your help."

"Wait, I told you it's not really a lie. It's more of a big misunderstanding. And despite how it all may seem, I don't really enjoy misunderstandings." I'm frantically shaking my head, pleading with him now. "So, it's probably better if you just keep your secret."

His nostrils flare, a muscle in his jaw tightening as he registers my words.

"Well, the thing is, you're engaging in academic dishonesty. Now that you've gone and told me about it, I should probably report this to your department. Or, at the very least, I should warn the baseball team."

"I haven't even met with them yet." My posture tenses. "Warn them how?"

"I don't know, tell them some groupie is masquerading herself as an intern." He clears his throat, gaze drifting to an unknown spot above my head. "She's not really there to do her job; she just wants to flirt with the players."

"I . . . you wouldn't . . . *seriously*, Luca?"

"Like I said, I need you," he echoes, no hint of apology or

regret in his tone. "If you aren't willing to trade a favor for a favor, then I'll do what's necessary."

"You know, this is blackmail," I tell him with an indignant huff. "It's wrong."

"So is lying to your professor."

I stare back at him, long and hard, a wild mixture of disappointment and frustration warming my cheeks. "An eye for an eye leaves the whole world blind."

"Okay, Gandhi," he mutters. "Here's the deal—do you agree to keep my secret if I keep yours? I mean, it'd have to be completely secret. You can't tell your friends, your parents, hell . . . keep it from your dog, even."

"I don't have a dog."

"Not my point." He clasps his hands together, forearms visibly straining from the pressure. "Just, Harper, do you agree?"

"Yeah, okay." I finally let my shoulders drop, resigned to his thinly veiled threat. "I agree. Just tell me what's going on, please."

There's a vein pulsing in his forehead now. "I'm injured."

"How so?"

"I was tackled in our preseason game, and my left knee popped in on itself," he explains, nervously wringing his hands together. "This was weeks ago now, and it's still not fucking healed. I need you to evaluate me and treat the injury. Under the table. Coach can't know about it, or he'll keep me off the field."

"Oh, Luca." Sympathy melts an ounce of my residual anger. "Wait, this could be really dangerous. You should schedule an actual MRI to assess the severity."

"I don't need an MRI," he argues. "I need you to just look at it, okay?"

"Okay, um, I suppose I can try," I offer, gaze dipping down toward his left thigh. "Could you roll up your pant leg for me?"

"Jesus Christ, Harper." His scoff echoes off the pier. "Not here, in front of the whole goddamn beach in broad daylight. What part of *secret* don't you understand?"

"Wow, no need to fly off the handle." I reel back, grimacing at his harsh tone. "When and where do you want to do this, then?"

"I don't know." His sigh is heavy. "Somewhere private, your place or mine. After work tonight?"

"Okay, and what am I supposed to tell my roommate? I can't just hide you in my bedroom and sneak you out in the middle of the night."

"We'll just tell her the same old lie," he insists. "That you and I are together, dating. It's the most believable excuse. And if you came to mine, my sister would go for it."

"You live with your sister?"

"I do." There's an uneasy crease between his eyes. "So, what do you think? Tonight?"

"Yeah, give me your number, and I'll text you my address."

"Great." He rattles off his number, patting his back pocket as I shoot off a text. "Now, if you'll excuse me, I have work that needs to be done."

"I'll see you tonight, okay?" I offer him a kind smile, my attempt at a peace offering. "Seven o'clock?"

"Okay."

"And for what it's worth, I'm sorry for my part in all this," I tell him earnestly, self-consciously shifting on the balls of my feet. "I didn't mean to drag you into my business."

His nod is silent, final, lips pressed into a flat line. There's no apology from his end, no sense of remorse or shame for the ensuing blackmail. I don't know what I expected from him, but it certainly wasn't this.

Luca Reynolds is in desperate need of my help. Luca Reynolds is my fake boyfriend. And I—*we*—have a big, ugly secret on our hands.

Chapter Six
LUCA

SOMETHING LEADS me to believe that Harper is an actual woodland fairy.

The front door to her fourth-floor apartment is wrapped in muted pink wallpaper. Tiny sparkling lights are tucked along the frame, with her unit number scrawled in painted gold script across the middle. It's a stark contrast to the stained gray carpet beneath the soles of my shoes.

If Harper hadn't already texted me the number, I think I would've inherently known this was it. The girl lacks subtlety. It's not an intrinsic personality flaw—and I certainly don't fault her for it—but it sure does raise a red flag.

I'm beginning to think this was all a terrible idea; enlisting Harper's help was an ill-fated decision made out of pure desperation. She's not the type of person who can harbor a secret from her friends. She hates lying. Or, rather, she won't admit that she's willing to deceive others for personal gain.

Unfortunately, she's my last resort.

My hand is poised to knock, knuckles tucked tightly against one palm, when the door swings open in my face.

"Oh!" Harper's brows scrunch together. "I'm so sorry, Luca. Are you okay?"

She takes a step closer, gently brushing one thumb across my jawline. Her fingertips caress my chin as she tilts my face to examine the damage. Left. Right. Center. My head rests entirely in her open palms now. Her tongue peeks out between her lips, and a steady look of concentration fills her gaze.

I clear my throat, resisting the urge to flinch away from the featherlight touch.

"Harper," I mutter gruffly, jaw clenched against her small palm.

Those blue-gray eyes widen, a sense of panic washing over the last ashes of a fire. I picture the gears ticking away inside her head. It's like she's suddenly realized exactly where she is and what she's been doing for the last few moments, as if she needed a verbal reminder to maintain personal boundaries.

"So sorry." She takes a timid step backward. "Are you—did I hurt you? I mean, your face looks completely fine. Good, even."

The corner of my lip twitches. "I'm fine."

"Great! Well, you should come in." She motions toward the open doorway, and I take her lead. "My roommate, Stella, she's still at work right now. Actually, she waits tables down at the Surfbreak Grill. You may have seen her there. Beachy blonde hair, wildly beautiful, about five foot nine or so?"

That must be the same waitress from the bonfire. I recall spotting the two of them drunkenly stumbling down the beach together. They were wrapped up tightly in each other's arms that night. And now, safely tucked inside this apartment, dozens of their pictures line the walls.

My gaze flits across the gold-framed photographs. Stella and Harper are smiling wide in every shot—happily embracing, nuzzling close, gazing fondly at one another.

"You two are open?" I ask, brows knit in confusion.

"Open?"

"In an open relationship?" I clarify, smoothing a hand over my forehead. "You agreed to tell your friends we were dating."

"Oh! Stella and I aren't together like that." Her lips curve into a full-out grin. "She has a girlfriend, actually. Lai'Lani. They've been dating for a few months now. But Stell and I are just best friends. Well, not *just*. Our friendship is really important."

"Yet you're completely fine with lying to her?"

"I mean, I'd really prefer not to." Her grin fades, fingers twisting into an errant strand of hair. "Not with Stell, anyway. So maybe I could just tell—"

"No, Harper," I harshly cut in. "This was our deal. Your secret for mine. No exceptions."

She's bouncing on the heels of her feet, gaze nervously shifting from my face to the wall of picture frames behind me. "But Eden and Stell, they already know about the *miscommunication* with Professor Gill. They know that you and I aren't actually together."

"Then tell them you came clean with me and we've started talking." There's a heavy note of exasperation in my voice. "Tell them I asked you to spend time with me, and one thing led to another. I don't care what story you make up, just as long as it's not the truth."

Her shoulders droop. "I'm a bad liar, Luca."

"You can solve that problem," I insist impatiently. "Just stop telling yourself that you're doing something wrong."

"But it *is* wrong."

Her gaze meets mine. In an instant, I'm swept up by the raging swirl of emotion in her eyes. The minor hints of color— all the various hues of blue—seem to fade away, revealing the thick, gray clouds of a thunderstorm.

"Tell me right now, Harper." I push the harsh words past the sudden lump in my throat. "Are we doing this or not?"

She breaks eye contact, fidgeting with her fingers in silence. "Yeah, we're doing this. I said I'd help you, Luca. I won't go back on my word."

The lump clears. "Then it's case closed."

"This is Harper St. James, officially locking her lips now." She mimes the action with her hands, tossing away a fictional key. "Come on, let's go to my room, and you can take your pants off."

"What?" I sputter.

"I need to properly examine the muscles and joints in your leg." She grasps tightly to my wrist as she drags me down the hallway. "Those bulky jeans are in the way."

My fingers involuntarily clench together. "I'll just roll them up past my knee."

"Won't work the same." She drops my wrist, pressing both hands flat against my back. With one solid push, I'm shoved inside her open bedroom door. "Come on, it's all good. This is strictly professional."

"Fine."

"I'm just gonna grab a few things." She sweeps an arm out, wildly gesturing toward her unmade bed. "Take a seat and make yourself at home."

As she bounces out of the room, my eyes hopelessly trail across her floral bedspread. She has a queen-sized mattress set on top of a white wrought-iron frame. Her bedding is chaotic, with twisted cream sheets, a tangled duvet, and more throw pillows than one person could possibly require.

Sitting amongst this mess feels like an invasion of privacy.

"Okay!" she chirps, bounding around the corner. "I've got

my goniometer, some ACE wraps, and . . . you've still got your pants on."

"Right." My gaze dips, the tips of my ears tinging with heat. "I didn't . . . did you want me to take them off now?"

"That would be great." She sets a few items on the dresser by the door, slowly shifting around to make her bed. "Sorry, I'll just fix this up, and then you can sit down."

"Okay, so I'll just—" My fingers are fumbling, thumbs awkwardly tugging at the button on my jeans. "—get undressed, then."

She smooths two hands across her duvet, patting down the wrinkles and fluffing her pillows in size-descending order. "Would you like me to turn around? Or I could step out and—"

"Yeah, if you could just give me a minute."

"Sure, of course." Her cheeks tighten with a gentle smile, eyes soft as they flit across my face. "Just let me know when you're ready."

The door lightly closes behind her. Taking a deep breath, I unfasten the button of my jeans and hastily tug them over my hips. Now I'm standing here half-naked in Harper's bedroom. It's a vulnerable place to be—alone in my boxer briefs and T-shirt—bruised knee ready and waiting for exposure.

At least now that the bed is made, smoothed over and situated, it feels slightly more acceptable to sit on. It takes me a few long moments to finally position myself, though. I shift my hips once or twice, going from the middle edge to the far corner and back again.

Once I'm mildly comfortable, I loudly clear my throat. "You can come in now."

"Okay, great." She swipes a measurement tool off her dresser. I sit back as her eyes sweep over me from head to toe, just once, before she takes a few steps closer. "We're all set, then. Could you please describe your pain to me, level and type, while I take a few measurements?"

"It's about a six out of ten." I wince as she settles in beside me, the sudden offset in the mattress jolting my knee. "At this specific moment."

"Okay, and at its worst?"

"Could be an eight or nine. Honestly, it feels like my entire shin is ready to dislocate at any moment. The pain is dull and aching at times; other times, it's a constant throb. Feels like one wrong move could send me reeling to the ground."

"I see." Her fingertips gently brush against the side of my thigh as she lines up her plastic tool. "This is a goniometer. I'm just gonna use it to quickly measure your range of motion, so could you please extend your knee for me?"

I carefully kick my shin out, eyes pinching shut as I fight through the pain. "That's end range," I mutter through gritted teeth.

"Okay, thank you." She sets the goniometer behind us. "I'm gonna need to palpate the muscles around the joint, so this part may hurt."

"Go ahead."

Her index and middle fingers carefully press against the knotted muscles on my inner calf, slowly stroking their way past the top of my thigh. A moment later, the pressure increases. There's an instant jolt of pain like nothing I've ever felt before, so profound that my vision turns hazy.

Sweat breaks out across my brow. My hand shoots out, grabbing hold of her wrist before I can stop myself. "Fucking hell, Harper."

"I'm sorry!" She withdraws both arms, frantically shaking them in front of her chest. "I'm all done now."

My spine stiffens, eyes downcast. "Did I hurt you?"

"No! I was just surprised. Did *I* hurt *you*?" Her voice is low, frantic, and stilted as she rambles on. "Shoot, that was a silly question. Of course I hurt you. Um, is there . . . is there ever a time when the pain disappears for you?"

"Directly after an ice bath, when everything else is fucking numb."

"Hmm," she murmurs.

"Look, I did my own research, and I'm fairly certain this is just an MCL tear."

"You're right, Luca." She flashes me an impressed smile, one brow slightly raised. "It's definitely an MCL tear, probably a grade two partial. You'll need to tread lightly for at least three more weeks."

My head snaps up, determination steeling my resolve. "Not possible."

"If you don't, you could end up needing surgical intervention." She's shifted away from me now, hands stuffed under her pockets. "Then you'd be out for, like, six months."

"That's bullshit."

"I know this must suck, Luca." Her shoulder twitches, and I know she's itching to reach out. Harper uses physical touch as a source of comfort, that much is clear. But she's trapped her hands beneath her thighs now—almost as if she needs a physical reminder, a clear-set barrier, to stop herself tonight.

"Yeah," I mutter.

"I honestly can't imagine what you're going through. Unfortunately, this is just the reality of the situation. I'll help you with your rehab, but you need to take it easy, or there's not much I can do."

"I need to keep showing face at practice." A heavy sigh pushes through my lips. "And I need to be on the field to generate a top-quality highlight reel."

"Okay, how about this: when it's not practice or game time, you just stay off your knee completely." She pulls her hands free, eagerly clasping them together as if she's made a grand discovery. "Then you can rest and rehab whenever you're off the field."

"That's all well and good, but I also have to go to work."

"Luca, you can't have it all. You have to give up something here and—"

"No."

She pushes off the bed, hands perched on her hips as she stands before me. "No? Just no?"

"I can do this. All of it," I insist. "Give me the exercises and your recommendations. I'll make everything else work."

Her eyes narrow as she assesses me. There's a long silent pause, a soft shrug, and then, "Okay."

"Where do we start?"

"For tonight, we'll do some massage and gentle stretching. Then I can write you a tailored home program and just . . . just do your best to rest when you can, I guess."

"Then let's get started."

"Could you please lie on your back and bridge your knees?"

An odd feeling passes through me at her request. There's a sudden realization that I'm sitting alone on a woman's bed in my underwear, but I push through my discomfort and carefully lie back. This is what I asked for, after all.

As I shift my hips, awkwardly wriggling into place amongst her sea of pillows, Harper manages to flash me an easy grin. For some inexplicable reason, her complete lack of concern puts me at ease. She barely bats an eye as I release a strained moan, the pain in my knee reverberating through my body.

"Okay, Luca." She moves into place beside me. "I'm going

to press my hand against the side of your hip here"—her finger-tips graze my outer thigh—"to massage your TFL."

"TFL?"

"Tensor fascia latae," she clarifies, kneading her thumbs into the thick tissue.

"Oh *God*." A deep, involuntary groan rolls out from the back of my throat. "Why does it feel like that?"

"You've been overcompensating, using the other muscles in your thighs to pull tension from your knee." Her thumbs continue to press deep into the muscle belly, and it's so fucking incredible I could cry. "Basically, your entire back and lower extremities are wound up tight. Seems like you're desperately in need of release, in more ways than one."

My brows shoot up, fists clenching at my sides. "Harper," I warn.

"Oh, not . . . not *that* kind of release." She's avoiding my gaze, cheeks flushing the lightest shade of peach. "Although, that might not hurt, either. Just maybe don't top anyone for a while. Could be bad for your recovery."

"Harper, stop," I finally manage to grit out.

"Oh, sorry," she murmurs, continuing her assault on my upper thigh muscles. "I didn't . . . are you uncomfortable talking about this?"

"With you?" I barely suppress another groan. "Yes."

"It's okay, Luca." Her voice takes on a matter-of-fact tone. "It's actually part of my job to advise my patients about safe positions and post-injury intimacy."

"I'm good." My body is both stiff and relaxed. Conflicted and subdued. I want to melt into this fucking bed, but Harper's line of questioning is seriously rocketing my heart rate. "We don't need to . . . let's just not go there."

"Okay, sure. Just know the conversation is always on the table, though, in case you have any questions later."

"Great," I mutter.

Her hands gently slide across my thighs, slowly caressing and pressing against the overworked muscles. I can't help the small, satisfied groans that slip from my lips as she massages away the pain. And I certainly can't help when my eyelids flutter shut, Harper's gentle hands lulling me to sleep on this perfect, flowery bed of mismatched pillows.

Chapter Seven

HARPER

THE SOUND of Luca's moaning and groaning isn't altogether unpleasant. In fact, it's kind of a nice soundtrack for my impromptu study session.

He's still in my bed now, two hours after he fell asleep during our massage. The MIKE linebacker, D1 athlete, and full-time overachiever seems to be at peace resting amongst an ocean of floral pillows. He's still fairly restless when he sleeps—shifting and drifting from one side to the next—but his eyelids are gently fluttering, so I think he may just be lost in an endless dream.

Something soothing, I hope.

My fingers tap against my thigh, drumming carefully as I sketch the tendons of a human hand. Anatomy is a difficult subject; the hand alone is filled with over thirty muscles and one hundred ligaments or tendons. Drawing them out is meticulous, but the sequence—the steady loops and twirls of my pencil on paper—helps with the organization inside my head.

It's nearly ten o'clock when I hear the front door of my apartment click open. I set my sketchpad on my desk, carefully tiptoeing out of my bedroom and down the hallway.

"Blue Fairy," Stella exclaims, face lighting up as I approach. She's removing her apron now, wadding it up to toss onto the kitchen counter. "How's my girl?"

"Shh." I drop my voice to a whisper. "I've got a sleeping boy in my room."

Her brows shoot up, cheeks tightening with an eager smile. "What sleeping boy? Did we finally bag Nate?"

"No, it's not Nate." My voice dips low. "It's Luca, actually."

"Luca Reynolds?"

"Mhm," I mumble, palms dampening with a thin sheen of sweat.

"No shit?" Her eyes are filled with a mixture of pride and confusion. "The infamous Reynolds is asleep in our apartment?"

"Yes." My heart patters wildly in my chest. It's officially lie time, folks. "So, let's keep our inside voices on, please."

She plants both hands on her hips. "Baby girl, did you seriously bone Reynolds tonight?"

"We didn't *bone*, Stell. He just fell asleep while I was giving him a massage," I tell her, the words tumbling out before I can manage to properly filter them. "I mean, while I was rubbing his back or whatever."

"You rubbed . . ." She trails off, one brow crinkling in suspicion. "Harps, what's going on?"

"He heard about the miscommunication with Professor Gill. Um, and then, you know, he approached me and asked if I wanted to spend some time together."

"So you two are what?" she happily prompts, tilting her head as she peers down the hallway. "Talking now?"

"I suppose, yeah. We're talking."

Her eyes meet mine. "What about operation Date Nate™?"

"Oh, um, I guess it's on pause for a little bit. I mean, I'm still gonna get to know him and whatnot." My heartbeat kicks up a notch. I press one palm against my chest, discreetly attempting to still the thrumming. "It's not super serious with Luca or anything."

"I'd hope not." She eyes me, her lips cracking into a cautious smile. "Is this, I mean, this is the first time you two are hanging out, isn't it?"

"Yeah, it is."

"Wow, and he's already falling asleep on you," she teases, grasping my upper arm. "Who knew you were so boring, Harper."

"Oh, please." I shake her off, soft laughter spilling from my lips. "I'm just really good at back rubs."

"I'd ask you to give me one, but I have a feeling your hands are gonna be tired after Luca wakes up."

"Oh, uh, we're not hooking up tonight." My smile slips. I press one thumbnail against my palm, shutting out the pitter-patter of butterflies in my stomach. "I'm just gonna let him sleep, I think. Are you heading to Lai'Lani's for the night?"

"Yeah, I'm just gonna shower, and I'll be out of your hair. You'll have the place to yourselves, so you might wanna reconsider the whole hookup thing." She strolls right past me, her voice level picking up as she travels down the hall. "The Iceman could probably use a good stress reliever."

"Shh, Stell," I whisper-shout, following closely behind. "Don't wake him up with all your dirty talk."

"No, babe, that's your job." She winks at me, one hand perched on the doorframe to our shared bathroom.

"Stop it," I playfully chide. "I'll see you later."

"Sure, sure." Her voice drops to a whisper as she leans in closer. "By the way, I kinda like this for you. Maybe you can help defrost that frozen man in there. Spice up his life a little, if you know what I mean."

An unwelcome flush of heat rushes from the heels of my

feet all the way to the tip of my nose. Lying is already fucking impossible, and I've barely even begun.

"Good night, Stell."

"Night, girly." She perches a flat palm underneath her chin, blowing a soft kiss across the hall. "That one's for your new man."

I shake my head, turning to cautiously open my bedroom door. Luca's standing at the foot of my bed now. All that teasing, those hushed whispers in the hallway, must have accidentally woken him up. He's muttering a string of nonsense words under his breath, hastily attempting to slip back into his jeans.

His head darts up as I close the door behind me. His pants are bunched up, pulled halfway over his broad hips. When our eyes catch, the tips of his ears tinge a bright red.

"Why didn't you wake me up?" he mutters, yanking the jeans up and quickly fastening them into place.

I swallow thickly. "Oh, I, um—it looked like you could use the rest."

"I didn't come here to nap, Harper," he snaps, voice sleep-drunk and raspy. "I came here for therapy. I don't have time to just lie around in your bed."

"Sorry, I didn't think about it that way." My brow furrows in confusion, eyes darting to the alarm clock on my nightstand. "I just thought you were tired and wanted to let you sleep. It's pretty late."

"Yeah, it's late," he parrots, clearly unimpressed. "And I should be home right now, not sitting here wasting time."

I blurt out, "Lying here, you mean."

"What?"

"Nothing," I chirp back. "You know, you can just leave if you'd like. No need to lecture me, really."

"Look . . . I don't—I'm not trying to be harsh." His eyes flit to a space above my head, voice dropping to a low murmur. "I just . . . time is valuable to me. Next time, wake me up, okay?"

"Okay, I will," I tell him, injecting my tone with false bravado. "Here's your home program, by the way. I typed it up while you were . . . resting." I swipe the stack of stapled papers off my desk, jutting them out in his direction. "I'll need to see you again in three days for treatment."

He pauses for a beat. Then, slowly, he takes a step forward and gingerly plucks the papers from my hand. "Same time on Tuesday, then, after practice?"

"Works for me."

His eyes search my face, settling on a spot between my forehead and the bridge of my nose. I think I might have a freckle there. Or maybe it's a beauty mark. A mole, really.

"I'll be here," he says.

I spin on my heel, pulling my door open. "Okay, I'll just . . . walk you out, then."

We walk in stilted silence down the hallway, him following my lead through the open living room. Once we hit the entryway, he stills, shifting awkwardly on the balls of his feet.

"Harper," he murmurs, finally catching my eye.

"Yes?"

"Listen, uh, thank you for the . . . massage. And thank you for this," he adds, gesturing toward the slightly crumpled papers in his left hand.

A hopeless smile curves my lips. "Sure, a deal's a deal. I—"

"Hey, you two." My head swivels at the sound of Stella's voice. She's standing in the hallway, soaking-wet hair dripping onto the carpet beneath her bare feet. A white terry cloth towel is wrapped around her body—it's tiny, thin, hardly containing her curvy hips and chest.

Luca audibly clears his throat, head dipping toward the

floor. His jaw is tight, the apples of his cheeks a rosy shade of pink as he stares at his shoes.

"I'll see you Tuesday," he mutters, hastily pushing his way out of our apartment.

"Bye, Reynolds!" Stella calls after him, the door smacking shut behind him.

A giggle breaks free. "You're evil, Stella."

Her gaze flits down to her chest, then back up to meet mine. "God, he acts like he's never seen a naked woman before."

"Maybe he hasn't."

"You think?"

"Oh, um, I'm not sure, really." I suppose it could be true, but it's not my place to speculate behind his back.

"Nah, I bet he's secretly a freak in the sheets," she argues, a wistful look in her eye. "Standoffish during the day and wild at night."

"Oh God," I groan. "Go have sex with your girlfriend, you horndog."

"Don't mind if I do."

It's Monday afternoon, which means it's officially the first day of my internship.

The baseball boys are training in the gym today, lifting and running treadmill sprints. Unfortunately, their field is practically flooded, filled with a mixture of mud and standing water after last night's storm—a common occurrence in September.

Apparently, according to my supervisor, most of the early fall season is spent off the field, anyway. It's no sweat off my back. I get to spend the semester watching attractive men lift weights, *and* I get to stay out of the rain. It's a win-win situation, especially during hurricane season.

Minh Le, their assistant athletic trainer, has spent the last five minutes introducing me to the team. I spotted Nate right away, of course, that curly head of dark hair standing out like a shiny beacon. He's ungodly levels of attractive, from his full lips to his thick lashes to his veiny fucking forearms.

I doubt he caught me staring, though. I was discreet, professional even, as I secretly stalked him in the crowd. Now I'm standing alone by the water fountain, silently observing Minh at work. It's my first day, after all, like syllabus week in the field-work world.

"Harper St. James." That familiar voice sneaks up behind me, the sultry sound curling around me like a warm blanket. "Who knew our team could be so lucky?"

"Happy to be here," I say, turning to face Nate full-on. "I've been looking forward to this internship."

"Really?" His eyes light up with amusement. "Figured you'd be bummed to be stuck with us in the off-season."

"I mean, you guys are still training hard," I assure him, a soft smile playing on my lips. "Plus, I really like the whole idea of preventive medicine."

One corner of his mouth tugs up. "Do you?"

"Mhm, it's important to be proactive. You know, prep for any self-inflicted torture."

He sizes me up, his dark brown eyes dragging across my small frame. "So, you think you're gonna shield me from future pain?"

"Something like that."

His chest steadily rises and falls as he takes one step closer. "And what if I enjoy a little pain every now and then?"

My brow quirks. "I guess that's your prerogative."

"How about you, Harper?" He tips his water bottle to his lips, taking a deep swig while his eyes stay locked on mine.

"Do I enjoy pain?" I release an amused huff of laughter. "Nope, can't say that I do."

"Hm, noted." He licks a dribble of water off his bottom lip. "You're looking good, by the way. I think this is the first time I've seen you out of your lifeguard uniform."

I make a crack at sarcasm. "I was thinking about wearing it today but wasn't sure it was professional enough."

"Nah," he agrees, eyes sparking with mischief. "I suppose there's nothing professional about it, is there?"

"Right, yeah, it's pretty tight." I push past the gravel collecting in my throat. "Doesn't, uh, leave much to the imagination."

"No, it really doesn't. Listen, do you—"

"Miss St. James," Minh cuts him off, hands cupped around his mouth as he calls me from across the room. "I need a moment."

I silently mouth a quick "sorry" in Nate's direction, nearly stumbling as I shuffle toward my supervisor. His soft gaze seems to follow me across the room. I'm fairly certain he's still watching me, minutes later, as I attempt to pay attention to Minh's incessant rambling.

I'm handed a roster of team files, the training schedule, and contact information for the coaches. Minh gives me a full rundown of our semester game plan. When I finally turn back, Nate's distracted himself with the lat pulldown machine.

Like a moth drawn to a flame, I can't help that my eyes settle on his muscular frame. His T-shirt is drawn tight, his upper back and lats bulging with every rep. Those strong hands wrap tightly against the bar, knuckles blanching a paler shade of brown.

It's been a while since I've gotten laid, so my mind easily wanders to places it shouldn't. Namely, Nate's fingers tightening around my thighs. But I've kind of, sort of, got a fake boyfriend now. And if word gets around to Nate, I'm sure he'd feel complicit in my phony affair.

Plus, I may have a real-life crush here. If Nate is the type of guy I think he is, then I'd want more than just a bed warmer out of him. A one-night stand. An itch-scratcher, if you will. I've got enough vibrators for that in my nightstand drawer.

Chapter Eight

LUCA

IT MAY SIMPLY BE a placebo effect, but I swear to God, my knee has already started feeling better. Since Sunday night, I've been icing and resting and following Harper's home program to the letter.

If I'm being honest with myself, I've been counting down the hours until I can lie down in her bed again. My gold-standard ice bath isn't cutting it anymore. I'm craving a full-fledged deep-tissue massage, but I have to wait a few more hours until I can have what I want. What I need, really.

As long as I can stay awake this time.

I can't afford to spend my Tuesday night lounging in Harper's bed. Not when I could be studying, or picking up an extra shift at the pier, or helping my sister with Bentley. I only have one hour to spare tonight. That's the allotted time I've given myself, preceded by team practice drills and a weekly phone call with my best friend, Danny.

My only friend, I guess, if I'm excluding my siblings.

Daniel Moreno has been my friend since before I can remember. In reality, we met on the playground way back in preschool. Danny kicked a load of sand in my shoe, so I punched him square in the nose. He cried, I felt bad, and the rest is history.

Now, Danny's a fellow linebacker at our rival school, Dayton University. It was always the plan to leave our small hometown together. But when it came down to it, I couldn't afford the early deposit and lost out on my scholarship. Thankfully, Coastal U made me an offer I couldn't refuse—a full ride within a twenty-mile radius of home.

Besides, I have no problem staying close to my family. Taylor and my parents need me around. And so do my three little sisters and delinquent brother. At least, they need me financially, which is why I'm counting on the draft this spring.

I'm nearly two hours into our nightly practice regime when I hear Coach call my name. His tone is sharp, gritty, and harsh on my ringing ears, and it's likely because I've been leaning to the right for the last twenty minutes.

What more does this stubborn man want from me? I suffered through his conditioning program this morning, got taped by our interns before hitting the field, and now I'm on my last set of bag and tackle drills.

"Reynolds," Coach calls again, one hand waving erratically in my face. "You're unsteady on your feet today. What's going on?"

I grit my teeth. "Nothing, Coach."

"Yeah? No joint pain?" He scrutinizes me, eyes slowly dragging from my shoulder pads down to my dirt-stained cleats. "You're leaning, son."

"We're all good here."

Maybe it's my imagination, but I swear his gaze lingers on my knee for a split second too long. Then, before I can even blink, he gives me a tight-lipped smile followed by a heavy pat on the shoulder.

"Why don't you have one of our interns look over you after practice today?" he suggests with a definitive nod. "Give 'em some practical experience."

My brain scrambles to invent a reasonable excuse.

"I, uh, I've got work tonight," I finally manage to spit out.

"I'm asking you for fifteen minutes, Reynolds." He cocks a brow, tapping the end of his pen on his clipboard. This is no suggestion, that much is clear. "You told me you were dedicated to the team. That's why I made you defensive captain this year."

He's right, in the end. I need to face the harsh reality that Coach Reid is the one in charge here. If I want to stay on his good side, then I need to keep up appearances and quit with the fucking back talk. God knows I'm not winning any popular votes with my teammates, either.

"Right." I clear my throat, flexing the fist I've been clenching to my side. "Yeah, I suppose I can spare fifteen minutes."

"Great."

I manage to finish my last set of drills fully upright, with minimal lateral lean and a phony-ass grin for Coach. By the time I make it back to the athletic training room, my muscles are crying out for that promised massage.

Harper must have magical hands or something, I swear to God. The fucking woodland fairy.

As I step further into the room, the sound of hushed whispers catches me off guard. Along the back entrance, Eden and Fletcher are standing awfully close, their faces an inch or two apart. It's difficult to judge Eden's expression, though, as Fletcher has her caged in with one arm.

I clear my throat, taking a few solid steps closer to the pair. "Everything good here?"

Eden's head ducks around Fletcher's tall frame, cheeks flushed a warm shade of pink. Her eyes widen with recognition when she spots me. It only takes a brief moment before she's scrambling away from her companion. Fletcher, on the other hand, is much slower on the uptake. His arm gently falls from the wall, spine visibly stiff at the sound of my voice.

When he finally turns to face me, his expression is plainly dejected.

"Sorry, Reynolds," Eden squeaks out. "How can we help you?"

I raise one dubious brow, eyes locked on Fletcher. "Actually, Harper's gonna look me over when I get to her place. If Coach asks, just tell him we're all good here."

"Sure thing." Eden's gaze flits from me to the wall, to Fletcher, and back again. She's chewing on her bottom lip so roughly that she's bound to draw blood. "See you later, then."

She waves one trembling hand before darting out the back entrance. With a crestfallen shake of his head, Fletcher trails closely behind. I swear I hear the word *princess* followed by the heavy slam of an automatic door.

By the time I've ventured home, showered, and dressed for Harper's, I only have about five minutes left for a phone call. It's not a huge deal, but we've been cutting our conversations short for months now. There's always something in the way, whether it be my schedule or Danny's.

He answers on the first ring with a cheerful "Hey, man."

"Practice ran a little late," I tell him, scrubbing a towel over my damp hair. "I only have a few extra minutes tonight."

"No worries. I'm going out to dinner with . . ." He clears his throat, an awkward lilt invading his tone. "I mean, I'm about to go out for dinner anyway, so it's no big deal."

I scrub an irritated hand across my forehead. "Alright then. How's uh, how's your team doing this season?"

"You little fucker." The playful timbre of his voice returns. "You know we got our asses handed to us last weekend."

My eyes roll back. "Yeah, you and your guys couldn't block Miami's offense for shit."

"And you still think you're hot shit because the Ospreys beat them last season. News flash, their best player was just medically disqualified."

"Yeah, and what's your team's excuse this year?"

"You're still such an ass, Reynolds." His warm chuckle reverberates through the phone. "Glad to see Coastal hasn't changed you too much."

"I'm a few miles from home, D. What is there to change?"

And that's the damn truth. While I've been stuck in this town for the past four years, Danny's been the one changing over at DU. In fact, he spent this past summer galivanting around Europe with his girlfriend. I doubt he's even been home once since last Christmas. At least, that's the last visit I'm aware of, anyway.

"Yeah, you're right," he says earnestly. "How is everybody over there, anyway? Little Giorgie?"

"Giorgie and the twins are good." I can't fight the grin that lights up my face. "Taylor's working her ass off, and Elio is himself, as per usual."

"I need to get back there soon for a visit. I think Sof . . . I mean, I think I'm gonna head back for fall break here in a few weeks or so."

"You know you can say her name, right?" I ask the question through gritted teeth. "I'm not gonna spontaneously combust if I hear it."

"Yeah, man, I know," he says somberly. "I just . . . it still feels a little weird."

"It's been two years."

"I know."

"Look, I need to go anyway." I straighten my shoulders, the next words unintentionally slipping from my mouth. "I'm, uh—I've actually started seeing someone."

"Oh?" His tone is pleasantly shocked. "That's fucking great, dude. What's her name?"

"Harper," I blurt out. "Yeah, she's . . . great. A sweet girl. I'm heading to her house now, actually."

"I guess I'll talk to you next week, then. I'm really happy for you, Luc."

"Sure," I grumble. "Have a good night with Sofia."

There's an awkwardly long pause, and then, ". . . yeah, thanks. Night, then."

When I finally hang up, my mind is reeling. Now, I've got a headache to go along with my body aches, and I'm jonesing even harder for that coveted massage. For Harper's magical healing hands.

I drive at least seven miles over the speed limit the entire route to her apartment. My knee is shaking as I take the stairs two at a time. With one solid knock, I plant myself directly in front of the sparkly, pink entrance.

The front door swings open in the same fashion as the other night. I narrowly avoid another smack to the face as Harper exclaims, "You're here!"

"I am."

"That's great." She smiles wide, soft cheeks stretched across her lightly freckled face. "And look, I didn't even hit you this time."

I give her a pursed-lipped nod. "Right."

"Okay, well, come on in and make yourself at home." She holds out one arm, gesturing wide to the entrance of her living room. "Stella's out tonight, just so you know. She wanted to give us a little bit of privacy."

"Privacy?" I ask, stepping over the threshold before us. Harper trails in after me, closing the front door behind her with a gentle shove.

"Stella thinks we're hooking up," she blurts, fingers twisting into the ends of her sun-bleached hair. "Not that I told her we were having sex or anything. I wouldn't do that yet. I mean, unless you want me to. Should we come up with a story to cover that?"

A flush of heat rushes to my neck. "Can't we just . . . leave that part to the imagination?"

"What do you mean?" Her head tilts like she honestly has no clue what the fuck I'm talking about.

"Surely you don't need to share all the details about your sex life?"

"Oh, um, yeah . . . we usually do." Her brow crinkles, nose scrunching as she assesses me. "You know, like, favorite positions, best partners, how we like to—"

"Okay, that's enough." I hold up one hand, the heat rising further up the column of my throat. "I get the picture."

"Sorry," she squeaks out, shooting me an apologetic smile. "This is all pretty normal for me, Luca. I'm sure you talk about worse things with your guy friends."

"I don't," I say plainly.

Her eyes go wide. "Ever?"

"Never," I confirm. "That's . . . private."

Her head is still tilted, gaze fixed on mine as she gently rubs at her chin. Her teeth press into her full bottom lip. "Is it because you've never had sex before?"

"What?" I sputter, disconcerted.

"If so, that's totally normal." Her hands clasp together

underneath her chin, that sweet, innocent smile of hers stretching a mile wide. "You know, virginity is actually just a social construct anyway, and no amount of—"

I clap a hand to my forehead, my headache returning in full force. "Stop."

"I promise, you have nothing to be embarrassed about." Her voice is soft, reassuring as she reaches out with one hand. Before she can make contact with my skin, however, she draws her arm back, clasping it tightly against her chest. "At least, not in front of me."

"I'm not a virgin, Harper." The words are biting, irritation slipping through. "I just have boundaries."

She's nodding emphatically now. "Boundaries? Like, in the bedroom?"

"Like, in my conversations," I correct. "I know the concept might seem foreign to you, but I don't need to share every intimate detail of my life."

She waggles her brows. "Intimate, huh?"

"We're done talking about this. Let's just get to work, because now I only have—" I pull my phone from my back pocket, checking the time. "—fifty-three minutes to spare tonight."

"Okay, well, you know the drill, then." She prances off down the hallway, tilting her head back to shout, "My bed! Pants off!"

An unhappy groan slips out as I mutter, "Is it your personal mission to make me as uncomfortable as possible?"

"Quite the opposite, Luca," she calls out, beckoning me toward her with both hands. "Now, come on, slowpoke. We're wasting time."

Chapter Nine

HARPER

"Luca," I whisper-shout, fingers wrapped gently around the upper half of his bicep. I give him one solid shake, then two, careful not to jostle him too much. "Luca, wake up."

His eyelids flicker, soft lashes fanned across his sun-kissed cheeks. His nose crinkles, a tiny twitch to the left and right before I whisper his name for the third time.

A heavy, displeased groan slips from his lips.

"Hey, sleepyhead. You told me to wake you up," I murmur, using both hands to shove at his large frame. "Wakey-wakey!"

He swats at me with a heavy hand. I swat him right back. The cycle continues until he releases an unhappy grunt, grasps my wrist, and twists to his side. I topple onto his chest with a heavy "Oomph." My arms are trapped between us, breasts crushed awkwardly against the side of his torso.

His eyes snap open with the force of my landing. I glance up, wincing as I take in his shell-shocked expression.

"Shit," he mutters in a sleep-torn voice, wide-eyed as I scramble away.

"Sorry!"

"What the fuck just happened?" he rasps, scrubbing a hand over his flushed face. An awkward, forced cough fills the room. He shifts onto his back, pushing up to rest against the wrought-iron frame of my bed.

I smooth two hands over my wrinkled shirt. "You, uh, you fell asleep again."

"I see that."

"You were only out for a few minutes, I swear." I nibble at the inside of my cheek, uncomfortably aware of his irritation. "I woke you up right after I noticed."

"Right." He shakes his head, rubbing at his temples for a few long moments. "Is, uh . . . are we done already?"

"No, no. It's just after seven thirty." I tap my imaginary watch. "We have some time, but the next part is active stretching. You need to be awake for that."

"Right, sure. Let me just . . ." He trails off, gaze drifting from an unknown spot on my bed to the door behind me. "I'm gonna use the restroom for a minute."

"Sure, go right ahead. It's just across the hall, but, um, there might be some bras hung up on the towel rack. Stella likes to air-dry them."

"Of course she does," he grumbles.

His long legs swing over the edge of the bed, sock-clad feet hitting the floor with a heavy thud. A shocked wince twists his features. It's so easy for him to forget, to throw around his weight like this injury doesn't control him, as if it doesn't rule every facet of his life.

By the time he's back from the bathroom, I've already remade my bed. I'm still working on fluffing the pillows in perfect order. Of course, the tiniest yellow puff sits right on top.

When I finally glance up, Luca's standing awkwardly in the doorway. His expression is carefully neutral, but the tips of his ears have gone red again. Yeah, he definitely got an eyeful of lacy cups and tiny, delicate straps.

"All good?" I ask, an amused smile curving my lips.

"All good," he says gruffly.

I barely suppress a giggle. "Okay, we'll start out your exercises in a gravity-eliminated position."

"Meaning?"

"Hop back on my bed, sunshine." I pat my mattress, smiling as he cocks one dark brow.

"Did you just call me sunshine?"

"It just popped out." I slip a strand of beachy hair between my fingers, absentmindedly picking at the split ends. "It's kinda funny, 'cause you're always so . . .'"

"Cold?"

My eyes widen at his harsh tone. "I was gonna say testy."

"Testy?"

"Mhmm," I drag out my confirmation. "You have a little bit of an attitude, you know. Actually, you remind me of this cat I used to have growing up. His actual name was Finch, but I called him Mr. Tickles. He died when I was nine, though." My palm splays over my heart, gaze drifting to the ceiling. "Rest in peace, Mr. Tickles."

A muscle in his jaw ticks. "I remind you of your dead cat?"

"Mhm. He was always swatting at everyone. But at the end of the day, he loved to snuggle in bed with me." I reel back when I catch his bemused expression. "Not that you . . . I mean, not that you want to snuggle with me, in particular. But you do seem to like my bed."

"It's comfortable," he agrees, one shoulder lifting in a shrug.

"I think it's all the pillows."

The corner of his lip twitches. "Probably."

"Okay, well, anyway . . . you can just lie down on your right side and face me." I pat my mattress again, gesturing to the foot of my bed. "That way, you won't be fighting the resistance of gravity."

He plops down, grimacing as he shifts both legs into place. "Like this?"

"Mhm, just a little bit closer." I motion with both hands as he shimmies and shifts toward the edge. "Yep, that's perfect."

"Great."

"So, I'll just move your limb passively to show you the action." My palm makes contact with his outer thigh, pushing against his IT band. "Then you can repeat it on your own, okay? Five sets of ten."

"Sure."

I slowly slide the surface of my palm down the side of his leg. My fingertips gently glide across the bridge of his knee, resting directly below his patella.

"I'm going to move you now," I warn.

A tiny groan escapes him at first range, shallow breaths puffing from his lips with every twitch of his joint. It doesn't take long for him to adjust to the feeling, though, and pretty soon, he's got the rhythm down himself.

I step back, carefully monitoring his expression, breathing cycles, range of motion, and patterns of movement. "So, how's practice going with your knee?"

"Just fine," he mutters.

"Yeah? No one's caught on to your injury yet?"

"Actually, uh, Coach asked me about it today," he admits through gritted teeth. "I was leaning, favoring my right side at the end of practice."

"Aw, shit." I plant both hands on my hips. "What did I say about overcompensating?"

His shoulders visibly tense. "Uh, that I . . . that I need to relieve some stress to avoid doing it?"

"Exactly."

His left leg kicks out again, just a tad too forcefully this time. "Yeah, well, I don't see that happening anytime soon."

"I can set you up with someone," I offer. "If you want."

"For Christ's sake, Harper. Is sex all you think about?"

"I wasn't talking about sex this time! I just meant . . . a date might help you relieve some stress. A dinner out with a nice girl or guy or whoever you want."

He finishes his last set of reps in silence; every breath is shallow, steady, and carefully measured. As he shifts back into a seated position, he finally says, "No."

"You don't want to date?"

He levels me with his stony gaze. "I'm dating you, aren't I?"

"Very funny."

"I don't have time, Harper. That would just add stress, not relieve it." He leans back on his palms, eyes pinched shut for a brief moment. "Besides, this is complicated enough between us."

"Oh," I mutter, dejected. "I'm sorry if my lie added more stress for you."

"No, Harper, that's not . . . I don't mean to blame you for anything." He shifts awkwardly on the edge of my bed. "I'm the one who dragged you into this twisted bullshit with my knee. I just meant that I'm focused on healing right now. That's it."

"Got it." I nod my head emphatically. "That's probably a good idea anyway. And look, we're pretty much done for the night."

"Oh? Okay, great." He pushes off the bed, his tall frame towering over me as he stands. "I'll, uh, I need to get going, then."

I offer a tiny smile as he shuffles around me, beelining for the exit. I take a step to my right, he takes a step to his left, and then we're both awkwardly bumping and brushing against one another as we leave my room. In the end, I quietly trail behind him down the hallway.

Once we've passed by the living room, he turns on his heel, eyes meeting mine. We're standing in the empty foyer now. His hands are in his pockets; mine are tangled in the ends of my hair.

"Thanks for all your help." His gaze flits around my face for a moment, settling on that singular freckle above my nose. "I honestly think I'm making progress."

"Of course, a deal's a deal."

He frowns, wrinkles his nose. "Just because we made a deal doesn't mean I can't be thankful for you."

"In that case, you're welcome." An unexpected smile cracks my lips. "We can probably just stick to one session a week from now on. Does Tuesday still work for you?"

"I'll request time off from the pier."

"Perfect."

His lips part, close, and then part again. Something unspoken sits on the tip of his tongue, but all that comes out is "See you next week."

"See you then."

It's my second week of interning, and I'm practically in love. Working for a professional sports team, or hell, even a collegiate sports team, is my lifelong dream. All I've done so far is review training schedules with Minh, discuss common baseball injuries, and develop imaginary treatment plans.

But I don't really care. I'm having fun learning from the team. Not to mention, spending more time with Nate is an obvious plus. I swear I caught him checking me out on more than one occasion—once when I bent over at the water fountain and then again when we made eye contact by the lockers.

It's the sole reason I wore this tight black athletic outfit today. I slipped my jacket's zipper down a little extra, exposing just enough sports bra cleavage to still be considered appropriate.

I mean, come on. This is the athletic training department, not an office setting.

"How's my favorite intern?" Nate's voice is smooth like honey as he sidles up next to me. It's the third time I've caught his attention this afternoon, so I'm planning on taking full advantage of it.

"Actually, I'm pretty excited." I clasp my hands together, an unfiltered smile spreading across my cheeks. "Minh's letting me develop next week's conditioning program."

He scratches the back of his neck, the muscles in his arms bunching and contracting with every tiny movement. "Are you gonna make us bust our asses in the weight room?"

"I was thinking about it."

"Anything I could do to change your mind?" His lips turn up in a smirk. "You know, I'm not opposed to begging."

"Oh?" I size him up, gaze drifting from the top of his forehead down to the soles of his shoes. "I think I'd like to see that. *The* Nathan Gunderson, begging on his knees."

"For you? That could be arranged."

Shocked laughter slips out. "You're so full of it."

"Yeah, that may be true." He folds his thick arms over his chest. "But I still think you should come out with me this weekend."

"What?" I blink, a warm mixture of giddiness and confusion bubbling in my stomach.

"Yeah, a few of us are going out to the bars on Saturday

night." His fingertips graze the crux of my arm. "I want you to be there."

For some reason, a million thoughts race inside my head. Imaginary plans are taking root, settling in the once-vacant spot on my calendar.

"Oh, um, yeah. I could probably make that work."

"Probably?" His brow raises in amusement. "I'm looking for a yes, Harps."

Holy shit. The boy I've been crushing on for months now is kind of, sort of, asking me out. And I'm . . . trying to invent a reason to say no. Fuck that.

"Could I bring some friends along?"

His smirk melts into a full-out grin. "The more, the merrier."

"Then count me in." My gaze darts around the room. I quickly spot Minh in the back corner, fully engrossed in a conversation with their head coach. "You can just text me the details."

He plucks the phone from my outstretched hand. "I will."

When he passes it back, his warm palm grazes mine. Those long, calloused fingers gently tap against the back of my hand. With one last caress along the side of my index finger, he slides his arm back to his side as a tiny shiver dots up my spine.

There's officially no doubt about it; this man knows exactly how to use his hands.

Chapter Ten

LUCA

THE PIER IS a slippery fucking disaster today. It's as if the universe is hell-bent on destroying any last semblance of my recovery. The slick combination of sand, salt water, and rotting wood has officially taken its toll.

Suffice it to say, I've eaten shit twice already this afternoon.

Now, my knee is a throbbing, swollen knot inside my jeans. My hands are shaking from the pain. And my head, it's a swirling vortex of frustrated energy. By the time I'm finished with my shift, I foresee a long night of suffering. Not to mention, tomorrow's game is likely to be a shitshow.

I'm in desperate need of an emergency session with Harper. I don't understand how she forces me to relax so easily —to fall asleep beneath the gentle, unyielding pressure of her fingertips. Believe it or not, it's typically impossible for me to feel comfortable in someone else's space.

With Harper, it's like I don't have a choice. I'm entranced by that sea of pillows and her soft, nimble hands. Plus, I appreciate the way she responds to my . . . *attitude*. Because apparently, that's what I have. The feisty, ripe attitude of her deceased family pet.

"You look like shit, son," Pawel calls out in his matter-of-fact tone. "Why don't you head out early, and I can close up?"

My boss isn't usually this perceptive, but it's painfully

obvious that I'm reeling. My brow is filled with sweat, my cheeks are burning with heat, and the bottom half of my jeans are fully drenched by the high tide.

Regardless, I ignore his offer. With one final shake of my head, I heave another box of equipment over my shoulder. This time, I make sure to brace myself on the rough polymer-coated pilings. Each one is spaced a few feet apart, so I grit my teeth and shuffle between them, careful not to lift up and slip on my ass again.

"I know you heard me, Luc."

I carry on with my task, gathering a mixture of trash, old equipment, and tangled lines into their respective places.

"I'm not leaving early," I mutter, wiping a stray bead of sweat from my eyelid. "I need the money."

"I'm still paying you for the shift, boy." Pawel shuffles behind me, clapping one hand on my shoulder and another on the crate. "But if you don't leave, I'll find a reason to dock your pay."

"Bullshit." My gaze drags over his weathered frame, with his frail hands, slumped posture, and graying tufts of hair. It's no secret that the man is well past retirement age. "You need more rest than I do."

"Do you forget that I'm a sailor?" He levels me with a harsh stare, his ocean-blue eyes swirling with tender resolve. "I've lived a thousand lifetimes, and I'll live a thousand more. Plus, I'm not the one who's injured."

I wince, wildly unprepared to execute damage control. "But I-I'm not—"

"If you think I don't see you, then you're wrong."

"Okay, it's true," I finally relent, puffing out a breath of panicked air. "I may be injured, but it's more so just a temporary bruise. I'll be fine, and I really need the hours, Pawel, so please don't cut me out of the schedule because—"

"Calm down, boy." He shrugs his windbreaker over his shoulders, flipping his hood at the first signs of rain. "No one's cutting anyone out of anything. Get on home, and we'll pretend this conversation never happened."

I flinch as a lone raindrop lands on the bridge of my nose, a tiny wet splash flickering against my hot skin. "Don't do me any favors."

"I'm doin' myself a favor," he argues. "You're no good to me if you're out of commission."

"Fine, I'll leave." I toss the damp equipment back into the crate, staring at the knotted pile of fishing line. "But I'm back Sunday morning, no excuses."

"I'm tired of watching your mouth move," he grumbles. "Get outta here."

The rain gathers steam as I hobble away from the pier. Warm, fat droplets fall from the clouds, pooling in my hair and slipping down the sides of my face. My feet drag, knee twitching as I yank the door closed on my old Subaru. Right in time, too, as rainwater pelts down in heavy torrents against my windshield.

After a full day of late summer heat, this downpour is as predictable and cyclic as the tides. It's hurricane season, after all, but it doesn't mean I have to tolerate the interruption.

My head tilts back against the headrest, eyes squeezing shut as I take a deep breath. The rain has mixed and melded with the dry sand, filtering in through my nose with every tiny puff of air. It's a syrupy, earthy scent that serves to piss me off.

Rainstorms always coincide with an atmospheric drop, meaning the soft tissues in my knee have begun to swell. It's a surefire way to prolong my inextricable pain. And if I wasn't certain before, now I know the universe is actively conspiring against me.

I allow sixty full seconds of self-pity before I dig my phone out.

"Luca!" Harper answers on the first ring, her voice a familiar chipper tone. "Hi, how are you?"

"Just fine," I mutter, the phrase absentmindedly leaving my mouth. "Actually, I fell at work and tweaked my knee. I know we're not supposed to meet again until next week, but I was wondering if I could come over tonight?"

"Oh, no," she murmurs. "I'm sorry, Luca. I can't have you over tonight."

"Right, of course not." A pit in my stomach hollows out. "It's fucking Friday night, I don't know what I was thinking. I'll just—"

"No, silly, I just meant . . . could I come to your place instead?"

"What?"

"I promised Stella and Lai'Lani they could have the apartment to themselves. I was actually just headed out for a bite to eat."

My shoulders relax, a sigh of relief filtering through my lips. "Oh, okay."

"So, is that alright, then? I'll come to yours?"

"I mean . . . uh," I sputter, racking my brain. I have no clue how long it's been since I last cleaned. I think my bed is made, and my laundry is done, at the very least. "Yeah, that'd be fine."

"I'm just gonna grab some tacos on the way," she says happily. "Would you like me to pick up some extra?"

The pit in my stomach groans at the thought, a sudden reminder that I haven't eaten since this morning. "I, uh, I'm not hungry."

"You just got off work, didn't you? I'm sure you're at least a little bit hungry. I'll pick you up some chorizo and egg," she rambles on. "Those are my favorite."

"That's really not nec—"

"You said you live with your sister, right? Does she like tacos? If she's vegetarian, they have cactus and potato as an option. I could also just pick a big variety."

"We're good, Harper," I protest, the grumble in my stomach growing louder. "We don't need any tacos. Taylor's probably out tonight, anyway."

"If you say so." Her tone is flippant, dismissively cheerful. "Text me the address, and I can be there in about thirty if that works?"

"It works."

"See you soon!"

I SPEED home through the rainstorm, my twenty-year-old Outback sputtering and hydroplaning through the newly formed puddles. By the time I make it back, I only have about five minutes left to spare. Of course, Bentley comes crashing into the living room to greet me—no signs of his mother in sight.

My palm runs through his silky fur, scratching behind his ears. Content, he trots behind me, panting and slobbering as I rush around the house. My swollen joints continue to ache and groan. Ignoring the pain, I toss the trash out back, stuff a few dishes into the wash, and wipe down the dining table.

The kitchen is my top priority at the moment since Harper might need a clean spot to eat her tacos.

When the doorbell finally sounds, I take one last look around the empty house. I suppose it's presentable enough for an outsider. There are no obvious messes or stains or discarded items lying around, but I wish I had a few more minutes to tidy up. If it wasn't immediately obvious, I'm not used to having visitors.

I release one heavy breath before I pull open the front door. The sight of a half-drenched Harper greets me, her beachy waves dripping onto the doormat beneath her feet. She's struggling to balance three paper bags in her arms. Her clothing is damp, small droplets of rain clinging to her exposed skin.

"Hey there, stranger." Her voice is soft, pleasant despite the circumstances. Her cheeks tighten with a carefree grin. If I were to make an educated guess, I'd have to assume that this girl enjoys the rain.

"Come in," I say.

As we step inside, I make a subtle move to reach for her bags. Unfortunately, Bentley comes bounding in behind me. His seventy-five-pound frame nearly knocks Harper off her feet as my hands instinctively move to steady her, fingers wrapped loosely around her upper arms. She sways and stumbles a bit, but we manage to effectively right ourselves before toppling over.

"Shit," I swear under my breath. "He's a little aggressive, but he means well."

"It's okay," she says cheerfully.

Once she's steady on her feet, I gather the bags into my arms. As she follows behind, I guide us toward the kitchen, corralling the dog to my side with a low whistle.

"What a beautiful baby," Harper coos, softly stroking Bentley's fur. "Luca, what's the puppy's name?"

"He's full-grown, but his name's Bentley."

She tsks. "I'm pretty sure all dogs are puppies forever."

I acknowledge the comment with a humorless snort.

Once I set her bags on the dining table, she steps forward to

SPRING TIDE 79

rifle through. First, she pulls out handfuls of hot-sauce containers. Then taco after endless taco. There are at least twenty
greasy white pouches on the table now.

I cock one brow. "This seems like way too much food for
one person."

"It's not for one person, you goof." She crumples up the
now-empty bags, spinning around in search of a trash can. "I
brought you and Taylor some. I got lots of hot sauce, too. Do
you like things spicy?"

"I told you this wasn't necessary."

"It's all good, Luca." She waves a dismissive hand. "I
can't just eat in front of you without offering anything.
Besides, I wanted you to try this place. It's one of my
favorites."

I can feel the warmth gathering in my cheeks. "Okay."

"So, you'll have some?"

"Since it's here, yeah, I probably should." I clear my throat,
gathering the trash from her hands. "We don't want it to go to
waste."

"Of course not." She glances back at me, waiting patiently
as I stuff the paper bags under the sink. "And your sister, is she
around?"

"She might pop in later. I think she's working on a project
in the circuits lab."

"Circuits?" Her brow quirks as she settles into a dining
chair.

I grab a few plates from the cupboards, joining Harper at
the table. "She's a master's student in electrical engineering."

"That's kinda badass."

"Yeah, it is." One corner of my mouth turns up. "Taylor, uh,
she works really hard."

Harper gathers a few tacos onto her plate, carefully

unwrapping them one by one. She drenches them in hot sauce before she says, "Must run in the Reynolds family."

"Yeah, maybe." I clear my throat, unwrapping a few tacos for myself. "Speaking of—if Taylor comes home soon, what do you want me to tell her?"

"Hm?" she mumbles on a mouthful.

"Your friend Eden, she originally called me your boyfriend." I nearly stutter over the word. "But I know that's not what you've been telling your roommate, so I'd like to make things clear. My sister and I are straightforward people. Should I tell her we're together?"

Her chewing is slow, deliberate as she ponders my question. "You, um, you could tell her we're just seeing each other for now. Nothing serious."

"Okay." I finally stuff a taco into my mouth, quickly discovering that it's pure fucking heaven.

"Actually, about that. I wanted to run something by you."

"Go ahead," I mutter, moving on to my second taco.

Damn. This delicious combination of meat and hot sauce is killing me slowly. In a good way, if that's possible.

"That guy I had a crush on . . . ya know, the baseball player?"

I take a moment to pause my incessant chewing. "What about him?"

"Well, he kind of asked me out. Or, he asked me on like a group hangout at a bar, but it was definitely flirty," she rambles, avoiding my gaze. "And I'm planning to go."

"You don't need to run that by me, Harper."

"It's just . . . if people really think we're together, then it wouldn't be great for me to be seen in public with Nate. So we'll just have to make sure everyone knows we're taking it slow, right? That we're totally free to see other people?"

Now, that gets my attention. "Are we talking about Nate Gunderson?"

"Aw, shit." She slaps both palms over her face, shaking her head. "I said his actual name, didn't I?"

"You did."

She drags her hands down her face, stretching her heated cheeks. "Um, well . . . yeah, it's him."

"Interesting," I say plainly, devouring my third taco in a matter of seconds.

She perks up. "Interesting how?"

I swallow. "Doesn't seem like he'd be your type."

"And you know him that well?" she asks, eyes narrowed in suspicion.

"I think I do."

No, I know I do. From the few interactions we've had, I know for certain that Nate's a conceited little prick. And Harper? The girl is . . . pure as gold. There's not an arrogant bone in her body.

"And you know *me* that well?"

I shrug, swiping my greasy hands on a napkin. "I'm starting to."

"Then you should know that I don't have a type." She blinks down at her mountain of food, absentmindedly picking at a piece of egg.

"Everyone has a type," I snort.

"I don't." She rips off a small corner of tortilla, dipping it in hot sauce before popping it in her mouth. "I like so many different types of boys, honestly. And the occasional girl. I'm really not picky when it comes to love."

"Hm," I murmur, flipping through the small white bags in search of one labeled "C." That's the chorizo and egg, I'm fairly certain. My new favorite.

"Hm?" She tosses her hands up. "That's it? Are you saying you don't believe me?"

"No further comment."

"Okay, wise one." She leans back in her seat, folding both arms across her chest. "If everyone has a type, then what's yours?"

"Oh, it, uh, it doesn't really matter."

"Of course it does." She gives me a teasing glare. "I want to know, so it matters."

My throat constricts. "Well, it's not really . . . it's more so a feeling."

"Okay, now you really have to tell me."

"Fine," I groan, pushing my plate away, wincing as it scrapes against the table. "My type is just someone who's content with—"

"Luc!" I'm cut off by the sound of my sister's high-pitched yell. "You in there?"

"It's me," I call back, breathing a sigh of relief. "In the dining room."

I flash Harper an apologetic smile. She playfully rolls her eyes, palms pressed against the edge of the table. Her heels are shaking, tapping off the leg of the chair while she waits.

As Taylor's footsteps grow closer, I scrub a nervous hand through my hair. When she finally enters the room, her eyes go wide, darting between Harper and me. "Who do we have here, little brother?"

"Taylor, this is Harper." I gesture across the table. "My, uh . . . we've been seeing each other for a few weeks now. Harper, this is my sister, Taylor."

Harper pushes out of her seat, scrambling to embrace my sister in a hug. "It's so great to meet you." She pulls back, gaze darting to the table. "Do you like tacos? I brought a bunch from this great place down the street."

"I love tacos." Taylor flashes me an impressed grin, wide-eyed and giddy as she settles in beside me. "Did you bring any hot sauce, by chance?"

"Loads of it," Harper says.

"Just my kind of girl."

Chapter Eleven

HARPER

Taylor is one of the sweetest, funniest people I've ever met. The two of us clicked right off the bat, like long-lost friends who both share an affinity for tacos, hot sauce, and teasing Luca until he's red in the face.

Not to mention, we're both women in STEM. There's some sort of power in that, I think, a sort of kinship between two of the most important women in Luca's life. Not that I'm conflating my own sense of self-worth.

Believe me, I know this is only a temporary relationship. A mutually beneficial agreement. I know I'm just providing a service or a simple swap of secrets, but I'd like to think we're building a real friendship here.

Luca's a cool person. And I enjoy being around him, even when he's a little agitated and a lot flustered. It's funny. And sweet. I initially thought he was just a shy person, that he might need some extra time to warm up, but I'm starting to understand him differently now.

Luca isn't shy, necessarily. He's just careful and private and sensitive. He clearly works himself to the bone, yet he opts to suffer in silence. When push comes to shove, Luca never pretends to be someone he's not. Those are all qualities I admire, regardless of how outwardly standoffish he might seem.

I consider him a friend now, and I'm sure hoping it lasts past this little arrangement.

"I'm gonna take Harper back to my room," Luca announces, pushing himself from the table. His hands fold in front of his waist, pressing together before dropping to his sides. "We're, uh—we have plans to watch a movie tonight."

"Well, don't let me stop you." Taylor chuckles softly, tilting back in her chair and rubbing both hands across her stomach. "Thanks again for the tacos, Happy."

"Happy?" I ask, cheeks scrunching with a smile.

"Thought it was fitting." She lifts a brow in her brother's direction. "Harper—*Happy*, 'cause you're just a little ball of joy. Not to mention, you clearly make my brother—"

"*And* that's enough of that." Luca clears his throat, fingers cautiously looping around my elbow. He meets my gaze. "You ready?"

"Of course," I murmur. "Let's go . . . watch that movie." I lift up from the table myself, drifting around the back of Taylor's chair. My fingers curl around her shoulders as I impart a quick, gentle squeeze. "It was great to meet you, Taylor. I'd love to do this again."

Her head tilts back. "Please, bring me tacos anytime," she says with a wiggle of her brows. "Nothing would make me happier."

"You got it," I promise.

Luca silently nods down the hallway, beckoning me to follow his lead. I trail behind him until we reach the last door on the left. Once we push inside, I carefully survey my surroundings.

It's surprisingly bright inside his bedroom.

The walls are a soft, pale shade of blue. His bedspread is a crisp white, with two perfectly placed pillows at the head. He even has a bed frame with a full-on headboard; it's a pretty, beachy mix of natural driftwood.

"Your room is very nice," I say earnestly.

He shakes his head, the tips of his ears tinging pink as he shuts the door behind us. "The furniture came with the room," he explains. "It's a temporary rental arrangement, on lease from one of Taylor's graduate professors. She's on an extended sabbatical, so . . . yeah. That's why my room's this way."

"Ah, I see." My eyes drift around, honing in on the three-dimensional figurine displayed on his dresser. "And I suppose you don't have a thing for seagulls, either?"

His gaze darts to the large plaster model. "That was also just . . . here."

"How long have you lived here, exactly?"

He awkwardly wraps a hand around the back of his neck. "A little over a year."

"You didn't want to personalize your space at all?" I ask, giggling. "You know, stuff the seagull in a drawer or something?"

"It's fine how it is, and this is just easier." He crosses his arms in front of his chest. "We should get started, though. Should I . . . do you need me to be in my underwear again?"

I tap my chin, lips twisting in a coy smile. "That would be ideal."

"Okay, well, Taylor's still out there." He wildly gestures toward his door. "And I don't have a bathroom in my room. So I'll need to get changed in here if you don't mind."

I raise a skeptical brow. "Do *you* mind?"

"At this point, does it really matter?"

"Of course. You should always be comfortable." My nose wrinkles as I soak in his stiff posture. "I can still turn around while you take off your pants."

He scratches at the back of his neck again, carefully flattening his weary expression. "No, it's . . . we're all good. This is a professional setting, as you say."

I nod my agreement, plopping squarely on the edge of his mattress. My gaze drifts around the room until our eyes catch. I place my palms flat against my lap, fingers twitching as we maintain eye contact. I don't know why, but it seems like it'd be wrong to look away now.

Luca said I didn't have to, after all. In fact, he nearly insisted that I don't. So, instead, I stare straight at him as he slowly undoes his belt buckle. Out of the corner of my eye, I notice the steady rise and fall of his chest.

Before he pushes his pants over his hips, his eyes narrow. "Harper, can you not just stare directly into my eyes while I do this?"

"Sorry, I didn't know where to look," I squeak out, quickly diverting my gaze to the floor. "I thought if I obviously looked away, then that would also be weird. You said you didn't need me to turn around this time, so I wanted to respect that. But then we just made eye contact instead and—"

"It's fine," he grumbles, cutting me off. In the last fifteen seconds, he's managed to remove his jeans, fold them, and place them in a neat little pile on top of his dresser. "See, pants are already off. We're good."

"Great," I chirp, patting the spot beside me on his bed. "Perfect! Saddle up, then!"

He coughs, choking back a sudden lump in his throat. "Saddle . . . up?"

"I meant, uh, get on the bed?" I try again, cheeks flushing as I shake my head. "Yeah, I don't even know where that came from. This is what happens when I do something awkward."

His eyes meet mine, one brow raised as he soaks in my

embarrassment. The corner of his lip twitches once, twice, before he breaks into hearty laughter. It's a sudden, unexpected sound—a loud, happy melody that echoes around the room.

"Okay, okay! We have work to do," I huff, feigning a pout. "Are you done?"

"Sure thing." He clears his throat, expression suddenly serious as he adds, "Giddy up, partner."

I groan, swatting him on the shoulder with a pillow. "Who knew you had jokes?"

"Only when they're at your expense."

I roll my eyes, stifling a secret smile as he shuffles onto his bed beside me. As he lies back, carefully settling against the mattress, I put my healing hands to work.

It's Saturday night, meaning it's almost time for my pseudo-date with Nate.

There are four of us crowded around the bathroom mirror, touching up our makeup and combing through our curls. I somehow roped my two best friends into joining me tonight. Naturally, Stella convinced her girlfriend to tag along, too.

Now, the two of them have their arms wrapped around one another. Lai'Lani leans in to press a soft kiss against Stella's cheek, leaving a faint outline of plum lipstick. Stella snaps a quick selfie and then swipes at her face with a tissue.

"Look at you two being so cute," I gush.

"That we are. But you know who's even cuter?" Stella singsongs, nudging me on the shoulder. "You and Reynolds."

"Me and Luca?" I ask, confusion coloring my tone. "I thought you all wanted me to go for Nate tonight?"

"We did. I mean, we do." She lets out a soft laugh, eyeing Eden in the mirror. "We want you to go for whoever you want, of course. We just think you and Ötzi are super cute together. She makes him blush, you guys."

Eden tries to hide her smirk, but I catch sight of it out of the corner of my eye. "You have something to add?"

Her smirk melts into a teasing grin. "Well, he does get really flustered when I bring up your name."

"Probably because he thought I was lying about him." I shrug, careful to keep my tone impartial. "And now that we're . . . doing whatever we're doing, he doesn't know how to act around you."

"I think there's more to it, though," Eden urges, adding the final row of bright purple clips to her hair. "I think he really likes you. Although he is easily flustered, like the other week when he caught Fletcher and me—"

"Fletcher and you, what?" I cut in, eager to be let in on the secret.

Eden's head tilts back, a heavy sigh floating from her lips. "Grant kissed me."

"*What?*"

Eden's eyes squeeze shut, nose wrinkling as she continues. "We were arguing about our schedule in the athletic training room, and he just . . . I don't know, somehow backed me against the lockers, and we kissed."

"Did he force you?" Lai'Lani butts in, a gentle undertone to her words.

"No, no it wasn't . . . I was definitely giving him signals," Eden wearily admits.

"Signals? Or consent?" Lai'Lani clarifies, lips pressed into a tight line.

"He knew I wanted him to," Eden argues. "I, um, I was staring at his lips, and then I leaned forward. Plus, I kind of kissed him back."

"Wow," I breathe out. "Do you want to get back together?"

While I don't know the exact details of their breakup, I know that it was quite nasty. There was lots of arguing, drunkenness, and lingering toxicity until it finally fizzled out before the summer.

Eden snorts, hands absentmindedly smoothing down the pleat in her trousers. "No, he's still a huge dick."

"He *is* a huge dick, or he *has* a huge dick?" Stella asks, waggling her brows.

"Both, unfortunately," Eden mutters in return.

The rest of us break into a fit of laughter, Eden rolling her eyes as I clutch Stella's arm. Then, naturally, we spend a few minutes discussing relative dick sizes. When the topic inevitably circles back to Luca, I expertly avoid the subject by calling us an Uber.

It's not long before we arrive at the Triangle Lounge. The four of us girls shuffle inside together, hands clasped in a tight chain as we weave through the crowd. This bar has a nightclub-type vibe, with glowing lights and dancing and off-the-wall music.

Thankfully, it doesn't take too long to spot Nate's perfect head of curls. Perhaps it's because he's surrounded by a group of tall, muscular baseball players. Or maybe it's because he's in the midst of laughter, head thrown back as his shoulders shake.

When he spots me, I swear something in his eyes lights up. "Harper!" he shouts, waving me over.

Once I slide in next to him, it takes a few minutes to get our introductions out of the way. Fortunately, I've already met most of the baseball players myself, but Nate does his due diligence by introducing them to my friends. Once we've all made the initial obligatory small talk, my friends break off to grab drinks at the bar.

And *his* friends, well, they all seem to slowly disappear.

"Can I get you a drink?" he asks, gaze drifting down to my empty hands.

"Good idea." I flash him a grateful smile. "I'll come with you."

Without warning, he cups his palm around mine, deftly navigating us through the crowd. The pads of his fingers are rough, but the feeling of his hand is warm and gentle and comforting. Before I realize it, we're standing at the end of the bar together. He orders us a few beers on tap, letting my hand slip from his as he reaches for his wallet.

He passes me a pint, guiding us to a nearby cocktail table. "You look great tonight."

"Thank you." I take a sip from my glass, stifling a wince as I do. The beer has a sour, tangy taste that sizzles on the tip of my tongue. It's not that I don't like it, necessarily. It's just not something I would've typically ordered myself. "Sorry that it's not my uniform again."

"It's all good." He chuckles, tipping back his own beer. "You look hot in anything."

"Oh, thanks. You, uh, you too."

I blush. He laughs. And then he asks me about my friends: where we live, how we met, and what we usually like to do on the weekends. He tells me that he lives at the baseball house and that he absolutely loves it. He says he doesn't know what he'll do when they all graduate, cracking jokes about the profound lack of communal living in the major leagues.

And by the time he's done, we've both managed to finish every last sip of our beers.

"You want a refill?" he asks, tapping my empty glass.

I muster up a single ounce of courage, glancing toward my friends on the dance floor. "Actually, would you maybe want to dance?"

"I'd love to."

This time, I'm the one that takes his hand, fingers weaving together as we slide into the middle of the room. My arms slowly snake around his neck, his hands settling somewhere between my ass and my waist. Our hips slot together. As I press against him, that self-assured smile slips from his lips.

There's an unmistakable heat behind his eyes now. It doesn't take long for his grip to tighten around me. The rough pads of his thumbs caress a small sliver of exposed skin, stroking me. "You know, I've thought about touching you since that first time I saw you on the beach."

"How come you never approached me?" I murmur, tangling my fingers into the soft curls at the nape of his neck.

"You're sweet, Harps. Soft," he adds, gripping my hips. "I'm usually not."

I press even closer. "Mm, you're not . . . you're not into being sweet?"

His head dips, the corner of his lips tugging into a smirk. "No, but I can be."

"Oh?"

"Yeah." One hand moves from my hip, trailing up the side of my body until he's caressing my jaw. "I'm gonna kiss you now."

"Okay," I whisper, neck tilted back as he gazes down at me.

He leans forward, and his lips press against mine, soft and sweet at first. The man is true to his word. But then his fingers tightly grip my hips, pressing us together as he caresses my tongue with his. He's sucking, kneading, pulling me in.

I can undoubtedly feel the bulge in his jeans throbbing through my skirt.

The feeling is . . . nice. More than nice, I guess, considering there's a slow, steady fluttering in the pit of my stomach. I'm definitely turned on. And I'd like to hook up with him tonight, especially since it's been a hot minute for me. Or two.

But after we inevitably come up for air, I make an excuse to rejoin our crowd of friends.

Nate and I spend the rest of the night innocently flirting and drinking and decidedly *not* making out again. He does kiss me once more, a quick peck, before the four of us girls stuff ourselves into another Uber.

I probably would've invited him back to my place, but I have an early morning shift at Amber Isle.

Plus, that wasn't even a real date, not that you need to wait for an actual date to hook up with someone. I don't subscribe to the antiquated "third date" rule or anything. When it comes to consenting adults, we should be free to jump each other's bones whenever the feeling strikes.

I guess, for some reason or another, tonight simply wasn't our night. But maybe next weekend will be. Nate invited me out again, so I suppose you could consider our first pseudo-date a real success.

By the time my head hits the pillow, my phone lights up with an Instagram notification. It's a follower request from @nategundy. I gleefully hit Accept and follow him right back.

Yeah, I'd say tonight was a definite success.

Chapter Twelve
LUCA

Sunday mornings at the pier are usually peaceful, especially in this late-summer heat. They're quiet, little slices of life, interrupted only by the calm sounds of the ocean and the pattering of footsteps ticking along the sand.

There are no families splashing in the water, no college students playing beach volleyball, and the sunrise surfers have already cleared out. There's still a lifeguard on post, though, on the off chance that some straggler might take a dip.

It's my favorite day to work.

There's a distinct lack of pointless interruptions and irritating noises. It's just me and this big empty pier, sorting fishing gear and minding my own business. At this pace, I could finish cleaning and prepping an entire stock of loaner rods in under an hour.

But as I tack a new photo onto the catch board, I'm distracted by the sound of my own name. Someone's eagerly calling for me in the distance, their voice growing louder with the sound of their impending footsteps.

"Luca!" Harper's chipper voice knocks me out of my trance. She's bouncing on her heels as she approaches, a wide-lipped grin pulling at her features.

"Hi, Harper," I murmur, soaking in her appearance. Her golden-brown hair hangs in wet, beachy strands that drip across the swell of her chest. Her damp suit is skintight and cherry red, clinging to her body and tucked beneath a set of tiny draw-string shorts. "You're wet."

"I went for a swim before my shift." She takes a few deep breaths, gesturing toward the open ocean. "It's so nice out there this morning."

"Seems like it'd be cold."

"It was surprisingly warm." Her flushed cheeks settle into a softer form of her signature smile. "How was your knee after the game? I was worried about you last night, especially because I couldn't watch in real time."

"That's right. You were out last night." I clear my throat, tucking a few more photographs onto the board. "Your big date with *Nate Gunderson*."

"It wasn't really a date," she clarifies, bouncing up to my side. "And can you not say his name so loudly, please?"

"You afraid that old couple's gonna hear me?" I tease, nodding about a hundred yards down the beach. "Or are you concerned about the seagulls?"

She snorts, eyes flashing with a hint of genuine surprise. "You really *are* obsessed with seagulls."

"You know what?" I fold my arms over my chest, turning away from the catch board to face her full-on. "Just for that, I'm not gonna tell you how our game went."

"Oh no, please tell me." She chuckles softly, planting both hands on her hips. "I'm dying to know. You don't look like you're in any pain right now, so I guess that's a good sign."

"The game went fine. I think our emergency session really helped."

There's a quick sigh of relief. "Oh, that's so good to hear because—"

"Uh, sorry," I cut her off, the incessant buzzing from my pocket serving as an unwelcome distraction. I take a subtle peek, noticing my best friend's name flashing across the screen. "I need to take this call."

"Oh, no worries." She shrugs, waving and smiling as I press the phone to my ear. "I'll see you later, Luca."

My gaze follows along as she bops back to the lifeguard stand. There's a definite pep in her step this morning. She seems more high-spirited than normal—refreshed—and she was apparently worried about me last night.

While Harper was on her date with Nate Gunderson, she couldn't help but worry about my performance in the game. Or she was worried about my knee, at the very least.

That would make sense, considering she has a personal stake in my recovery.

Of course.

"Hey, man," I mutter into the phone, attempting to keep the frustration from my voice. "Everything okay?"

"What?" Danny releases a derisive snort. "I can't call you if it's not Tuesday at six o'clock?"

"Nah, it's not that. It's just . . . what's up, Danny?"

"I'm thinking about coming down to visit this weekend." There's an air of awkwardness in his tone. "Our team has a bye week. Thought we could grab dinner or something Saturday night."

"We're playing the Eagles on Saturday."

"Fuck, that's right." I pin my cell phone against my shoulder, finishing up the catch board as he jabbers on. "What about Friday? We're only gonna be back for two nights."

A muscle in my jaw ticks. "We?"

"Oh, yeah. I'm bringing Sofia with me," he cautiously admits. "It's just, she hasn't been back much since her parents moved to Greece."

"Right."

"I mean, you already knew that. Sorry," he manages to spit out. "It's uh, she's just gonna stay with my folks while we have dinner. If that's fine?"

There's a deep pit forming in my stomach. The contents of my breakfast threaten to spew out, but I take a few seconds to swallow them back.

"She should come with us."

A long, piercing silence follows my suggestion. "What?"

"Yeah, she should come. We can make it a double date." My words are nonchalant, but there may be a hive or two that's developed on the back of my neck. "I've been wanting you to meet Harper anyway."

"Yeah?"

"Yeah," I confirm.

"Alright, Luc. That sounds great." His words are eager, rushed as he carries on. "And what about Saturday before the game—could you spare a few minutes to swing by your parents' place? I'd like to say hi to the fam, especially Giorgie."

I massage my left temple. "I don't know that I'll have time for that."

"Ah, come on," he urges. "When was the last time you saw them all in person?"

"Yeah, it *has* been a while," I admit, the guilt settling deep inside my chest. "But I've been busy as hell."

"No worries, I guess I can catch them next visit. Are they at least going to your game, then?"

"No." This time, I don't bother to restrain my frustration. "You know my parents can't bring Giorgie to the games. She's not big on crowds. All the noise and people."

"Damn, I thought she might have grown out of that by now."

If I wasn't already irritated beyond recognition, his offhand comment would've thrown me over the edge. "Is that a joke?"

"No, man, I'm sorry." He swears under his breath. "That wasn't a joke . . . don't know why I said that."

I pinch the bridge of my nose. "Giorgie's perfect the way she is."

"I know." He speaks slowly, carefully selecting his next words to keep my temper in check. "I wouldn't want to change anything about her, you know that. Your family's my family."

"I've gotta get going, anyway. I'm actually at work right now, so we'll just see you Friday."

"Friday, it is." There's a quick pause, then, "Love you, man."

"See ya." I end the call, stuffing my cell phone into my back pocket. Now I'm frustrated with both myself and with Danny —me for making that shithead suggestion and him for making that shithead comment.

I scrub both hands across my forehead and tug at the ends of my hair. Good going, Luca. Now I'm stuck spending Friday night with both my fake girlfriend and my ex-girlfriend.

It's a two-in-one special.

THERE's nothing like the heady anticipation of asking your fake sort-of girlfriend on a fake sort-of date.

I couldn't bring myself to approach Harper directly after that phone call, so I waited. It's only been two days, but Danny's already given me three reminders about our upcoming rendezvous: two texts and one scheduled phone call.

My best friend is fucking eager, that's for sure. And I'm . . . rightfully freaking out. I haven't asked a girl out on a first date since I was seventeen years old. Not that this is an actual date, but the stakes are just as monumental.

If Harper says no, if she says it's not part of our deal, then I'll be spending my Friday night looking like a lonely asshole. I'll be forced to suffer through an entire evening with the loved-up couple because there's no way I'm telling Danny to uninvite his girlfriend. Not at this point.

That would make it seem like I still care when I really don't.

I mean, I *hardly* do.

Harper answers her front door at the first sound of my knocking. Her face lights up with that happy-go-lucky smile, we exchange a quick greeting, and she guides us back toward her bedroom. I'm sweating bullets as I trail behind her, even though I've thrown on a thin T-shirt and athletic shorts tonight.

I decided not to bother with the jeans this time, considering my pants are coming off in a matter of minutes. As soon as she closes her bedroom door, I strip down to my boxers and settle onto her mattress.

She blinks a few times in my direction, lips curling in subtle amusement. "Someone's eager to get started."

"Yeah, that's me." I awkwardly chuckle, heat warming the back of my neck.

"Great, I thought we could add in some more resistance exercises tonight. I brought some light ankle weights and these exercise bands." She's a ball of excited energy, bouncing on her feet as she gathers up the equipment. "I think you might be up for the challenge."

"Okay." My eyes squeeze shut, word vomit spilling out before I can restrain it. "Will you go out with me on Friday night? On a date?"

She's quiet for a few long moments, during which I spend

every painstaking second contemplating my own existence. When she finally opens her mouth, all that comes out is a very confused "Umm . . ."

"Not a real date," I quickly clarify, pressing my sweat-damp palms against my thighs. "My best friend is coming into town with his girlfriend, and he wants to meet you. I told him I'd ask, but if you already have plans or you think it's too—"

"I kinda do have plans," she cuts in, a strange quirk to her brow. "I'm supposed to meet Nate for drinks again."

"Right, *Nate*." I clear my throat, spine stiff as I perch on the edge of her bed. "Just thought I'd ask. No worries. We should get started, though."

"That's not what I meant." She settles into the desk chair, her gaze soft as she assesses me. "I can always reschedule with Nate. I mean, we can do drinks anytime. You're my friend, Luca. If you need me on Friday, then I'm coming with you."

"Yeah?"

"Duh." She laughs, and it's a soft, musical sound that softens my rigid posture. "I think it sounds fun. What's your bestie like?"

"My *bestie*?" I snort, rubbing some tension out of my shoulder. "He's a decent guy. We've been friends for ages."

"But he doesn't live here?"

"He goes to Dayton. He's there on a D1 scholarship."

She tilts her head, brows drawn back together in confusion. "If he doesn't go to Coastal and he doesn't play for the Ospreys, why'd you lie to him about us?"

My brain scrambles to generate a believable excuse, something that sounds a lot better than the truth. First, that I'm a desperate fool. And second, that I wanted to show my best friend and my ex that I don't give a fuck about their relationship.

That I've moved on to greener pastures.

"I told you it was between us," I carefully admit my partial truth. "I made you lie to your friends, and I don't do double standards."

"I guess that makes sense." She leans forward in her chair, elbows propped on her knees as our eyes meet. "So how are we gonna do this?"

"What do you mean?"

"You know you have to at least pretend to like me on Friday, right?"

My gaze trails across her face, taking note of the open vulnerability in her features. She's joking with me now, but there's an underlying sense of insecurity behind her words. "I do like you."

Her lips curve with the hint of a smile, a dusting of peach coloring her cheeks. "You do?"

"Is it not obvious?"

"I mean, I thought we might be friends now. But I wasn't one hundred percent sure how you felt, 'cause you're always so ..."

"Unfriendly?"

She taps her fingers against her chin, resting it in the palm of her hands. "Broody, contemplative, private."

"Well, I like you, Harper," I repeat, the words rolling easily off my tongue. "There, now you don't have to doubt it. You're one of the few people at this school I actually enjoy being around."

That earns me another blush, a hint of warmth camouflaging her freckles. "I like you, too, Luca."

"Well, good, then." My chest feels lighter, weightless now that she's officially agreed to be my date. "We shouldn't have any trouble faking it."

"Except for the physical part, right?"

"What?"

"How much PDA do you like to do when you're in a relationship?" she asks, that weightless feeling suddenly disappearing. My chest is tight again, heart pattering against my breastbone. "Just so I know how much to touch you on Friday."

"We don't . . . I mean, none?" I sputter, subtly pushing against my sternum. "Like you said before, I'm a private person. We don't need to worry about how much to touch each other in front of my friend and his girlfriend."

"Not even holding hands? Or, like, a quick kiss on the cheek?"

"Maybe . . . maybe the hand thing," I relent. It doesn't seem like a terrible idea, holding hands with Harper in front of Danny and Sofia. I'm sure they'll be doing much more than that themselves. "I don't know, can we just play it by ear?"

"Sure, Luca," she says brightly, popping up from her seat and nudging me on the shoulder. "Friday night. Me and you, playin' it by ear."

"Great."

"Enough chitchat." She rubs her hands together, grabbing a few bands and gesturing for me to lie down. "Let's get to work."

I shake my head, attempting to relax my erratic heartbeat. This is what I'm here for—relaxation, rejuvenation, and recovery. Harper's my wellness coach, my physical therapist, my fake girlfriend, and I guess now . . . one of my only friends outside of Daniel.

And she already touches me all the fucking time, so that was a fairly innocent question. There's no reason, none at all, that it should've rattled me down to my bones.

Chapter Thirteen

It's BEEN ages since I've slipped into something this fancy. In fact, I can't recall the last time I wore this tight satin dress or these little black heels. I even curled my hair and spent more than ten minutes on my makeup. Sure, it's only some extra lipstick and eyeliner, but I swear I feel like a whole new woman.

I may be anxious as hell for this fake date—for another evening filled with lies—but at least I'll look good while we're at it.

"Are you okay?" I ask Luca, taking note of his stiff posture. His grip on the steering wheel is tight, knuckles blanching a stark white as we pull into the lot behind the restaurant.

"I'm fine," he says, as expected.

"Are you sure?" I try again, attempting to break through his aloof outer shell. I know he's not fine because he's been jittery and distant the entire half-hour drive. "Because I'm feeling pretty nervous myself."

He cuts the engine and shoves the keys into the pocket of his black trousers.

"Why?" he asks without turning to face me.

"I'm about to meet someone important to you, plus I have to lie straight to their face."

"Harper, if you don't want to do this . . . I can take you

home right now." His fingers clench against the sides of his thighs, eyes squeezing shut as he pastes on a phony half-smile. "I'll just tell them you weren't feeling well."

"No, no, it's not that," I reassure him, reaching for my door handle. "I just . . . you know I'm not the best liar."

"Just be yourself. That's all I need from you tonight."

His words instantly relieve some of the tension bubbling in my gut. Be myself? I guess I can manage that.

"Okay."

He pushes his door open, walking stiffly around to the passenger side. When he pulls open my door next, I swing my legs out and keep my knees clenched together, hoping to God I don't flash him in the process.

"If they ask us for any details, just leave it to me." He stands beside me, brushing out the wrinkles in his button-up shirt.

"I can do that."

He finally spares me more than just a quick glance, eyes subtly shifting over my outfit. His gaze doesn't linger too long, but I think I notice at least a single spark of appreciation. "Okay, you ready, then?"

My fingers tap against the sides of my thighs, that nervous energy returning in full force. "Maybe we should do that hand-holding thing we talked about?"

He pauses for a beat, taking a step or two closer until we're standing side by side. Without another word, his hand slides into mine, strong fingers interweaving through my slender ones.

I smile up at him, an immediate sense of comfort warming me from the inside out. "Okay, now I'm ready."

As we enter the restaurant, hand in hand, I spot a young couple seated in a booth directly across from the entrance. I assume they must be who we're meeting since Luca's gaze inconspicuously narrows in that direction. His grip on my hand tightens, his left thumb pressing sharply against my trapezium bone. I can almost hear the first joint pop before I'm wincing in pain.

"Ouch," I whisper-shout, wiggling my arm in some sort of distress signal.

His vise grip loosens, but he keeps ahold of my hand. "Sorry."

His fingers flex twice before he gently rubs his thumb against the outside of mine. It's a silent form of apology that seems to soothe the sudden jolt of pain.

After a few quick words with the hostess, we maneuver toward the back booth together. The two lovebirds are seated on the same side, heads ducked as they whisper and laugh and sneak in a kiss or two. It's sweet, really. Luca's best friend and his girlfriend seem like they're so in love, at least from a distance.

Once we reach the table, both of their heads abruptly shoot up. It's as if they were lost in their own little world and we've somehow interrupted. When our eyes connect, there's an awkward hint of tension that fills the room.

They've been staring at us for a beat too long, wide-eyed and silent, as I attempt a casual smile. Luca's friend shakes his head, a grin of his own finally taking hold. He hastily scoots away from his girlfriend, sliding out of the booth to wrap both arms around us.

The hug is short-lived, but he squeezes us tightly, patting both of our shoulders before he steps back. I've never seen a man so excited to meet his friend's newest fling.

"Danny, Sofia." Luca tosses a quick nod in her direction. "This is my Harper."

"It's nice to meet you both," I offer, finally dropping Luca's hand.

Danny reclaims his seat, and we join them in the booth. Now that Sofia's sitting directly across from me, it's nearly impossible to ignore her beauty. She has striking features—a perfectly angular nose, light brown skin that seems to glow, and long, dark hair that sits in waves across her shoulders.

There are a few more friendly introductions before our server appears. Luca and I both order different iterations of some fancy burger, while Sofia and Danny opt to share a pasta dish. Apparently, it's some cutesy tradition they co-opted during their summer abroad together.

I think it's sweet, mostly because it reminds me of *Lady and the Tramp*.

"Luca mentioned that you've been friends since pre-K," I say, directing my attention toward Danny. "I think that's really cool."

"That's right." Danny chuckles, a smirk tugging at the corner of his lips. "And now he's stuck with me for the rest of his life."

I shift my attention toward Sofia, nodding between her and her boyfriend. "And how did the two of you meet?"

"Actually, the three of us have all been friends since middle school," Sofia chimes in, a sudden quirk to her brow. She looks confused, unsettled as she bites down on her full bottom lip.

"Oh, wow," I murmur, impressed. "So are you high school sweethearts, then, or did that part come later?"

"No, we, uh . . . we didn't get together until sophomore year of college."

"I think that's so sweet," I reassure her with a soft smile. "Your relationship's built on the foundation of a strong friendship."

"Yeah." Danny coughs into his fist, quickly gulping down a drink of water.

Luca awkwardly clears his throat beside me. All three of them seem stiff now, somehow uncomfortable with the current topic, so I opt to change course.

"So, um, you two go to Dayton?" I ask, shifting in my seat until my thigh makes contact with Luca's. It grounds me a little bit to know that we're physically connected. "How's that?"

"We love it," Danny says, instantly perking up. "I wish Luc was able to join us there, but it seems like he's pretty happy at Coastal these days. Especially since he met you."

"Oh, you were supposed to go to Dayton?" I nudge Luca with my elbow, tilting my head to gauge his expression. "You never mentioned that."

"Oh, yeah." He shrugs, a distinct lack of emotion on his face. "I was planning on it a long time ago."

"But you changed your mind?"

"They actually gave away his scholarship," Danny cuts in after a stilted pause. "It was pretty fucked-up when it all went down. I mean, he was only, like, one day late on putting down his deposit. Right, Luc?"

"Right," Luca confirms, jaw tight.

"Oh man, that really sucks," I say, attempting to provide him some comfort with my words. My hand itches to rest on his knee, to press a soft squeeze against his thigh, but I fold my hands together in my lap instead. Just because physical touch gives me reassurance, it doesn't mean it's the same for Luca. "I guess, selfishly, I'm happy you ended up at Coastal."

"It worked out the best for everyone, didn't it?" He mutters the question to no one, but his gaze seems to be pinpointed on Sofia. I glance from Luca's stony expression to Sofia's soft blush to Danny's obvious embarrassment.

There's clearly some unspoken tension between these three. Honestly, I'm starting to regret my decision to join Luca tonight. I canceled on Nate because I wanted to help my friend. But now, I'm the odd one out, wading through a decade of unresolved issues that don't belong to me.

"Excuse me," I murmur, sliding out of the booth. "I'm just gonna go freshen up."

As I make my way toward the back of the restaurant, my heels click loudly against the linoleum. My body is jittering, hands shaking as I turn the lock on the restroom door.

I lean against the back wall, the cool tile pressing into my neck and shoulders. It's alerting at first, but then it works as I intended. All my attention is suddenly refocused on the sensation. It's uncomfortable, but it rewires my chaotic thoughts.

I can finally stop fretting over all the ways I've blundered tonight. It's not even my fault, considering I have no clue what's got them all in a funk. If I said the wrong thing, then that's on Luca.

He should've warned me.

Once I'm calm, I slowly push myself away from the wall. Sighing, I turn the faucet to its warmest setting, scrubbing my hands and forearms under the steaming water.

When I finally finish up, Luca's waiting for me in the hallway, his back pressed against the adjacent wall.

"You okay?" he asks, gaze locked onto the heated, pink blotches that decorate my arms.

"I should be asking *you* that question, don't you think?"

He schools his expression. "I'm fine."

"Really?" I cross both arms over my chest, brows raised in disbelief. "Because I feel like there's some big, unspoken secret that I'm not a part of. Why is everyone so tense tonight?"

He releases a heavy sigh, pinching the bridge of his nose. "Probably because Sofia's my ex."

"What?"

"We dated first, before she and Danny got together," he quietly explains, scrubbing a hand through his hair. "Two years in high school, then we broke up during our first year of college. We tried the long-distance thing, and it didn't work."

"Why didn't you tell me this before?" I toss my hands up, frantically glancing toward our booth. "I just sat out there and asked them all those embarrassing questions."

"You're right, I should've told you."

"Luca . . ."

He winces, a clear apology in his eyes. "I'm sorry."

"How did those two even end up together?"

His gaze shifts from my face to a spot on the wall behind me. "We should probably get back to the table."

"So you're just not gonna tell me?"

"Not tonight," he urges, stepping a fraction of an inch closer. "Not here. I promise to tell you some other time, okay?"

"Did you ask me to come here because you wanted to make your ex jealous?"

His eyes meet mine. "No."

"Are you sure about that?"

"It's not about jealousy." His lips purse together as he wrestles with the truth. "I guess, I just, I wanted them to know that I've moved on. That I don't care that they're together anymore so Danny can stop treating me like I'm some sort of wounded animal in a cage."

"Yeah?"

He gives me one sheepish nod, his posture finally relaxing as if he's been holding back these feelings all night. I suppose I could hold a grudge, but I know this wasn't intentional.

I didn't ask, so he didn't tell.

In Luca's mind, it's as simple as that. Plus, I think he's a little embarrassed by the truth. No matter what happened between them in the past, his best friend is now dating his high school sweetheart. That shit has to hurt.

"Then we'll have to do a better job of proving it," I say earnestly.

It's true. I want to help Luca because that's what I'm here for. If we have to amp up the lovey-dovey stuff, then that's what we'll do.

"You're not upset?"

"I wish you'd been honest with me from the start, but I'm here for you. And I think we can do better than this." I link our hands together in a silent form of solidarity. "You do have to let me touch you, though."

He chuckles, gently squeezing my hand. "Whatever you need."

"And you also have to stop acting like you're constipated."

There's a shocked snort of laughter, followed by a contented half-smile. "I might be able to do that."

I tug him behind me as we weave through the restaurant. Once we slide back into our seats, I release my grip on his hand, shooting an apologetic smile across the booth. "Sorry we took so long. He just won't keep his hands off me."

Danny's uneasy smile melts into an ear-splitting grin. "Oh, that doesn't sound like the Luc we know."

"Hm, he's always been like this with me." I lean against his side, pressing a gentle squeeze to his upper arm. "Right, baby?"

"Uh-huh," he murmurs, visibly flustered. "Harper just, uh, she brings out a different side of me, I guess."

"That's so sweet," Sofia chimes in. "Your parents must really love her, huh?"

"Oh, they don't, uh—we haven't—"

"You *have* met Gia and Greg, right?" Sofia asks, one perfect brow quirked in my direction. "They're the absolute best."

"She hasn't met the whole family yet, actually," Luca cuts in, patting the back of my hand. "Just, er, we've just had dinner with Taylor so far."

"Oh my gosh." Sofia's eyes light up, her tone filled with excitement. "So you haven't met the twins or Elio yet, either? They're all just so funny. And little Giorgie—she's gotta be, what, at least seven years old by now?"

"She is," Luca confirms.

"Aw, and does she still call you Lucky?"

"Yes."

"I miss her so much. So does Danny. He talks about your family all the time." Sofia nudges her boyfriend. "Right, babe?"

"Yeah." Danny nods his agreement. "We both miss them."

"Right," Luca murmurs. I can sense another oncoming flash of irritation. This time, I don't hesitate to curve my palm around his thigh, urging him to mask his temper. "Well, my family can't wait to meet Harper. I talk about *her* all the time."

The couple is quiet, seemingly stunned by his response.

"You two seem like a great match," Danny says, finally managing to find the right words. He's being sincere, but it comes out as slightly condescending. "We're so happy for you, Luc."

Our attempts at chitchat finally die out, replaced by the sounds of quiet chewing as we enjoy our meals. I take every opportunity to touch Luca during this time—to act like a truly domesticated couple—just to rub it in their faces.

I swipe the corner of his lip with a napkin. I hold his hand on top of the table. I lean against his shoulder and take a bite off his plate. And to top it all off, I take a long sip from his fresh beer, stealing the thin layer of foam. We both ordered the same type of ale anyway—something smooth, sweet, and fruity.

I usually wouldn't be so over-the-top, but the circumstances have propelled me into action. It's too difficult to give these two the benefit of the doubt. Not after what they've done to Luca. Not after how they've made him feel.

By the time we finish up our dinner, it's nearly nine o'clock. The four of us shuffle out of the restaurant together, lingering under the awning as we say our goodbyes.

Sofia pulls Luca aside, right out of earshot, as she wraps her arms around him. She leans onto her tiptoes and whispers *something* into his ear. It may be painstakingly difficult, but I manage to tear my prying eyes away to focus on her boyfriend beside me.

"I'm so glad we all got to do this tonight," Danny says, pulling me into a friendly side-hug.

"Me too."

"I hope we can come back and visit sometime soon," he says eagerly, balancing on the back of his heels. "Maybe you could help convince Luc to let us visit the fam?"

I raise one brow. "If he wants to do that."

"Right, yeah, of course." Danny nods his head emphatically, as if I simply misunderstood his meaning. "He seems really happy, you know?"

"We both are."

"I'm glad to hear that."

It's not long before the ex-couple rejoins us. Danny gives his friend the ultimate bro-hug, and Sofia wraps me up in her slender arms. They're very touchy-feely people, these two, at least in comparison to Luca. It's usually my MO, but something about all this hugging tonight is making me cringe.

While I'm lost in my own head, Sofia takes that as her cue to whisper some nonsense into my ear. "Treat him right," she says, and I almost spit up my entire dinner on her designer dress.

As we break apart, Danny and Sofia head across the street while Luca and I wander toward the back of the building. I'm not sure why, or who initiated it this time, but we're holding hands as we walk through the parking lot.

"Well, that was really something," I murmur, cutting the silence.

"Thank you for that," Luca says, squeezing my hand as we stand in front of his car. "For tonight. For everything."

I squeeze back. "What are friends for?"

"Yeah."

"Hey, um, did you know that it's only nine o'clock?" I prompt, unsure of where I'm headed with this. Maybe I could ask him to come over tonight, to watch a movie or something, or maybe we could even get a drink downtown.

Just as friends, to debrief this wild night.

Before I can offer up a useful suggestion, he drops my hand and takes a step back. "Right, I forgot you had plans with Nate. Did you want me to drop you off at the bar or something?"

"Oh," I sputter, confused.

I honestly had forgotten about my second pseudo-date with Nate. Plus, I already canceled on him at the last minute, so I'm not even sure the offer still stands.

But maybe I should try and honor my original plans? At least, Luca seems to think I should.

"Yeah, um, okay," I murmur, moving toward the passenger door. "Thank you."

"What are friends for?"

Chapter Fourteen
LUCA

My headlights illuminate the bay window as I pull into our driveway. Bentley is waiting for me there with his tail wagging and tongue flailing as he perches on the back of the couch.

He always greets me as though it's been years since I've last seen him. That excitement—his eager anticipation—makes me feel a little better after this disaster of a night. At least Harper helped make this experience bearable for me.

She willingly lied her ass off to make me look better. She went above and beyond to bridge the awkward gap between us, pushing this false narrative I'd created. And then, after the charade was finally over, she let me thread my fingers through hers in the back parking lot, unaware that she was holding my last thread of patience together.

After listening to Sofia's parting words—that endless string of bullshit she whispered into my ear—I nearly snapped. And now, I'm grateful this fucking night is over.

As I clamber out of the car, awkwardly shuffling my stiff leg in the footwell, my phone buzzes in my back pocket. There's an incoming call from Harper, even though I only dropped her off at the bar fifteen minutes ago.

"Harper?" I murmur, pressing the phone to my ear. "Everything okay?"

"Everything's fine." Her voice is uncharacteristically quiet, somewhat somber as she continues. "I was just wondering, um, are you pretty far away already?"

I gently shut myself back into the car, perking up in the driver's seat. "Did you need me to pick you up?"

"Only if you aren't too far. I just . . . I could probably call an Uber, so—"

"I'll come and get you," I cut in, turning the key in my ignition. "I'm just around the corner anyway."

"Okay, thank you."

"Did you have trouble finding Nate?" I ask, pressing the speakerphone button and docking my phone into the dash mount.

"No, no," she mutters, voice low. "I found him just fine."

"Okay." I scrub a confused hand across my left temple, rubbing out the lingering frustration from earlier. "I'll see you in less than ten minutes, alright? I'll pull up to the front."

"See you soon."

Once we end the call, it takes me seven minutes to make it back to the Triangle Lounge. Harper's waiting alone out front, arms crossed over her chest, shivering in her tiny black dress and heels. She's not necessarily frowning, but she still doesn't look like her usual happy-go-lucky self.

As soon as I pull over, she scrambles toward the passenger door and stuffs herself inside. "Thank you for coming back for me," she mumbles, readjusting as she pulls the seat belt across her lap.

My brows furrow in confusion, unsettled by her sudden change in demeanor. "Are you okay?"

"Yeah, I'm okay." She manages to muster a smile, but it doesn't quite reach her eyes.

I take a deep breath, flipping my turn signal as I pull back onto the main road. We sit in silence for a good thirty seconds before I start spitting out questions.

"Was it Nate? Did he do something to hurt you?"

Out of the corner of my eye, I catch her twisting a strand of hair between her fingers, anxiously twirling and pulling it taut. "Not intentionally, I don't think."

My fingers clench against the steering wheel. "What did he do?"

"Well," she sighs, dropping her hands to her lap, "when I first walked into the bar, he wasn't too hard to find. Unfortunately, he already had his hands full."

"What does that mean?"

"He was dancing with some girl I didn't recognize. They were kissing, touching, um, I don't know, having sex on the dance floor, essentially." She laughs, but it's a humorless, lifeless sort of sound.

"You've got to be fucking kidding me."

"It's not a big deal, really." She lifts one shoulder in a careless shrug, fingers drumming against her lap. "I thought we kinda liked each other, but it's not like he owes me anything. I guess it just wasn't meant to be."

"Not a big deal? Are you kidding?"

"No?"

"Harper, he asked you to come out with him tonight. You took a rain check, sure." A muscle in my jaw ticks, irritation crawling up my spine. "But he told you to come out if you changed your fucking mind, didn't he?"

"He did."

"So you ended up changing your mind." I shake my head, gritting my teeth. "You come out to see him, yet he decides to stick his tongue down some other girl's throat. Fucking asshole."

"It's okay, Luca." Her hand comes to rest against my shoulder, reining in my temper. "We didn't know each other that well, anyway."

"You've had a crush on him for a long time, Harper." I pull up to the stoplight, glancing to my right until our eyes connect. "You fucking switched your class assignment to get closer to the guy. What are you even talking about?"

She nibbles on her bottom lip. "It was just a silly crush. I only know, like, three things about him at this point."

"Is one of them that he's a fucking dickhead?"

"Noo." She drags out the word, half suppressing a snort. "I know that he's handsome, he likes to play sports, and he really likes it when I wear my lifeguard uniform."

"Wow, what a well-rounded guy."

"You really don't like him, do you?"

"No, I don't, especially not after tonight. And you shouldn't, either." I turn one last sharp corner, angling into the parking space in front of her apartment complex. "He doesn't fucking deserve you."

We both turn quiet as we sit together in the lot. It's a comfortable sort of silence, I guess, one that's filled only by the sounds of my idling engine.

When she finally decides to speak, her voice is cheerful again. "Do you want to go grab some ice cream?" she asks with that light and airy tone I've come to expect.

"What?"

"Ice cream? Do you want some?" Her lips curve into a wide grin. "There's this great place not too far from here. They're open late."

"You want to go out for ice cream? Right now?"

"Yeah, I do." She nudges me with her elbow. "I think we both deserve it after the night we've had, don't you?"

My brow furrows in confusion, but I nod my agreement nonetheless. "Alright, let's go."

I shift out of park, following her wayward directions to the Golden Cone, Harper's favorite ice cream shop. It's convenient because it's only five blocks from her apartment, and they happen to have a drive-through window.

We both order plain chocolate ice cream, but Harper opts to top hers with gummy bears. Apparently, she likes it this way because it adds a splash of color. It's a disgusting combination, yet somehow, it makes sense to her.

It's all just sugar, anyway.

"Can I ask you a question?" she asks, mindlessly swirling her ice cream around.

We're sitting together in my car now, engine off, spoons scraping against paper bowls in the parking lot.

"Will you ask me even if I tell you not to?" I mutter, shoveling in a quick spoonful.

Damn. She was right. This ice cream *is* fucking delicious, so at least there's that.

"Yes."

"Then go right ahead."

"What did Sofia say to you?" she carefully asks, licking the edge of her spoon. "Before we left the restaurant tonight?"

My shoulders tense. "It honestly doesn't matter."

"Please, tell me," she pleads, unraveling my resolve with her puppy-dog stare. "You said you'd be more open about this stuff. Actually, you promised you would."

"She said—" I swallow hard. "She said sometimes she wishes we had never dated. That it would make it so much easier for us all just to be friends again."

Her eyes go wide, a gasp of air slipping through her lips. "She didn't."

"She did." I give her a tight-lipped smile. "Three years, Harper. I was with her for three fucking years, and she wishes it never happened?"

She drops her spoon into her bowl, body shifting to face me full-on. "I'm really sorry."

I take a deep breath, contemplating how much I want to share with Harper tonight. I've never really opened up about this shit before. I've told Taylor some, but there's only so much you can share with your older sister.

"You know," I murmur, throwing caution to the wind. "She's the only person I've ever been with."

"You mean . . ."

"Yes, Harper." I roll my eyes, one corner of my mouth tugging up. "I mean, she's the only woman I've ever had sex with."

"I knew there was something evil about her," she mutters, stabbing her spoon into her ice cream, jabbing at each individual gummy bear. "How could . . . how could she just betray you like that?"

"It was a long time ago. And while she might want to forget that we were ever together, I don't." I take another spoonful of my own ice cream, waiting for the chocolate to melt on my tongue. "I spent three years of my life with her. It didn't work out, but it still fucking happened."

"How did she even end up with your best friend in the first place?

"Freshman year, when she went off to Dayton, I guess we weren't doing so great. She told me that I wasn't 'providing for her emotionally.' I don't know, I thought everything was fine, but it wasn't."

She stabs another gummy bear. "So she just ended things?"

"She came to visit me near the end of the school year to tell me it was over." I wince, remembering that soul-crushing conversation. "But she and Danny didn't get together until months later. They grew closer after the breakup, I guess. And I didn't want to hold them back, so I gave him my blessing to go for it."

"But he knew how you felt?" she huffs the question, indignant. "That you weren't over her back then?"

"I didn't say that."

"You didn't have to."

"Yeah . . . yeah, he knew how I felt," I admit, scooping up the last bites of my dessert. "And now, two years later, things are still fucking awkward between us. That's what tonight was about, Harper. I just . . . I wanted to take a step in the right direction. Get some normalcy back in our friendship."

"Why are you fighting so hard to keep this friendship going, anyway?" she asks, stacking our empty containers together on the center console. "Danny, he just doesn't sound like the greatest friend."

"At times, he hasn't been. But I grew up with the kid." I run my fingers through my hair, pushing back the discomfort. "And he's a part of my family now, so I can't just let him go. I don't know if you've noticed, but I'm not really the greatest at making friends in the first place."

Her lip twitches. "You don't say?"

"He's always stuck up for me. He's a social guy—an extrovert—he could have left me in the dust a thousand times, but he never did."

Her brow crinkles, button nose scrunching. "What do you mean?"

"I mean, I got teased as a kid. I was quiet, or just kind of shy, I guess. I don't know, other kids thought I was standoffish or something. But Danny never gave a shit." My voice is sincere, steadfast as I attempt to affirm my best friend's loyalty. "He stood up for me, no questions asked."

Her eyes are soft, alight with interest. "Yeah?"

"Yeah," I confirm. "There was this one time when we were about nine years old. Some kid dumped water down my pants. He told all our classmates that I pissed myself on the playground. And you know what Danny did?"

She's smiling now, fingers absentmindedly running through the ends of her long, beachy hair. "Beat him up?"

"Nah, he poured water down his own pants. Told everyone he peed himself, too."

She breaks into a tiny fit of laughter. "Wow."

"Yeah, so there's that," I say, a chuckle of my own slipping out. "Danny and Sofia may be together now, but that guy will always be my best friend. And I can't blame him for this shit anymore. Sometimes, we can't choose who we fall in love with. It just happens . . . or so I've been told."

"Who knew you were such a romantic?"

"Hey, I've got layers," I say, feigning offense.

"Like a croissant."

"Sure, just like a croissant." I release a humorless snort, shifting in my seat as my gaze narrows in on the cup holder. "Hey, I, uh. I actually have something for you."

I fish out the tiny circular object, placing it in Harper's outstretched hand. She inspects it for a long moment, brows drawn together, bottom lip pulled between her teeth.

"What is it?" she finally asks, gazing up at me.

"It's a poker chip, from casino night at the Surfbreak," I explain, awkwardly scratching at the back of my neck. "I found it wedged between the slats on the pier. There's a—"

"Seagull on the back," she cuts me off, smiling wide, eyes crinkling at the corners as she flips it over.

"Yeah, I don't know." I lick my dry lips, one shoulder lifting in a casual shrug. "I saw it and thought of you."

"Really?" Her smile is contagious, eyes shining as her gaze darts back to meet mine.

"Uh, yeah," I mumble, a sudden tightness in my chest. I think I'm anxious or something, but there's no fucking reason for me to feel that way. "Now that you're holding it, I realize I've just given you a piece of literal garbage."

"No, no." She emphatically shakes her head, caressing the chip in the palm of her hand like it's some sort of precious object. "I love it."

"Yeah?" I nearly choke on the question. "We can toss it if you want. I just thought it was kind of funny. You know, uh, seagulls?"

"I'm keeping it," she declares, carefully tucking it into her purse.

My chest deflates, that anxious feeling settling in my gut. "Okay."

"You wanna know something?" Her hand slides against the side of my forearm, fingers curling until they make contact with my upturned palm.

"Hm?"

"She didn't deserve you, either," she says, thumb tapping mine. "Not by a long shot."

Chapter Fifteen

HARPER

THE FOUL SMELL OF SWEATY, male athletes and dirty gym socks permeates the air around me. Before last weekend, the weight room used to be a welcome reprieve. I looked forward to tallying reps and tailoring workouts each week, to building skills that would propel me toward my future career.

Now, I'm mildly irritated to be here.

Nate is sprawled across a weight bench on the other side of the room, his bar racked with three plates on each side. He's pumping his chest and slamming the weights around like some kind of wild animal. And I'm standing here, arms crossed, pretending not to notice him sneak glances in my direction.

I spend nearly two hours skirting around him, distracting myself with other players, and sucking up to my supervisor, Minh. Unfortunately, I can't escape Nate forever. Once training is over, he lingers around while the rest of his teammates clear out.

This week, I'm supposed to monitor their progress and present an alternative program to my class. As all forty-two players pile out, they leave their workout logs in a haphazard stack near the locker room entrance. Well, everyone except for Nate, who decides to personally hand-deliver his.

He approaches me with that familiar swagger in his step.

His expression is guarded, but there's a tight half-smile that curves his lips.

"Need some help getting these to your car?" he asks, lacking his typical suggestive tone.

"I'm good," I say softly, preoccupying my hands by tidying the stack. "Thank you, though."

His eyes narrow. "What's with the cold shoulder, Harps?"

I tap my fingers against the plastic binders, anxiously debating my response. Nate's unabashed question caught me off guard. But I guess he's chosen to take the straightforward route, so it's only fair that I meet him with the truth.

"I'm just wondering why you asked me out if you were planning on kissing someone else?"

"Seriously?" His expression slides into a frown. "You told me you had to bail. Understandable, sure, shit comes up. But then I find out you're on a double date with two linebackers?"

I wrinkle my nose. "What?"

"Some girl tagged you in a photo. I saw it before I even showed up at the Lounge."

"Oh," I murmur, my false bravado fading as he furrows his brow.

"Yeah." He jerks his binder forward, tossing it onto the stack I just straightened. "Probably should have told me you were dating Ötzi before I put my tongue in your mouth."

"We're not—it's not . . . I didn't mention it because we're not serious or anything."

"So, what, then?" He waves a dismissive hand, lips twisting into a mocking sneer. "You just wanted to bag football and baseball captains at the same time? Makin' your way through the NCAA roster?"

I rear back, irritation gnawing at my chest. "You're not being very nice."

"Yeah, well, I didn't realize that's what kind of girl you were."

I let my shoulders slump. "Then I guess we were both wrong about each other."

"Yeah."

My pulse pounds in my throat, aching to bite out a scathing retort. It's not my fault that Nate's clearly insecure. He can use that as an excuse to justify his behavior, but it's a waste of energy to argue with him now. So I flip around instead, gathering up the binders and tossing them into a rolling bin.

"Can you just leave?" I mutter, back turned in his direction.

"Shit, Harper . . . wait." He grasps ahold of my wrist, gently whirling me back around to face him. "I'm sorry for being a dick. It's just, the whole Ötzi thing is really throwing me off. If you two have something going on, then I should probably stay out of it."

"Yeah, I think that's for the best."

"Fuck, you must really think I'm an asshole now." His forehead creases with worry. "Don't you?"

I lift my shoulder in a half-shrug. Do I think Nate's a complete and total asshole? No, I can't make that decision yet. I try not to judge a person's character based on one anger-fueled encounter, but I still don't feel like nursing his bruised ego right now.

"Trust me, it's not about you." A shadow of doubt creeps over his face. "I'm just not interested in being the *other guy*. Been there, done that. I really did like you. Or do, I do like you."

"Okay," I say, rattled by his sudden attitude shift.

"Maybe if things don't work out with Ötzi, we could try this again?"

"Um, maybe," I say softly, even though operation Date Nate™ has already melted inside my brain, disappearing like an ice cube on a hot summer's day. "Look, I should probably finish collecting these binders. I have a lot of work to catalog tonight."

"Sure, okay." He scrubs one hand across the back of his neck, gaze sheepish as he retreats into the locker room. Before the door swings shut behind him, he shoots one last apologetic smile over his shoulder.

It's already been over a month since Luca first tore his MCL. Over the last few weeks, we've been slowly building his tolerance for resistive exercises. He's worked his way up to the heaviest black TheraBand that our department carries, and tonight, I've moved him on to weighted tubes.

I can tell he's been consistent with his home program, following through with his nightly stretching and massage routine. The thought makes me unbelievably proud. It's pretty rewarding to see all our hard work pay off like this.

"You're doing so well with the added resistance," I tell him, my smile stretching from ear to ear. "I think you'd be clear to go back to a full weighted routine soon."

He answers me with a noncommittal grunt. My head cocks to the side as he loops the red tube over his foot, grimacing while he pushes through his heel.

"What?" I ask, eyes playfully narrowed. "Aren't you excited?"

"Uh, yeah." With a flick of his wrist, he waves away the question. "That's great news."

I plop onto the mattress beside him. "Okay, what's your deal?"

"What deal?"

"That's great news," I mock, lowering my voice to match his gruff cadence. "Please, I can so easily tell when you're fibbing."

"I, uh, I may have already been doing my full weighted routine," he sheepishly admits, shoulders tense.

"You're joking."

"I have to, Harper." He pushes out a harsh breath, tensing as he flexes his ankle. "Coach has like . . . fucking eagle eyes or something. I have to pretend everything's normal for strength and conditioning days. But I've been squatting and deadlifting like half my weight otherwise. I just pick up the pace when he glances over."

"No wonder you keep tweaking your injury."

His gaze angles toward me. "You just said that I'm doing better."

"Yeah, but you could've been fully healed by now!" I shoot him a half-assed glare. "It's been five weeks since your initial injury, and you still haven't even hit fifty percent functional capacity."

"I'm functional enough," he says gruffly.

"Yeah, when you're not limping around on the pier or numbing yourself to death with ice after a game. I'd still say you need another three weeks of solid recovery training."

"Great, that's still a good month before the championship game." He carries on with his exercise, indifferent to my criticism. "I'll be back to one hundred percent by then."

"If you actually manage to listen to me in the meantime."

He reaches out, the sides of his fingertips brushing against my knee. "I listen to you."

"Partially," I murmur, unexpected heat staining my cheeks.

He tosses me a lopsided grin. "Are you . . . do you still have time to do this with me? I know you've got baseball training and work and—"

"I have time. Don't worry about that."

"It's just, I wouldn't rat you out or anything." His face falls the slightest bit, brows knit into a frown. "To the baseball guys. I'm not . . . I don't want you to feel like I'm still blackmailing you into helping me."

"No, I want to help you," I reassure him. "I like helping you."

"Okay. And I mean, now that you're not pursuing things with Nate anymore, there's not really a secret to tell anyway."

My eyes squeeze shut. "Yeah, about that . . ."

"You're not, are you?" His leg stops moving, an awkward stillness saturating the air between us. "Considering him still?"

I worry at my lower lip, unsure of the best way to respond in this situation. Luca barely knows Nate, yet he already despises him. If I spill the full details of our conversation, it might only add unnecessary fuel to the fire.

"Seriously?" He shakes his head, the question dry. "After he ditched you like that on Friday night?"

I pick at a frayed thread on my jeans, swirling the words around on my tongue. "Actually, *I* ditched him."

"What are you talking about?"

"I ditched Nate for you, remember?"

"Yeah, but that was—"

"Fake? Well, not from Nate's perspective," I say, unsure of why I'm even defending him now. "He saw the two of us in some picture together and wasn't too happy about it."

"So what, he kissed someone else to get back at you?"

"I don't really know what was going through his mind, but maybe?"

"Okay?" He bundles up the weighted cord, tossing it onto the mattress beside us. "So you *do* want to be with him now?"

"No, I don't think I do."

"You don't *think* so?"

"He wasn't too nice when he confronted me. And honestly, I didn't like how he acted about the whole thing. But, I don't know, he just thought I was a two-timer or something. He actually said that maybe we could try things later on. You know, if you and I don't work out in the end."

He leans back on his hands, lips pursed for a beat too long. "Okay."

"Okay?"

"Yeah, Harper." He leans forward, rubbing a hand across his forehead. "You already know what I think of the guy. But if he's who you want, then I guess that's all I can say."

"Oh no, that's not—I-I don't really think I want that anymore."

He snorts. "*That?*"

"Nate," I clarify, nudging him with my thigh.

He nudges back, a flicker of a smile finally passing his lips. "Okay."

We finish up the rest of our cooldown stretches in relative silence. Luca's oddly quiet, or at least quieter than usual, for the rest of the hour. Normally, I'd attempt to fill the silence with silly chitchat and small talk, but tonight, it feels more comfortable this way.

It's probably because I already put my foot in my mouth one too many times.

Once we're finished, I follow Luca to the front door. He lingers there, longer than usual, one hand curved around the doorknob.

"Everything okay?" I ask.

"Yeah." He turns to face me, hand dropping back to his side. "You know my sister, Taylor?"

"Of course."

"She was wondering if you'd want to come back for dinner soon. I wasn't gonna ask you because, well . . ." He shakes his head, a quick bobble back and forth. "It doesn't really matter. Taylor said she wanted to make you some risotto, our mom's recipe."

The idea of having dinner with Luca's family, even if it's only a singular member, has me feeling all sorts of giddy inside. After that disaster of a night with his friends, it'll be nice to spend some time with a person who loves him right.

"I'd love that."

"You'd have to pretend again," he says, expression drawn tight. "That we're together."

"That's fine. It wasn't so hard last weekend."

It honestly wasn't. In fact, it was one of the easiest lies I've told since we started this whole charade.

"Friday night, then, after practice?"

"I can make that work. Maybe I could head over early and help her out in the kitchen?"

"I don't know, Taylor's kind of a freak about cooking." His soft chuckle hits me right in the chest. "She'd probably swat your hands out of the way if you tried to help."

"Okay, nix that plan. Do you think I could at least bring something? What kind of wine do you drink with risotto, anyway?"

"Our mom usually cooks with pinot grigio but drinks half the bottle while she's at it." His expression shifts to something lighter, as if he's replaying the memory in the back of his mind. "I'm guessing that would work."

"Perfect."

I bounce on my heels, itching to throw my arms around him. But instead, I simply lay a soft hand on his shoulder, squeezing just once before he's on his way out the door.

Chapter Sixteen

LUCA

I'm scrambling around my living room, gathering up old magazines, dusting off shelves, and tucking ugly knickknacks into back corners. No matter what I do, the house doesn't feel ready for guests. But it's nearing seven o'clock, and Harper's bound to be here any minute.

My fingers flex, fists clenching together as I enter the kitchen. Taylor's happily stirring away at her risotto, clueless to my frantic energy as she dances and twirls to some LÉON song. The pungent smell of mushrooms, fresh oil, and pancetta wafts through the air, and I feel a little bit calmer.

It reminds me of home—my parents, Elio, Mia, and Vivia. And most of all, the earthy, almondy scent reminds me of little Giorgie, who used to pluck each mushroom out and feed them to Bentley under the table. It also reminds me that it's been weeks since I've FaceTimed with her.

She's only seven years old, and I'm her favorite sibling, yet I can't even spare a few minutes to see her through the phone. To watch her smiling face light up as she clicks that four-leaf clover on her iPad, greeting me with her special nickname.

Lucky.

"Luc, hellooo," Taylor singsongs, waving a wooden spoon in my face. "Earth to Luca."

"What?" I ask, rearing back as she smacks me upside the head.

"You've been zoning out for, like, five whole minutes." An amused expression quirks the side of her mouth. "You okay?"

"Just fine," I grumble.

She turns back toward the stovetop. "Then you should probably go get changed. Your girlfriend is going to be here any second."

"I wasn't planning on changing."

Her sudden burst of laughter echoes throughout the kitchen. When it's met by my unimpressed silence, she whirls back around to face me, waving that spoon in my face again.

"You can't wear that, Luc." Her nose scrunches in distaste, gaze quickly sweeping over me from head to foot. "You look like you're headed down to the pier for work, except you couldn't find your uniform, so you put on Dad's old, wrinkly, hand-me-down T-shirt from the eighties."

My head drops back with a displeased groan. "Jesus Christ, now I have to fucking change."

"Good," Taylor happily chirps. "Before you do, taste this real quick."

She scoops up a tiny bit of arborio rice from the pan, tilting the wooden spoon toward my face as she cups one hand underneath. I roll my eyes, leaning forward to accept her offer. The rice is piping hot, but *damn*, it might even be better than our mamma's.

"It's decent, Tay."

"Decent, my ass," she mutters, eyes widening at the sound of Bentley's frantic barking.

"Shit, that must be Harper." My fingers scrape through my half-styled, unruly hair, nervously pushing it back as the door-bell rings. "Can you get that while I throw on another shirt?"

She drops her spoon back onto the stovetop, nodding as she pushes me toward the hallway. "I bought you a couple of new outfits for tonight. On clearance. They're in the shopping bag hanging off your door handle."

"Dammit, Taylor," I mutter. "This isn't a fashion show."

"Yes, it is. Now, go, go!"

I jog down the hallway, listening for the signature sounds of Harper's animated voice. As soon as the front door swings open, I retrieve Taylor's shopping bag and shuffle into my bedroom.

Of course, the clothes Taylor bought me look fucking ridiculous. There's a pair of dark-wash jeans, charcoal trousers, a button-up, and this heather-gray sweater. An actual fucking sweater. I think it's been about fifteen years since I've worn something like this.

I shake my head, grimacing as I assess my appearance in the mirror. I feel like a complete phony, but I don't have time to fret over it right now. Besides, as if I needed the constant reminder this whole thing is fake in the first place.

But at least for right now, it's officially showtime.

"Harper," I greet, clearing my throat as I re-enter the kitchen.

She's on her knees on the hard tile floor, scrubbing her hands through Bentley's shaggy fur. Her chin tilts up at the sound of my voice, cheeks brightening with a sweet smile as she rises to greet me.

Her golden-brown hair is styled into a wild mix of braids and waves. She's wearing a muted green dress that stops midthigh. It's not tight, but it pools and dips along all the places where her body curves. At the mere sight of her, I swear something in my chest draws tight, a low and pleasant hum warming my blood.

"Hi," she murmurs, glancing over her shoulder for a beat. My gaze cuts in that direction, noting my sister's not-so-inconspicuous stare. Harper steps forward, fingers brushing across the side of my jaw, soft and slow, voice dipping as she says, "You look handsome."

I might assume the words aren't truly meant for me, that they're a mere cover-up for our lie . . . but she's whispered them. There's no way Taylor could even hear what she's said, not over the sound of King Princess playing in the background or the sizzle of our dinner on the stovetop.

I swallow back the lump in my throat. That ridiculous feeling from earlier, the one I had when I was staring at this godforsaken button-up/trouser combo, has suddenly disappeared.

It feels pretty fucking nice.

"You look great, too." I glide my fingertips from the top of her bare shoulder down to the crook of her elbow. "Beautiful."

A warm, peachy heat colors her cheeks. "Thank you."

"Hey, lovebirds," Taylor cuts in, her voice filled with unfiltered glee. "Our dinner's ready. Take a seat at the table so I can serve us up."

The food is great, the wine Harper brought is perfect, and she and Taylor get along like they've known each other for ages.

They've even developed some sort of inside joke about hot sauce. I won't try to understand it, but it's nice they've bonded this quickly. Even after three years, Taylor never formed a lasting relationship with my ex. In fact, Sofia was always much closer to my parents than she was to my siblings.

Now that we've been broken up for ages, Taylor always reminds me to move on and move up. In her words, that is. She always thought I could do better, but at the time, I thought Sofia was better. Or that she was the best fit for me, anyway.

My be-all and end-all.

Now I know that's not the case. Not that Harper is meant for me, either, considering we're not actually together. I haven't fully deluded myself into believing that much, but at least I've gained a real friend out of all this. Someone who understands me.

It's been a while since I could say that about anyone and truly mean it.

"I have a bartending shift in a half hour," Taylor says, swiping a napkin over her lips. "Do you think you could take care of this?"

Harper shoots out of her chair, already gathering up the dirty dishware from the table. "Of course! You don't even need to ask," she insists, prying used cutlery from my hands. "You cooked, so we'll clean."

"I knew I liked this one." Taylor pushes up from her chair, reaching out to pat my fake girlfriend on the top of her head. Harper simply grins at the affectionate gesture.

"She's not Bentley, Tay," I mutter, gathering up the empty wineglasses. "You can't just give her head pats for a job well done."

"Sure, she can." Harper giggles, soft and sweet, as she turns on her heel. The dishes are piled high into the sink—pans, cutting boards, plates, glasses, and bowls. It's a disaster, but I suppose it's a sign of a well-loved meal.

"Thank you for dinner," I tell my sister. "We've got this, no problem."

"Thanks, you two. I'll be home late, so—"

"Yeah, yeah." I wave off her concern, mouth curved with a knowing smile. "I'll play with Bentley and let him out right before bed."

Her eyes narrow. "I was going to say, so you'll have the

place to *yourselves.*"

"Oh." I choke on nothing, sputtering out a mixture of gibberish words before Harper comes to my rescue.

"Thanks, Taylor," she cuts in, wrapping her arms around my sister. "And thank you again for the risotto. It was the best I've ever had."

My sister cocks an amused brow in my direction. "Of course. You'll have to come by our parents' sometime and try the original recipe."

"I'd love that."

Taylor grins, her cheeks stretching wide before she traipses out of the kitchen, down the hallway, and into her bedroom. I wince at the heavy sound of her door slamming shut. Now Harper and I stand here alone, facing one another, and something has me feeling slightly unhinged.

"She'll probably leave in about five minutes. You know, if you want to head out after," I quietly suggest, gaze flitting to a chipped subway tile behind her head.

"No, thank you." Her brows knit together. "I'd like to stay and help."

"You don't have to. You already spent the last few hours playing house. You know, pretending for my sake."

She shakes her head, eyes brimming with warmth. "I wasn't really pretending tonight. Besides, Taylor's super cool."

"Okay." I clear my throat, folding up the sleeves of my button-down. "Let's get these dishes done, then."

I move toward the sink, Harper following closely behind. Together, we pile the dirty dishes into one side, filling the other with scalding, bubbling cleanser.

"I'll wash," Harper suggests. "You rinse and dry?"

"You got it."

We pass the first five minutes in comfortable silence,

washing and drying like two coworkers fulfilling an assembly line. It's not long before the front door opens and my sister calls out a quick goodbye. Once we're alone, Harper decides it'd be a good idea to splash me with dirty sink water.

"Woops," she murmurs, the sparkle in her eyes spelling mischief.

I set the last two glasses in the drying rack, silently running my hands under the faucet. My palms rub together—once, twice—before I shake off the excess, the wayward droplets flying in Harper's direction.

She playfully scoffs, gathering up a large scoop of bubbles with both hands. Her hips swivel toward me, palms flattening as she blows them directly into my face.

"Very mature," I tease with a low chuckle.

"Oh no." She swipes another handful of bubbles across the bridge of my nose. "I missed a spot."

"I'd spray you with the faucet, but I wouldn't want to ruin that pretty dress of yours."

"A bit of water never hurt anyone."

I scrub a clean hand towel across my face, clearing up the lingering soap residue. "So you do want me to soak you, then?"

"I'm sure you have something warm I could change into."

My gaze dips to her mouth, assessing the curve of her tilted smile before flitting back to meet her eyes. There's an unmistakable curiosity there, as if she's testing me with her words.

"Harper—"

My phone buzzes loudly on the counter beside us, rattling me out of my daze. A heavy breath heaves from my chest as I slide the device toward me. There are three iMessages waiting, all sent from Giorgie over the past hour—a string of angry emojis followed by a singular snake and clover.

"Do you mind if I call my parents real quick?" I step back

from the sink, wiping my palms down the front of my trousers. "My little sister's sending me some weird messages from her iPad."

Her smile is soft, gentle as she says, "Not at all."

"I'll be right back."

I step into the living room, dial my mother's number, and press the phone to my ear. She answers on the first ring.

"Ma, is Giorgie okay?" I ask before she can even manage to breathe a word.

"She's fine, *caro*. She had a meltdown earlier, but she's in bed now."

"She's been texting me for an hour, and I didn't see them until just now," I explain, gritting my teeth. "What happened?"

"Nothing for you to worry about."

I pace across the living room, frustration bubbling in my gut. "Mamma, Giorgie doesn't text me for nothing."

"She's just tired. It was her last day at the sensory gym and—"

"What are you talking about?"

"I told Taylor last week," my mom says softly, mumbling some nonsense words under her breath. "Papa and I are cutting some costs now that Elio is doing courses at the junior college. We have two copays for occupational therapy per week, and the gym is extra."

My heart squeezes inside my chest. "But she loves the gym."

"It's not a necessity."

"It *is* a necessity," I insist, gripping my phone tightly in one hand. "She's so much happier when she goes there. It makes her feel better. Here, let me talk to Elio."

My mom's voice is stern as she argues, "He needs the classes."

"I want to see why he can't pay for them himself."

She tsks. "Your brother is in high school."

"Taylor and I both worked in high school."

"Your brother is not the same." There's a rhythmic beating in the background, and I can almost picture my mother impatiently tapping her foot.

"Let me just speak with him, please."

"He's away."

I squeeze my eyes shut. "Fine, then I'll call him myself."

"You will not."

"Ma," I plead, only to be met by silence. "Fine, how much extra is the sensory gym? I can pick up some more shifts to cover it."

"Giorgie will be fine, *caro*."

"It doesn't matter," I say, carefully resigned. "I can send you one-fifty a week. I'll FaceTime Giorgie in the morning and let her know she can go back."

"Luca—"

"I have to go now, love you." I hang up before she can continue the argument, a heavy weight settling on my shoulders. I might love my parents, but they simply refuse to see how Elio takes advantage of them. With six kids in the family, it's impossible for me and Taylor to pick up the slack forever.

"Everything okay?" Harper asks, concerned as I slide back into the kitchen.

"Yeah, it's fine." I shake my head, attempting to clear the unwelcome cloud of fog settling in my mind. "I just . . . you should probably get going. It's late, and we're pretty much finished."

"Oh, okay. I mean, I could stay if you wanted to—"

"I'm tired."

"Okay," she speaks slowly, carefully inching out of the

room. Her confusion is so palpable that it's starting to scramble my brain even more. "I'll see you on Tuesday, then. My place?"

"Tuesdays aren't going to work for me anymore." I rub my face with both hands, frustration slipping through. "I'm gonna be picking up some more shifts down at the pier."

"Oh, should we reschedule, then? I can do any other weekday or on weekends after lifeguarding. Just as long as I know ahead of time."

"You don't have to do that."

"What do you mean?" A deep furrow tangles her brow. "It's no big deal for me to work around your schedule."

My thoughts are misaligned, tumbling and scattering into one another faster than I can manage. "It's just not fair, Harper."

"What?"

"It's not fair that you keep doing all this shit for me. You're busting your ass to help me after I blackmailed you—going out to dinner with my friends, faking it for my sister—and I'm giving you nothing."

"I don't mind. I—"

"You should go."

Her face falls. "What?"

"You need to go." I force my spine upright, attempting to clear the emotion from my voice. "I'm not . . . I think I need to just calm down and think for a minute."

We're backtracking, scrambling toward the front door together. My fingertips make contact with the small of her back, and I almost crack into pieces.

"Okay, yeah," she murmurs. "Call me when you figure things out?"

"Sure."

"I'll, uh, I'll see you later?"

"I'll text you."

Once she's out the door, I let the panic swell inside me, threatening to swallow me whole. Two more shifts at the pier, along with football practice, recovery training, midterms, and God knows what else.

But this is what's best for Giorgie.

My heart thumps against my rib cage, fighting for space with the frozen air inside my lungs. I draw in a long breath, willing all the anxious thoughts to subside.

I can do this. I know I can, because I have to.

Chapter Seventeen

"WHAT's GOT my girl so down in the dumps?" Eden asks, slinging one tiny arm around my shoulders. The two of us bump hips, swaying softly as we head out of our Friday lecture.

"Honestly?"

"No, lie to me."

My shoulders drop with a quiet sigh. "I think I just miss Luca."

"Trouble in paradise?"

"Kind of?" Eden's arm slips back down, fingers looped around her backpack straps. "He's been radio silent all week. I texted him to, um . . . reschedule our hangout, but he never replied."

"Did something happen between you two? I thought he'd be happy since you officially put an end to Operation Date Nate™."

"No, I'm pretty sure that made him happy." An amused smile quirks my lips. "For some weird reason, he can't stand Nate."

She stops in her tracks. "Some weird reason? Yeah, like the fact that he's in love with you."

"He's not in love with me," I insist, the truth bubbling in the back of my throat. Eden has no clue how off base she is.

"Please." A snort accompanies the dramatic roll of her eyes. "He totally clams up whenever your name is even mentioned. Have you seen how red his ears get? So adorable."

"If he was actually in love with me, then don't you think he would've reached out by now?"

"He's seriously been ghosting you?"

I clutch the hem of my sundress, smoothing the wrinkles out with a few anxious strokes. "I mean, I think something is actually bothering him. But of course, he's trying to deal with things on his own and shutting me out in the process."

"Maybe you just need to show him that you're really here for him. Prove that he can talk to you about anything that's on his mind."

"Maybe so."

"You really like him, don't you?"

My chest tightens at her suggestion. I glance around the quad, not quite sure what I'm looking for. My gaze flits toward the exposed brick buildings, across the rows of untended garden beds, and lands on a few seagulls huddled around a storm drain. They're picking at old, discarded food scraps and squawking at each other.

The sight instantly warms my blood, a sweet, honey-like substance trickling through my veins.

"I think I do, yeah," I finally admit.

Somehow, the revelation doesn't shock me. I like the way I feel when I'm around Luca. He's smart, handsome, dedicated, and surprisingly funny. He loves his family with all his heart. He may be guarded, but he's been revealing all the secret pieces that make him whole.

It's not a crush, per se, but I'm not really sure what to call it.

"Well, I'm definitely on Team Reynolds, that's for sure. Same with Stella and Lai'Lani." She skips over a jutting brick in the cobblestone pathway. "We've already discussed this in great depth."

I scoff, feigning offense. "What about Team Harper?"

"I heard she has enough cheerleaders."

"Speaking of—"

"Hey, Princess!" Fletcher's booming voice carries halfway through the quad. "Wait up."

Eden slaps a palm across her forehead, groaning as she turns on her heel. "Did you need something?"

"I was just wondering," he pants to catch his breath, planting both palms on bent knees, "did you already book your room for Hanford?"

"Uh, yeah, I did." She flashes me an odd look from the corner of her eye. "Weeks ago."

Fletcher clears his throat, returning to his full towering height. "Did you . . . would you want to drive up there together in the morning, then?"

There's an awkward pause. Eden shoots me a withering glance, gnawing at her lip while she scrambles for an excuse. "I'm already catching a ride with Harper, sorry."

His shoulders sag, gaze drifting to meet mine.

"Yup." I shrug, camouflaging my surprise. "Sorry, Fletch."

"Right." A solemn smile tugs at the corner of his mouth. "Should've figured you'd be there to support your boy."

"That's right," I choke out.

Someone should give me an award for fibbing, considering it's become my full-time occupation now.

"Well, I guess I'll see you two up there."

We both watch in silence as Fletcher retreats, his head hung in defeat. I nudge Eden in the ribs once he's officially out of earshot. "What was *that*?"

"I know, I totally just threw you under the bus." She

cringes, apology reflected in her eyes. "We're going to Hanford for the away game tomorrow. We'll be on the field all night, so you don't actually have to go with me. Obviously."

"Wait, that's a great idea." I pause for a moment, rescheduling the weekend inside my head. "I could get someone to cover my shift at Amber Isle. You said it yourself, I've gotta show Luca how much I really care."

She loops our arms together, a nervous smile playing on her lips. "So you'll actually ride up with me, then? Stay the night and everything?"

"Of course. It sounds fun."

"And you'll help keep me away from Grant's hotel room?" she asks in a quiet, pleading tone.

I can hardly suppress the soft giggle that escapes my throat. "Now, that one might be out of my hands."

"Pleeease, Harper," she begs, clasping both hands together in front of her chest. "He's being so goddamn sweet lately. It's getting too hard to resist. I mean, did you see that shy little act he put on just now?"

I clasp both of her hands in mine, leveling her with an ear-splitting grin. "Maybe it's not an act."

Her brows shoot up. "Have you met Grant Fletcher?"

"Very true."

We resume our walk, heading through the quad in search of the nearest café. It's a nice afternoon, but there are a few looming storm clouds gathering in the distance, the lingering heat from this morning dipping into sweater weather.

"So you gonna give your boy another call?" Eden nudges me again. "Let him know you'll be at his game this weekend?"

"I think I might just surprise him, actually."

. . .

I'M FAIRLY RATTLED by the time Eden and I arrive at the hotel. She's an erratic driver, the type who likes to duck between lanes to shave off a few extra minutes of drive time. I asked to take over on several different occasions, but according to Eden, I drive like a "retired grandmother who forgot her glasses at home."

I have great vision and a perfectly clean driver's record, so I highly doubt the accuracy of that statement.

Once we pull into the parking lot, Eden basically peels into the closest spot near the hotel entrance. The tires on her old Hyundai squeal against the pressure, the car lurches to a sudden stop, and I finally let my head drop back.

After a few calming breaths, Eden clears her throat beside me. "Hey, Harper?"

"Yep," I murmur, eyes still shuttered.

"Half the team is staring at us right now."

My head snaps up, gaze darting toward the hotel entrance. Nearly a hundred players and support staff are huddled along the expansive sidewalk, gear and duffles in hand as they await their shuttles.

I eagerly scan the crowd.

Luca's standing near the back of the flock, broad arms folded across his chest, attention planted firmly on the sidewalk in front of him.

"Go say hi before they get on the bus," Eden prompts, nearly shoving me out the passenger door. "I have to go catch up with our supervisor."

"Don't forget to tell her she's my idol," I say, scrambling for my bag in the back seat.

With one strap slung over my shoulder, I smooth down the tangles in my hair and square my shoulders. Internally, I'm freaking out. Externally, I've managed to muster up twenty-one years' worth of confidence.

As I carefully approach, footsteps quietly pattering against the asphalt, a few players nod in my direction. One of them lays a heavy pat against Luca's shoulder. His head snaps up, body jolting forward at the unexpected impact.

There's a quiet moment right before our eyes catch. A deep furrow tangles his brow, his warm brown eyes swirling with confusion. He glances around, once to either side, before nodding toward a nearby bench. I trail behind him, chewing at a cuticle as we settle onto the cold wooden slats.

"What are you doing here?" he asks, voice low and measured. It's not accusatory, but he doesn't exactly sound excited.

"I came up with Eden to watch you play."

"Ah."

"You didn't answer my texts." I bite off a tiny sliver of my fingernail, then carefully tuck my hands beneath my thighs. "I've been worried about you."

"I'm fine, just been busy."

"You sure?"

"Yes, Harper." He manages to plaster on a half-assed smile. "I'm okay."

"Do you have a room here?" I ask, voice dipping to a whisper. "I could help you with a postgame recovery session if you wanted?"

"I'm driving back tonight. I have an early morning shift at the pier tomorrow."

The faint, salty sting of disappointment settles in my gut. "Oh, um, yeah. I guess I should've realized that."

"You're staying, though?"

"Mhm, I'm rooming with Eden." I attempt a lighthearted chuckle, but the tone is brittle and hollow. "I promised to try and keep her away from Fletcher tonight."

"Good luck with that. That guy looks at her like a dog in heat."

I free my hands, tracing the worn initials carved into the bench seat. "You think so?"

"Definitely."

That brings a genuine smile to my face. "Maybe they should just stop fighting it and hook up again. Might cut some of the tension between them."

"Didn't you say they went through a bad breakup not too long ago?"

"Yeah, but—"

"And you think sex is the answer to their problems? Makes perfect sense."

"That's not what I—"

"Look, we're heading to the stadium in a minute." He avoids my gaze, zeroing in on the shuttles idling under the hotel awning. "I better get going, but thank you for coming."

"Sure." I swallow back my words of protest, tucking them into my back pocket for another time.

IT'S BEEN an ear-splitting rush of excitement for the past three and a half hours. The student section was small but mighty tonight, especially compared to our traditional home games. It also helps that the Coastal Ospreys decimated the Hanford Hawks, ending the game with a score of 42-14.

Throughout the entire game, I only caught one tiny glimpse of Luca stumbling on the field. I'm not sure how he pulled it off, considering my gaze was laser focused on his knee the whole time. If he was truly in pain tonight, or if he was holding himself back, then I surely would have noticed.

I wait until the majority of fans file out before attempting to find Eden. We agreed to meet near the press entrance to the locker rooms, but it's proving difficult to push through the media swarm.

I shuffle to the side, pressing onto my tiptoes and using a pillar as leverage.

It takes me nearly fifteen minutes to spot the familiar head of black hair bobbing through the crowd. I suppose I should've been looking for Fletcher in the first place, considering she's tucked against his side now, their hands carefully intertwined.

I clear my throat as I approach them, gesturing wildly to catch Eden's attention. Once she spots me, she shoves Fletcher out of the way, her cheeks flushing a brilliant shade of red. He leans down, brushing her hair back with a playful roll of his eyes.

They exchange a few hushed words before he turns and disappears into the crowd.

I'm giddy, bouncing on my heels as I ask, "Were you two just holding hands?"

"Kind of." She groans, rolling her shoulders back. "Okay, yes, we were full-on holding hands. Harps, he's just so . . . *ugh*. And he invited me back to his room tonight."

A teasing smirk lights up my face. "Of course he did."

"Don't worry, I told him no. I convinced you to drive up here with me on a whim, so—"

"Don't let me be the reason you turned him down. If you want to see where things go, I don't mind."

Her nose wrinkles with hesitation. "Are you sure?"

"Totally. I'm rooting for whatever makes you happy."

"Okay, then I think I might go for it," she says wistfully, pulling out her phone to shoot him a text. "We'll see where the night takes us."

I pat her on the shoulder. "Atta girl."

The majority of the stadium has cleared out by the time we call for our Uber.

We're standing near the front entrance as the first patter of raindrops starts to fall—thick, fat drops splashing into our hair—which quickly devolves into a heavy downpour. The two of us scramble for shelter under a nearby awning.

Eden swears under her breath, flashing her weather app in my direction. "It looks like there's an awful storm coming in."

"Really?"

"Yeah, there's a tornado warning and everything." She swipes the rain droplets from her screen, peering closely at the text. "Winds are predicted to be up to fifty miles per hour tonight."

I frantically yank my phone from my back pocket. "I'm gonna call Luca and tell him not to drive home."

His voicemail picks up at the same time as our Uber arrives. I leave him a panicky message and shoot off a quick text, piling into the back seat with Eden in tow. By the time we arrive back at the hotel, I've called him nearly a dozen times.

"I'm just gonna make one last-ditch effort to reach him," I tell Eden, eyes darting around the lobby. We're both soaked to the bone, clothes and hair dripping onto the vinyl beneath our feet. "You can head up to the room and get ready for your night with Fletch."

"You sure?"

"Yes, go shave and exfoliate and . . . oh my God, did you even bring sexy underwear?"

She gives me a sheepish grin. "I may have come prepared."

"Should've never doubted you." I shake my head, attempting a tiny smile of encouragement.

"Okay, I hope you get ahold of Luca. I'll text you when I get to Grant's room, okay?" She tosses her arms around me, the squelch of our damp clothes eliciting a chuckle from us both. "Love you."

"Love you more."

Fifteen minutes later, I'm pacing the lobby, repeatedly checking my phone as the first round of players trails inside. It looks like one or two of the shuttles have already returned, yet there's no sign of Luca in sight.

I'm giving up hope, wondering if he's headed straight to his car before coming in. I could venture out there, but I'd need something warmer and more waterproof than this thin sweater. Maybe if I run up to our room for just a quick second, then I could be back in time to—

"Harper?"

I whip around at the sound of Luca's voice. My heart skitters in my chest, relief flooding through every tiny crack and seam. There's nothing I can do to stop myself from rushing toward him, throwing my arms open, and wrapping myself around his giant frame.

"Oh, thank God you're here," I murmur the words against his chest, sinking into the warm feeling of his arms around me. "I thought you were gonna drive all the way home in this storm."

I pull back, brushing the wet strands of hair from my cheeks. He studies me with piercing scrutiny, eyes silently devouring me before he shakes his head. "Nah, half the team just got back, and the roads are pretty fucking terrible. I, uh, I decided to book a room for the night."

"You didn't answer your phone."

"I had it on silent in the locker room." He wrestles the device out of his duffle, clicking the side button to illuminate the screen. "Forgot to turn the ringer back on."

"Oh."

He glances down at his screen for a long, silent moment. A flush of red heat crawls up his neck and singes the tips of his ears. "You, uh, you called me seventeen times?"

"Yeah."

There's a crease in his brow. "You were really worried."

I tamp down my embarrassment, attempting a casual half-shrug. "It's . . . windy out there."

His shuttered expression splits into a lopsided grin. "Yeah, and we're both soaked. Let me go book a room, and I'll be right back. Y-you don't have to wait for me, though."

"I'll wait." I place a soft squeeze against his palm.

He returns a moment later, nervously running his fingers through his damp hair. "They're all booked up. I'm gonna have to call Coach or one of the guys, I guess."

"Or you could just stay with me."

"No, no, that's—"

"Luca," I cut him off, pleading with my eyes.

If he stays in our room tonight, then he can't escape me so easily. It's a chance for him to open up, to ask for help, to stop suffering in silence. It's also a chance for me to explore uncharted territory, otherwise known as my unresolved feelings.

"You sure Eden would be okay with it?"

"She won't mind," I assure him, wiping the hesitation from his brow. "She's staying in Fletcher's room tonight, anyway."

"So then, it'd just be you and me?"

"Just us."

He rubs the back of his neck, shoulders dropping. A tiny half-smile pulls at his lips. "Okay."

"Come on." I loop our fingers together, tugging him toward the elevator. "Let's go and get out of these wet clothes."

Chapter Eighteen

LUCA

IF MY CALCULATIONS ARE CORRECT, Harper's about thirty seconds away from walking into our room wearing nothing but a chintzy towel.

I know she didn't bring a change of clothes with her into the bathroom. Her bright yellow duffle bag sits on the singular queen bed beside me—taunting me—reminding me that I'm alone with a girl in a hotel room. And that it's not just any girl.

This is Harper, with her big, sweet smiles and her uncanny knack for bringing me comfort. She drove all the way up here to watch my game tonight, despite the fact that I ignored the shit out of her all week. It's not that I didn't want to see her or speak to her.

I'm just not used to having anyone to answer to.

"Luca," her soft voice calls from across the room, a tiny crack opened in the doorway. "I forgot my stuff out there. Do you mind if I come out in just this towel? Or could you maybe pass me my bag?"

I clear my throat, running an unsteady hand across my forehead. "Just the towel is fine. I mean, *no*, I don't mind."

Her gentle footsteps patter into the room. She's grinning, face flushed with heat from the shower, damp hair combed back behind bare shoulders. There are a few droplets of water gathered in the clefts of her collarbones. I attempt to divert my eyes from her body, subtly enough not to draw attention.

The feat is nearly impossible.

"I don't bite," she says softly, bouncing toward the spot beside me. She unzips her bag, rifles through the clothing, and yanks out a pair of pajamas. They're tiny, blush pink, with a hint of lace. If she truly plans on wearing those in front of me, I think I might have an existential crisis.

"Right, I just . . . anyway." I swallow back the lump that's wedged its way into my throat. "I'm gonna hop in the shower now. I called Taylor to let her know I'd be staying the night."

"Perfect. I'll call room service and ask them to send up a few more pillows."

I absentmindedly massage the back of my neck. "Could you ask for a cot, too?"

"A cot?"

"If they have one, just so that I don't have to sleep on the floor. I don't know that my body could take it after tonight's game."

"We can just share the bed, can't we?"

The muscles along my spine pull tight. "You want to . . ."

"Sleep together?" She busies herself, laying out a few more items on the bed—some lotion, a hairbrush, and one pair of big fuzzy socks. I do my best to keep my eyes trained there. "I think it'd be fine. We're friends, right? Plus, I can even set up a pillow wall between us if you want. A cot isn't going to be comfortable for anyone."

I contemplate my answer for a long moment, my frozen feet rooted to the spot. By some miracle, I effectively manage to spit out the words "yeah" and "okay" without choking on them in the process.

"So get your butt in the shower, and I'll give them a call."

Following a simple nod, I flip around, dragging one foot after another until I reach the threshold of the bathroom.

Pausing in the doorway, I pat one hand against the frame and tilt my head back in her direction. "Thanks, Harper."

She flashes me a warm smile. "You're welcome."

I attempt to clear my mind in the shower. My eyes flutter shut, my shoulders relax, and my brain melts into a puddle at my feet. The scalding water washes over my sore, aching muscles, pulling at the anxious threads that twist in my gut. It's the first time I've been alone all day.

I'm not used to this. Generally, after an away game, I'd spend the next few hours decompressing by myself on the long drive home. Now, I have less than ten minutes to get my act fully together.

It takes a great deal of effort to force myself out of the shower. While struggling in silence, I towel off and throw on a soft cotton undershirt with a pair of gray sweats. When I re-enter our room, Harper's bent halfway over the bed.

And it looks like I was right. That tiny pair of satin pajamas doesn't leave much to the imagination. Her bare legs are long and lean, sculpted from years of lifeguarding on the beach. There's a dusting of dark freckles spattered across her shoulder blades. Her skin is glowy—tanned and vibrant—from all the time she spends soaking up the sunshine.

My entire body buzzes at the sight of her.

"Hey, there." She pats down a stack of pillows, her soft gaze sweeping toward mine. "They brought up some more pillows and towels for us, so I thought we could prop up your knee with them. I also went out to the ice machine in case that might be helpful. Plus, I got you a Snickers bar and some chips, just barbecue Lay's. They didn't have very many options in the snack machine, and I didn't know how hungry you were."

"Jesus, Harper," I croak, unable to peel my gaze off of her. "Thank you."

"Sure. I figured the team didn't get to order any food due to the storm, and it's a little too late for room service, so—"

"You really didn't have to do all this."

"It's no big deal, really. I'm sure you'd do the same for me." She stretches one arm out, passing the ice bag from her hand to mine. "Here."

I tug at the thin collar of my T-shirt, regret swirling in the pit of my stomach. "I'm sorry."

"What are you sorry for?"

"I was overwhelmed this week, and I didn't know how to talk about it." I lower myself onto the edge of the bed, patting the spot to my left. She joins me there, one knee bumping against mine as we settle in together. "I feel like I'm being pulled in a thousand different directions, and I'm fucking exhausted. I'm not used to someone else caring about me, but I shouldn't have written you off the way I did."

She gently tugs my hand onto her lap. "It's okay."

"It's not. I'll, uh . . . I'm gonna work on it." I slide my thumb along the underside of her wrist. "I want to be a good friend."

"You already are." She shifts her hips and tosses her arms around me, face burrowed into my chest. A deep breath fills my lungs. I press my nose against her hair and soak up the faint scent of her peach shampoo. Before I can stop myself, my lips form a quiet kiss against her crown.

She pulls back. "Shoot, now I'm the one that's sorry."

"What?" I ask, a breathless sound.

"I know you're not a very touchy-feely person." There's a crease in her brow, a sheepish half-smile pulling at her lips. "I keep forcing you into hugs tonight."

"I don't mind hugs from you."

"You don't? I just figured, I mean, sometimes I've seen you flinch when people touch you."

"It's not so much the touching itself but who's doing it and in what way."

Her head tilts. "What do you mean?"

"It's different when it's someone I want touching me. Uh, I mean, if I'm close with the person, then I don't mind it. I just like to know it's coming, and it has to be the right type of pressure."

"Pressure?"

"Yeah, just a firm touch." I press two unsteady palms against my lap, praying that the perspiration doesn't leave a mark. "Nothing too light or unexpected—that's when I feel like crawling out of my own skin."

"So it's a sensory thing?"

"It is."

"I think I know what you mean, then." She offers a reassuring smile. "I used to get that same yucky feeling from stepping on sand. It's like my feet were on fire."

"But you practically live on the sand."

"I guess my body adapted to it somehow."

"Right. That's good."

She shifts course, pushing herself up from the bed. "So hugs from me are okay?"

"Yes." I join her with a slight wince, the pressure and swelling from tonight's game finally catching up with me.

"Good to know." Her gaze cuts to my knee. "How are you feeling now? Are you tired, sore, strung out?"

"I think a little bit of everything."

"Would you like a massage or just sleep?"

Although the former sounds most appealing, I might not be able to handle her hands on my body right now—pushing, prodding, kneading at my weaknesses. "Sleep might be best."

She agrees, lifting the covers to slide herself into bed. I cross to the other side and shuffle in beside her, careful to keep a neat foot of distance between us. My left leg is propped up on the stack of pillows she created.

It's all a bit awkward, but I try not to dwell on it.

Following an exchange of whispered good-nights, we simultaneously dim our bedside lamps. At first, the silence feels so loud. My breathing is erratic, my chest is heavy, and every tiny shift of her body sends a shock wave through my spine.

Five grueling minutes pass. Then, there's a bright flash of lightning, followed by the crack of heavy thunder. Our window illuminates, the sound of steady rain returns, and my body starts to settle.

"Luca?"

"Yes?"

"I'm glad you stayed tonight."

My voice sounds foreign to my ears, hoarse and unpracticed as I sputter a response. "Me too."

"You played a great game. It was fun to watch you in your element."

"Thank you."

She's quiet for a few long moments, then, "Luca?"

"Yes, Harper."

"I don't know if I can fall asleep in this storm."

I reposition onto my right side, kicking out the pillows as I prop myself on one elbow. "I gathered that."

"Sorry to keep you up." She shifts onto her side as well. It's nearly pitch-black in the room now, but I can still see the faint outline of her facial features—the gentle slope of her nose, the curved bow of her lips. It's difficult to make out her freckles in this light, but I can surely imagine them.

"It's fine," I whisper. "I don't think I can fall asleep, either."

"Maybe we should play a game, then."

"What kind of game?"

"How about two truths and a lie?"

"You start."

"Okay." She nibbles on her bottom lip as she contemplates a response. "I'm majoring in sports medicine. I've always loved the beach. And earlier, when I felt your lips press against my hair, I wish you would've just kissed me for real."

My mind is a buzzing mess of static. My heart, a pounding arrhythmia inside my ears. "You used to hate sand."

"I did."

"So the beach . . ."

"I used to hate that, too." Her hand reaches for mine under the covers. "You know you could still kiss me now . . . if you wanted to."

Desire burns a hot coil inside my gut. "I probably shouldn't."

"Why?"

My thoughts are racing, but my mind is blank. It's difficult to conjure up a reasonable excuse. All I know is that I'm Luca and she's Harper and we don't fit together, despite what I may be feeling right now.

"There are . . . so many reasons."

"Is it because you don't want to?"

"I didn't say that."

I want to. Of course I fucking want to.

"Luca, when was the last time you did something just because you wanted to?"

"I can't even remember how long it's been."

"Then take a chance." She presses her thumb against my palm, rubbing small circles directly against the center. "Right now. Kiss me just because you want to. Forget all the silly reasons why you think you shouldn't."

I release her hand, snaking my own behind her head. She shifts a half breath closer, and my fingers tangle into the damp curls at the nape of her neck.

"I don't want to keep begging you, but I might just be willing to."

"You don't need to beg me," I murmur. "Not now, not ever."

I release one last unsteady breath, shaking all remaining shreds of doubt from my brain. Then, slowly, with the smell of peaches filling the room and the sound of rain pelting against the window, I press my lips to hers.

Chapter Nineteen

From a distance, Luca is all hard ridges and lines, a six-foot-two package comprised of rugged, sinewy muscle and worn, calloused hands. He's aloof and carefully measured, seemingly immune to the pressures the rest of us mere mortals endure.

But up close, underneath these threadbare covers, he's all sorts of soft. His hands are gentle. His heart is full. And his lips, they move in a perfect, tender rhythm against mine.

He curls his fingers into the hair at my nape, tugging softly, dragging me closer toward his body. I mold myself against him with a breathless sigh. Between our chests, there are only two layers consisting of a thin cotton T-shirt and my silk camisole. The lower half of our bodies remain inches apart.

Too far apart for my liking.

So I push even closer, wriggling and writhing until our bodies are flush. One hand pushes at his shoulder, urging him to turn onto his back.

"Harper?" He rasps the question of my name into my mouth, thumbs caressing both sides of my face as I maneuver on top of him.

My thighs spread apart, straddling him on the mattress, our hips aligned. I can feel . . . everything from this position. My breasts brushing against his chest, nipples tight and pebbled. Breath mingling as our lips come together and fall apart.

The soft, sudden shiver that racks his body as I circle my hips. The rumble of his groan.

His hands drift from my cheeks, fingers cascading down my shoulders in a gentle caress. I disconnect our lips, dip my face into the crook of his neck, and kiss him softly in the tender spot just below his ear.

"Harper," he sighs my name again. This time, it's not a question.

His rough, calloused fingers move further down my body, cresting closer to the place I need him most. He traces the curve of my waist—down, down, down—and I can't mask the sigh of pleasure that escapes my lips.

But then he stops, his thumbs digging into my hips as I press against the hard length of him. His entire body grows stiff. Now, when his lips form my name for the third time, they carry a note of warning.

"Harper, wait."

I pull back, slightly shaken. My breath is heavy. I can hardly see the outline of his face in the dim light, but I know he's not smiling.

His hands drop to the mattress beside his thighs. He's no longer holding me in place, so I push upright and slide myself slightly forward, just enough so that my lower half isn't perfectly aligned with his erection.

"What's wrong?" My fingers twitch against my sides, desperate to trace the outline of his facial features.

Following a deep breath, he asks, "Could we . . . could we slow down?"

"Oh." I shift my body to the side and slide into the empty space beside him. "I'm sorry."

"Don't be sorry. It's just been a while for me. I wasn't expecting—"

"No, no, I get it." I shift another inch away from him, embarrassment creeping up my spine. "I asked you for a kiss, but then I took it too far. I mean, I practically mauled you there."

"You didn't *maul* me," he rasps, appalled. "And I'm sorry I stopped like that when we, well, when you . . . I know this probably isn't what you're used to."

"What do you mean?"

"Rejection," he murmurs, twisting onto his side. One hand props up his chin while the other palm presses flat against the mattress. "I don't want you to feel like I've rejected you because that's not what this is."

My chest deflates. "Luca, it's okay if you don't want to have sex with me."

"That's not—" He pauses, head shaking, lips pursed as he formulates a coherent response. "I do—I mean, I do want to. With you."

"You do?" My voice is small, a bare whisper in the three-inch space between our lips.

"Yes." His chin dips, gaze drifting toward the hidden bulge in his sweatpants. "I thought that . . . was it not obvious?"

A tiny crooked smile twists my lips. "I mean, it sure felt like you did a minute ago."

"I definitely did a minute ago. And thirty minutes before that." His voice is reassuring, gruff, with a hint of his normal shyness. I'm sure if I could see them, the tips of his ears would be burning. "Since I saw you come out of the bathroom in that towel, actually."

I breathe a soft sigh of relief, curling my knees back against him. "But you also want to take it slow?"

"Like I told you, it's been a while for me. A long while. And I'm still trying to wrap my head around the fact that you even wanted me to kiss you. But I do want you, just maybe not tonight." His palm presses against my cheek. "Is that okay?"

I lean into him, soaking up the warmth from his fingers. "It's more than okay, Luca. I had no expectations tonight other than honesty."

"I can do honesty. And maybe just . . . I'd like to hold you while we fall asleep." His hand drifts from my cheek to my shoulder, tucking me against his side. "If that's okay?"

"Please." I shift on the mattress, pushing back until our bodies are nestled tightly together. His arm bends around my waist, large fingers splayed across my stomach, his nose buried in the crook of my neck. With one last kiss against my pulse point, we both drift off to sleep.

"Shit!" The sound of muffled swearing jolts me awake. My eyes slowly blink open, heavy with sleep as I take in the sight of Eden's crouched form. "Sorry!"

Luca stirs beside me, grunting softly. The covers are strewn toward the bottom of the bed and tangled between our intertwined thighs. One hand caresses my bare stomach, pajamas askew, while his thumb dips a half inch below the waistband of my shorts.

"I didn't know you had company," Eden whispers again, her high-pitched voice carrying across the room.

"Shh!" I whisper-shout in return, an uncontrollable smile creeping onto my face. "You're gonna wake him up."

"Sorry, I just forgot my toothbrush," she says, holding up the slim piece of plastic. "Grant's taking me out for breakfast before we head back. He ended up riding the bus here, but do you mind if he catches a ride home with us?"

"I can just go with Luca. Give you guys some more alone time."

"You don't mind?"

"Of course not." Luca tightens his hold on me, a barely perceptible twitching of his fingers.

"Okay! I'll just see you in class tomorrow."

"Drive safe," I say with a wave.

"You too. Oh, and Harper, I'm glad your plan worked out." She smirks, yanking open the door to our hotel room. "Looks like we both got some much-needed action last night."

Luca's arms grow stiff around me. I shift on the bed, grabbing the nearest soft object to lob at Eden. Unfortunately, the door slams behind her with a violent bang, the cheap throw pillow falling limply to the floor.

Luca flinches in response. He pulls back, twists onto his side, and pushes himself into a seated position. His legs hang off the side of the bed, back facing toward me now.

"Morning, sleepyhead," I tease, shifting onto my knees behind him. I lean forward to place a heavy hand on his shoulder. "Were you pretending to be asleep that whole time?"

"No."

I scooch my hips even closer, replacing my hand on his shoulder with a soft kiss.

His spine is stiff, voice stilted. "So I guess I'm giving you a ride home, then."

"Is-is that okay?"

"Sure."

I maneuver myself beside him on the edge of the bed, leaving a small half inch of space between our thighs. "Are *you* okay?"

"Why wouldn't I be?" His gaze is trained on the window in

front of us. There's a subpar view of the pavement through the crack in the curtains. A tiny gray bird flies by.

"Because you're acting funny after we spent the night together." I knock my knee against his, gently jolting him back into the room. "It's a bit of a red flag."

He shakes his head. "It's nothing."

"You said you were going to be honest with me."

"What did Eden mean when she said your plan worked? I thought . . . you said you didn't have expectations last night. Did you come up here with the intention of sharing a room?"

I gnaw on my bottom lip, confused by the frustrated curve in his brow. "Are you asking me if I came to your game because I was trying to seduce you?"

"Did you?" he grinds out, face flushed with heat.

"No, Luca." I laugh, the sound empty and awkward. "I came up here because you weren't talking to me, and I wanted to show you that I care about you. That's it."

"Okay," he sighs, seemingly unconvinced.

"Okay? Even if I had wanted to sleep with you, completely premeditated, would that have been so wrong?"

"I told you I want to take things slow."

"I know." I shift to face him, waiting patiently until he meets my gaze. When our eyes connect, I feel the hesitation rolling off him in waves. "I'm just wondering . . . this seems like a big hang-up for you. Is there something else going on?"

His jaw is tight. "What?"

"You're acting like I committed a crime or something."

He gestures wildly toward the door. "I mean, you let Eden think that we slept together."

"I'm sorry? I didn't think it was a big deal since she believes we're a couple . . . because that's what *you* wanted."

He releases a humorless snort, eyes narrowed at a spot behind my head. "Right, because sex isn't a big deal. My bad."

"Luca!" My frustration finally wins out, voice growing weary. "Stop putting words in my mouth, please."

"Fuck." He leans forward on the mattress, palms resting against his knees before he runs them up and down his thighs. He jerks into a standing position. His fingers push through his sleep-tousled hair.

"I'm sorry, Harper. I think you're right. There is . . . *something* I'm hung up on."

"What is it?"

He's quiet while his jaw works back and forth, slowly releasing the tension. "You remember what I said about my ex?" he finally asks. "Why she broke things off?"

"She, um, she said you weren't providing for her emotionally?"

"Right." His eyes squeeze shut. "Like I said, I had no fucking clue she felt that way about us. We weren't together a whole lot after she left for school, but we would talk, *often*, and when we did see each other, she was . . . all over me."

I wince, rubbing an open palm against my thigh.

"Shit, I'm sorry. This is too much." He caresses my bare shoulder. "See, this is why I don't—"

"No, it's okay. I want you to tell me."

"Sof, *she* was more of the initiator than I was, I guess. That last weekend, when she came to visit, we slept together twice before she dumped me. I asked her why . . . why would she be with me that way if she knew it was over?" He squeezes my shoulder once, ever so gently, before his hand drops back to his side. "You know what she said? '*Sex was never the problem between us. It was everything else.*'"

My gaze is soft as I reach for his hand, his large palm sliding against mine. "Wow."

"Yeah, wow. And now, I guess I don't want to be confused again. Blindsided. If you and I are gonna be together physically, I want it to be clear where we both stand. I need to know this isn't just part of our original agreement. I need to know it's not fake."

"I get that." I grip his hand, using it for leverage as I pull myself to stand.

"So if you're not sure how you're feeling, or if you don't want more for us, then—"

"I do want more." My other hand comes up, slides into his hair.

"Yeah?"

"I like you. For real." I press onto my tiptoes, find the pulse in his neck, and press the tiniest whisper of a kiss just there. "Was it not obvious?"

He gulps, chuckling, Adam's apple bobbing as I kiss along the column of his throat. "And I like you."

I detach my lips from his neck, tilt my face, and smile up at him. "No more hang-ups?"

His body relaxes, head dips. Our lips meet again, grazing at first and then pushing and bruising as he murmurs his response. "None."

"Good."

"Harper, can we . . . will you come over tonight?" One arm wraps around my shoulders, the other hand still clutching mine. "Once we get back? I'd like to take you on a real date."

I fall back onto the balls of my feet and tuck my head into his chest. "I thought you'd never ask."

Chapter Twenty

I DROPPED Harper off at her place earlier this afternoon, spent the remaining hours attempting to study, and now I'm scrambling to find something presentable to wear tonight. For our date.

Our first real date.

It still feels like I fell asleep after the game last night and dreamed up this entire scenario. Harper likes me. She asked me to kiss her, practically begged me to, and then we slept cuddled up in bed together. Not once did I have the urge to push her away or take up space solely for myself.

Now, instead, I've been thinking about how it felt to be with her all day, during our car ride home, during the short walk up to her apartment, and especially during my numerous attempts at memorizing physics flash cards.

After waking up with her in my arms, I can't seem to keep my brain straight no matter what I do.

All we did last night was share a kiss—a heated kiss with some minor fondling—but I was too chickenshit to move things forward. Harper was warm and soft and perfect in my hands, pressed against me in all the best places, yet I was paralyzed by my past. She says she understands that I want to take things slow, but I can't help but feel like I'm always the one she's making sacrifices for.

She's been my helper and healer since the beginning. We

both used each other, sure, but I was gaining the most out of our arrangement over the past few months. To move forward with our relationship, I want us to start off on the same foot.

I want to be everything for her that she is for me—a best friend, a confidant, a source of motivation. The reason that I feel like smiling when I wake up in the morning now. For the first time in a long time, I have something to look forward to at Coastal other than football.

It feels really fucking good.

"Taylor, does this look okay?" I ask, one hand perched on the doorframe of her bedroom. She's typing away on her laptop, a stack of engineering textbooks and scattered papers lining her desk. At the sound of my voice, her head darts up.

"Lookin' good, bro." She flashes me a toothy grin. "But I thought you were just taking Happy to the beach tonight?"

"Sure, but I want to seem like I put in at least a little effort." I gaze down at my outfit, a simple button-up rolled at the forearms and a pair of nice shorts. It's not much, but I tried. "You think this is overkill?"

"Not at all. I'm just used to your old, faded jeans and T-shirt combo."

"Yeah, well, thanks."

She draws her attention back to her laptop, scrolling aimlessly through her notes. "Did you get the flowers like I told you to?"

"Yes, Tay," I say through pursed lips. "I got her some flowers."

"Good." She types another few sentences. "I'm staying at Meera's tonight, by the way. All-night study group."

"Good to know."

As I stand in her doorway, a soft knock signals Harper's arrival. I swipe a bead of moisture from my forehead, rubbing my hands down the side of my thighs. After I back out of Taylor's room, I grab the small bouquet of peonies from the entryway table. They're pale and pink and pretty, the perfect fit for Harper.

Plus, according to Taylor, these flowers symbolize happiness and healing.

Bentley joins me to greet her at the front door, his tail whipping back and forth in excitement. He's always antsy for visitors, but he's taken a special liking to this girl in particular.

It seems as though we all have.

With one final deep breath, I pull the door open to find that familiar, heart-stopping smile. Harper's cheeks are pulled tight, freckled and rosy from the late-afternoon sun. She's wearing another simple green sundress with some strappy sandals. Her hair is a mixture of wild curls, two thick braids framing either side of her face.

She's absolutely stunning, as usual.

"Hi," I mutter. It may be pathetic, but it's all I can manage to squeeze out at the moment.

"Hi!" Her eyes spark as she glances down, the forgotten bouquet hanging limply beside my thigh. "Are those for me?"

"Oh, uh, yes." My hand juts forward to pass them off. "Peonies."

"I love them." She brings the flowers to her nose, grinning as she sniffs them. Beaming, she lifts both arms, leans onto her tiptoes, and slowly wraps them over my shoulders. "Thank you so much."

"You're welcome. You look beautiful, by the way."

"You too."

I shake my head, one corner of my mouth lifting into a lopsided smile. "You ready to head out?"

"Is Taylor home? I want to say hi before we leave."

"Yeah, she's just in her room studying. Why don't you head back there, and I'll grab our stuff for the car?"

"Meet you out front in five." She presses a small peck to the side of my jaw, prancing off down the hall, stopping to greet Bentley with a few quick pets.

I rake my fingers through my hair, attempting to suppress the full-out grin that's taken residence on my face.

It takes me a few minutes to gather up the basket of food I picked up earlier, plus a small cooler of drinks and some blankets for the beach. I pat Bentley on the way out the door before I move to toss the items in the back of my trunk. In case Harper gets cold tonight, there's an extra sweatshirt waiting for her in the back seat.

She rounds the corner as I finish propping open the passenger door. Her fingers interlock with mine before she asks, "So where are we headed?"

"I thought we'd go to Amber Isle to watch the sunset. I packed some food and stuff. If that's cool?"

"Food and stuff? Like for a picnic?"

"You could call it that."

"Then I will. Luca Reynolds is taking me for a sunset picnic on the beach. How lucky am I?"

"It's nothing elaborate, Harper."

"No, but it's perfect."

With one final squeeze of my hand, she tucks herself into the passenger seat of my Subaru. I'm tempted to kiss her again as the lingering sunshine strikes the side of her cheek, but I'm not sure if we've reached that level of casual intimacy yet.

Are you allowed to kiss someone unprompted on the first date, simply whenever the mood strikes, or is there some kind of unspoken etiquette to follow?

Fuck it.

I duck my head, grazing my lips over hers. There's the tiniest flush of heat in her cheeks when I pull back, a slight curve to her lips, and it all makes me wish I kissed her for just a little bit longer.

WE TAKE our time finding the perfect spot on the beachfront, yards away from any lingering tourists. It's still warm for an October evening on the coast, but there's a slight breeze that kicks up our blanket as we flatten it over the sand. While we settle in next to each other, shoulder to shoulder, I grab our basket of food.

"You hungry?" I ask, a small shiver racking my body as she leans against me.

"It depends on what you brought."

"What if it's tacos from that place you love?"

"Then I'd probably say I'm starving."

I flip the lid open on our basket, lifting out the familiar foil packets and a set of paper plates. "That's good, then, because I picked up a shit ton of chorizo and egg. They still feel pretty warm."

"Oo, our favorite."

I stifle a grin. "Yeah."

She leans across my lap and fills her plate with a few wrapped tacos. "Hot sauce?"

"Don't think I forgot," I say, rifling through the cooler for the stack of plastic containers. "There's also some beer here if you want. Dos Equis. Or wine since I already knew you liked pinot grigio. It doesn't really go with tacos, but I wasn't all that sure you liked this beer. Or water if you're not into alcohol tonight. I know it's our first . . . *date*, so don't feel like you need to—"

"I'll take a beer." She sets her full plate to the side, grinning as she pats the side of my thigh. "Thank you."

I sort through the cooler for two beers, popping the tops off and passing one to Harper. She clinks hers against mine and takes a deep sip, smiling as she gulps back the cool liquid.

"Good choice," she says, wasting no time as she unwraps her food and applies a generous heap of salsa verde. "I honestly wasn't that hungry, but now I think I could eat like ten of these."

I tip back my own beer, an easy smile stretching my face. "Go for it."

"I will."

We eat our tacos in relative silence, pausing here and there to chat about work and classes, crumpling up foil wrappers as we go. We've made it through a handful of tacos each by the time we're on our second beer. In the distance, the sun has officially started to set.

"Sometimes I forget how beautiful it is out here," she murmurs, stacking our dirty plates and empty beer bottles into the now-empty basket.

"Yeah, I don't think I've actually stopped to watch the sunset in years. I'm out here four days a week, but I never take time to enjoy it."

"Well, thank you for bringing me tonight. I'm glad we can enjoy it together."

"Of course."

Now that our little picnic is cleared out of the way, I spread my legs across the faded blanket. Harper pats my left thigh, hinting for me to make some extra room. With a contented sigh, she shifts herself between my open legs, crawling into the space and leaning her back against my chest.

"You know what's kind of sad, now that I think about it?"

"What's that?" I ask, wrapping one arm around her waist and propping us both up with the other.

"I only have two more weekends of lifeguarding left in the season. Come November, I'll probably only come here to see Stell at work."

"You think I could get you to visit me at the pier?"

Her fingers brush against the side of my thigh. "You'd want that?"

"Of course. Pawel would probably lose his mind over it."

"Then yeah, I'll visit you."

I press a kiss to her hair. "Good."

"I've been meaning to ask, how's your knee feeling after the game last night? It seemed like you were completely fine out on the field."

"I put on a good show, huh?"

"Really?" She shifts in my arms the slightest bit, neck tilted up to gauge my expression. "You're not doing any better?"

"Nah, I am." I wrinkle my nose, plastering on an indifferent smile. "It's more of a dull ache now, mostly after a long practice or if I put too much pressure on it. It's completely manageable. Honestly, I probably don't need to keep up with our PT regularly. I, uh, I think I'm pretty much healed."

It's not that I'm lying, necessarily, but I could technically use all the help I can get. Still, a larger part of me feels like we need to stop blurring the lines in our relationship now. I'm mostly healed at this point. Plus, thanks to Harper's diligence, I know how to continue with her treatment on my own time.

"Oh, you think so?"

"Yeah, if that's okay with you? That way, our time together doesn't need to be focused on my healing anymore. We can just ... be."

"You're not just saying that because you want me to stop worrying?"

"That's certainly a perk."

"Luca . . ."

"No, I'm really okay now." I wave off her concern, tugging her closer. "Plus, I want us to put all that behind us. You can still give me massages if I really need one, though."

"Ah, see, I knew I was lucky."

"The luckiest."

She tilts her head back again, pressing a soft kiss to the underside of my jaw. "You know, I think this was a pretty perfect first date so far."

I gaze toward the shore. The bright vermillion hues have already faded into the subtle shades of the blue hour. There's a slight chill to the sea breeze now, but Harper seems content in my arms.

"You think?"

"Mhmm. Did Taylor help you plan it?"

I let out a hearty chuckle. "I'll take about half the credit, at least."

"You're so cute."

"Cute," I echo.

"Mhmm." She flips herself around in my arms, straddling my lap. Her fingertips trace the side of my face as she murmurs, "And handsome."

"Better."

Her lips press against mine. "Sexy."

I can't help my disbelieving snort.

"What?" Her tone is indignant, eyes playfully narrowed. "You are, to me and probably to everyone."

My hands wrap around either side of her body, sliding across the soft cotton of her dress. "Everyone, huh?"

"Yes."

"I know you said before that you didn't have a type, but I still wasn't sure you'd be into a guy like me." I squeeze my fingertips against her hips, avoiding the curious look in her eyes.

"What do you mean?"

"I don't know." There's an awkward clenching in my chest. "I guess I'm not all fit and lean with perfect hair like Gunderson. I think that guy has a six-pack on top of his six-pack."

Shocked laughter spills from her lips. "That's not why I had a crush on Nate."

"No?"

"No, you goof. I mostly liked him because he reminded me of a puppy."

"A *puppy*?"

"Yeah, like one of those little guys running around on the beach with their tongue hanging out, chasing birds and stuff."

"Wow, this is great. I feel loads better now. So I remind you of your dead, grouchy cat, and Nate reminds you of a cute, innocent puppy?"

"RIP, Mr. Tickles," she mumbles, glancing toward the sky. "And not anymore. Plus, like I said, that silly crush had absolutely nothing to do with this double six-pack you're referring to."

"Alright."

"I do love *your* body, though." Her fingertips fumble with the buttons on my shirt, slipping each one through its respective hole. Her hands slowly trail down past my waist, then slide back up to push at the fabric around my shoulders. "Definitely sexy."

"We're in public, Harper."

"We're at the beach, Luca." She swipes her tongue across her bottom lip, subtly, an action I would have hardly noticed if my eyes weren't glued to the spot. "People go shirtless at the beach, you know. Plus, it's practically dark, and no one's out here anymore."

"All of this is true."

"I'll take my dress off if that would make you more comfortable."

My grip tightens around her hips, brows lifting. "How would . . . you know, there's something inherently wrong with your logic tonight."

"I have a bikini on under this, silly. We could go for a little night swim before we head back."

"I didn't bring trunks."

"You have boxers on, yeah?"

"Yeah."

"Then let's go."

She pushes onto her feet, tugging at my free hand. There's a pleading smile and a hopeful glimmer in her wide-eyed gaze, as if I might actually deny her.

"Yeah, alright."

The next thing I know, she drops my hand, lifts her dress over her head, and bounds toward the open ocean. The soft, green fabric billows into a pile halfway down the shore. I've barely managed to unbutton my shorts by the time she's fully submerged underneath the shallow waves.

With one final shake of my head and the ghost of a laugh, I take off after her.

Chapter Twenty-One

My hair is still damp from the ocean. The lingering salt water seeps into the headrest behind me, soaks through the bottom of my dress, and pools onto Luca's faded leather seats. I'd normally be worried about the possibility of a stain on his interior, but he doesn't seem to mind.

"Seriously, Harper, don't worry about it." His right arm slings around the passenger seat, one corner of his mouth lifting in a reassuring smile. He glances behind us, shifts into reverse, and steadily pulls out of the beach parking lot.

My shoulders slump. "I feel bad since I made you go for a swim when you weren't expecting it. I didn't even think about towels or anything."

"First of all, you didn't *make* me do anything. And second, I've had this car since before I had my learner's permit. I seriously could not care less about a bit of sand and salt water. Trust me."

"That long?" Luca must have owned this car for six or seven years at this point. I find it admirable, considering I've gone through at least three vehicles since the summer I turned sixteen. Four, if you count my short stint with a Vespa last year. "Was it a gift from your parents?"

"Definitely not." He gives me a disbelieving snort. "I saved up for it from the moment I turned twelve, just working odd jobs around the neighborhood."

I've always known Luca was a hard worker, but the fact that he started earning a wage that young is impressive. When I was twelve years old, I barely had the drive to run my own lemonade stand.

"That's cool. Subarus are great starter cars, according to my dad anyway."

He keeps one hand on the steering wheel, patting his dash with the other. "Yeah, I'm sure I'll hold on to her until she dies on me. I'm not looking forward to that."

"Do you have a dream car, then? Something you want to buy when you go pro?"

An odd expression tilts his features. "Nah, I haven't really thought about it."

"What about something else? Something you want to spend your first paychecks on?"

We pull up to a stoplight, and his gaze cuts in my direction. He lifts one brow, the corner of his mouth ticking into an amused smile. "You seem really confident that I'll be drafted."

"Oh, without a doubt," I say sincerely, reaching for his hand across the center console. "I know you will be."

A grin splits his face. "I hadn't really thought about it too much, either, to be honest. But I guess a bigger house for my parents. I'd probably pay off Taylor's graduate loans and maybe college for Elio."

"That's your younger brother, right? He's eighteen?"

We round another corner into town, only a few miles away from his neighborhood now. The roads are mostly empty, and the sky is dark, but the steady glow of the streetlights splashes against his side profile.

His features are the perfect mixture of soft and masculine—

with his sharp jaw, the wide bridge of his nose, and the puffiness to his full lips, Luca is undeniably attractive, especially when he talks about his family.

"In a couple of months, he will be." There's a bitter undertone to his words, a flash of irritation setting his jaw. "He's supposed to be submitting college applications right now, but I'm sure he'll make up some excuse for not doing them."

I change course, pressing a soft squeeze to his hand. "And your younger siblings?"

"Yeah, maybe I'll start college funds for them, too. And pay for more therapy for Giorgie."

Ah, there it is. Another sliver of information about Luca's life outside of Coastal. I know it's not easy for him to confide in others—he admitted that last night—but I'm glad he's starting to open up to me now.

"Therapy?"

"Yeah, she's, uh . . . she's got a lot of sensory issues, communication differences, that sort of thing. That's actually why I've been picking up extra shifts lately. I want to help my parents out where I can."

I lift our linked hands to my mouth, pressing a kiss to his knuckles. "You're a good brother, Luca."

His cheeks tinge the slightest shade of pink. Clearing his throat, he squares his shoulders and says, "I mean, it's what you do for family."

"Yeah, but still."

"What about you? You've never mentioned siblings or anything."

I settle into my seat, tipping my head back against the headrest. "I'm an only child, so it was just me and my parents growing up."

"When was the last time you saw them?"

"Oh, it's been a few months or so. I think Dad has plans to visit in a couple of weeks, but we'll probably just grab dinner or something quick."

"And your mom?"

"Probably not until spring, actually. She's galivanting around Europe with her boyfriend for the next few months."

"Wow, that must be nice."

"Yeah, she's been sending lots of pictures, and it looks amazing."

"So your parents are . . ."

"Not together, obviously. It's only been a few years since they divorced." Or energetically split, as they like to call it.

I think it all happened, oh, about forty-five minutes after I left for Coastal. My parents called me separately, the week after I settled in, to share the news. They were obviously waiting until the exact moment I flew the coop, not that I minded.

"That sucks, Harper. I'm sorry."

He makes one last turn, steering us down the road toward his and Taylor's home.

"No, don't be. I was actually happy for them when it happened. I never thought they were a very good couple. Plus, now they're living their best non-married lives without each other. Dating lots of different people and traveling. It's great."

"Wow, I can't imagine my parents ever doing something like that." His eyes widen at the thought. "I can't even picture them leaving our tiny little hometown."

"Yeah, but it sounds like you have this big, happy family. I love both my parents, but they were never like that. I'm sure it must be pretty fulfilling."

"They're definitely happy, so far as I can tell."

"And your siblings, are they happy?"

"I think so." He cautiously flips his turn single with his only free hand. "Elio's pretty much always whining about something and getting into trouble, but that's expected from a kid his age."

We pull into the empty driveway, headlights flashing through the front windows of their home. I catch a quick glimpse of Bentley before Luca slowly drops my hand and cuts the engine.

"Do you think I could meet them someday?"

"You'd want to?" He flicks a mirthful glance in my direction. "They're kind of a lot."

"Of course I would."

His shoulders relax, the slightest smile tipping the corners of his mouth. "Then, yeah. I'll take you home whenever we can make time."

My heart swells. "Good."

"So."

"So . . ."

He nods toward his front patio. "Would you want to come inside? Maybe shower off and watch a movie or something?"

"I'd love to."

THERE's a pile of Luca's clothing waiting for me on the countertop—a crisp white T-shirt adorned with the Boyer Pier logo and a set of gray sweatpants. He's down the hall, finishing up his shower, while I peer at myself in Taylor's bathroom mirror.

I look beyond tired. My eyes are bloodshot from our late-night swim. My face is scrubbed clean, devoid of every last drop of tinted sunscreen. I'm worn-out from the eventful weekend, recovering from some mild emotional whiplash, but so happy at the same time.

As I gaze at my reflection, I take a moment to pinch some warmth back into my cheeks. I swipe the wet, tangled strands of hair from my eyes, pulling them back behind my shoulders.

I don't think I've ever looked so rough on a date before, but I can't bring myself to care.

"Everything okay in there?" Luca asks, his deep voice carrying through the wooden barrier. "You have what you need?"

"Your clothes are falling off of me, but I'm good." I attempt to re-cinch the drawstring on his sweats for the third time, shaking my head as they slip from my hips. "You said Taylor's out for the rest of the night, right?"

"Yeah, why?"

"I'm just gonna go without the pants, then."

I wriggle out of his sweatpants, scoop up my damp clothing, and toss the used towel over one shoulder. When I finally pull open the door, Luca's eyes go wide.

"Hey," he says evenly, his heady gaze scraping down the length of me.

"Hey." I glance down to my partially bare legs. It's not like the sight is obscene or anything, considering his T-shirt drapes at least halfway down my thighs. Besides, I spent the last few hours wearing nothing but a tiny string bikini. "Hope this is okay? I couldn't get the pants to fit without falling right off."

"It's good." His words are thick, rough with tension before he clears his throat. "I mean . . . you're good."

"So, what do you want to watch?"

He swallows, throat visibly bobbing. "What?"

"The movie?"

"Oh, right." He shakes his head to clear the fog, gesturing for me to exit the restroom behind him. "Yeah, anything. We can watch something in the living room or . . ."

I lift a brow. "Or?"

"Or I could set up the laptop in my bedroom?"

"Let's do your room."

With a soft smile, he takes my hand and guides me down the hall. His thumb nudges against the back of my hand, two soft little taps, before he drops it and starts to fidget around his room. While he preps his laptop, I slide underneath the covers.

His mattress is comfortable, his room is tidy, and his sheets are crisp and clean. There are more than enough pillows for us to use, which I prop into place while he slides in beside me.

"You want to pick?" he asks, one arm looping around my shoulders, laptop braced on his thighs.

I nestle against him, shifting so the sides of our bodies are flush. "Surprise me."

He scrolls through the homepage of Netflix for a few moments, stopping to click on some late-nineties thriller starring Matt Damon. I don't care what the movie is, honestly. I'm just here to snuggle.

As the film progresses, I slowly tangle our legs together. My head rests gently against his warm chest, and his heartbeat nearly lulls me to sleep. I manage to keep my eyes open, if only to sneak in a kiss or two.

We're about halfway through the second act when Luca's palm brushes against my hip. At first, I think it might be a simple accident, but then his fingertips press into my skin, dancing toward my inner thigh. His borrowed T-shirt rides up, exposing me, and my breath hitches in my throat.

"Luca, I'm not—"

"Fuck, I'm sorry." He pulls back sharply, as if burned by a lick of fire. "Was that too forward?"

"No, no." I slide his palm back into its rightful place. "I just know you asked to take things slow, so I wanted to warn you that I'm not actually, um, wearing any panties at the moment."

His nostrils flare. "Oh."

"It's just, I wore a bikini under my dress earlier. It was wet, and your shirt was long enough, so I—"

"Harper, you don't need to explain yourself." His chuckle is soft, fingers tightening against me. "You were just trying to be comfortable."

"Right."

"Besides, there's been something on my mind since last night."

"Yeah?"

He uses his free hand to pause the movie, voice dipping low. "I know we talked about slowing down, figuring this out together, but I've still been thinking . . . about what *you* might like."

"What do you mean?"

"What you like . . . or, I guess, what makes you feel good."

My brows furrow. "Oh, like in bed?"

"Yes, Harper." His eyes pinch shut, one hand rubbing his temple. "In bed."

A bubble of surprise fizzles low in my stomach. "Oh, well, I could always tell you if you want."

"Maybe you could show me?"

"Hm?"

His eyes meet mine for a few beats, chest rising unsteadily. It's clear that he's nervous, but he seems determined to plunge forward anyway.

"Harper, I'm asking if I can go down on you, because it's pretty much all I've been thinking about since you first asked me to kiss you. And now you're sitting here, in my bed, wearing nothing beneath my work shirt."

"Yes, yes." I scramble to sit up in the bed, already writhing against him. "Then let's do that. Right now?"

"Right now." He chuckles again, fingers playfully tugging at the hemline of my T-shirt. "And maybe, in the spirit of our honesty pact, you could show me exactly what you *do* and don't like."

"Yes, I can definitely do that." I move to kiss him, shoving my fingers into his hair. It's still slightly damp from the shower, but the strands feel soft and perfect against my hands. When he attempts to maneuver us onto the edge of the bed, I stop him, my rational brain making a brief appearance. "Wait, what about your knee? You probably shouldn't—"

"Oh, fuck my knee."

Chapter Twenty-Two

LUCA

My knees hit the floor as I drag Harper's hips into place. She's lying back on the edge of my bed, shirt riding up a half inch below her navel, elbows perched against the mattress. Our eyes meet—slate gray against warm cedar.

"Are you sure about this position?" she asks, worrying at her lower lip. "We could just lie on the bed head to foot? Or I could hop onto the bathroom counter, and then you wouldn't even—"

"No," I say gruffly. "This is just how I imagined it. Me on my knees for you."

"Jesus," she murmurs.

My hands slide up her body, pushing at the loose T-shirt until the undersides of her breasts are exposed. Goose bumps leave a trail beneath my fingertips. As I graze the hemline, her nipples pebble against the thin fabric.

"That feels good," she whispers.

I stretch my arms across the bed, palms moving to cup both breasts. They're so fucking soft—small and bell-shaped and perfect beneath my hands. On a deep exhale, my fingers sweep down to gently grasp her hips.

Although the top half of her chest remains covered, the rest of her body is bare to me now. Her freckled skin is warm to the touch. Her strong thighs are parted around my waist. If I'm being honest, it's a miracle I haven't come in my pants already.

Steeling my resolve, I shift back to press a kiss to her inner thigh. Her eyes flutter closed.

"So soft," I rasp.

"I shaved my legs just before our date." Her eyes shoot open. "Not because I thought anything was going to happen, I just—"

"Shh." My lips kiss a trail toward the center of her body. "Harper?"

"Yes?"

"I can feel how you move against me, hear how you sound, but I'm not the best at reading cues or body language. I'm gonna need you to tell me what you like, what you want, okay?"

"Using words?"

I smirk against her skin. "If you can?"

"I can."

With my fingers flexed, I slowly drag two knuckles against the seam of her. She's already soaking wet and warm to the touch, silkier and softer here than I could have imagined. On the second graze through, a sigh of pleasure escapes her lips.

"More," she pleads.

I use my thumb to push against the small hood covering her clit. There's another half sigh before I pitch forward and suck on the tiny bundle of nerves. Three slow, deep pulls before I slide an index finger inside of her.

"One finger or two?"

She squirms against me, her hips writhing against my hand. "Mmm," she moans in response, low and slow, but it's not the answer I'm looking for.

"Harper?"

"Right," she pants. "Just the one. Your fingers are ..."

"Big?"

"Mhm. Is the rest of you?"

Warmth spreads across my cheeks. "Big enough to fill you, if that's what you're asking."

I'm not huge or anything. I'd say slightly bigger than average and certainly nothing to be ashamed of. Judging by the snug fit of my finger inside of her, I'd bet money she'll be satisfied by my size.

"Luca, can you—" She pauses, whimpering as I hook my finger and drag it against her inner wall. "Can you . . ." She trails off again, interrupted by another tiny series of whimpers. My finger continues to pump, my thumb pushing and circling her clit.

"Can I what, Harps?"

"Can you use your tongue?"

I kiss the side of her knee, smile against her skin, moving to circle her clit with my tongue. There's a breathy moan. A soft sigh. I drag my finger out and grip her hips, yanking her another inch closer to my mouth.

The flat of my tongue slides across her slit, a gentle pass-through before I push inside of her. As she cries out my name, her fingers slide into my hair.

"Yes, yes, yes," she murmurs the mantra, bucking her hips into me. Her body grinds and twists as she wrings out her pleasure. The low, steady pulsing of her clit throbs against the bridge of my nose.

I remove my tongue and draw the bud into my mouth—a few pulsing sucks—before I pull back and ask, "Fingers now?"

"Uh-huh." She nods frantically, her body quivering and shaking above me. "Please."

At the hum of her pleading, I plunge two fingers inside of her, curl them softly, and suck her clit one last time before she comes apart. A rush of sweet, earthy liquid coats my fingers, my tongue, then slicks across my palm.

She collapses onto the bed, her own fingers sliding out of my hair as I revel in her taste. At this point, I'm so hard that it's almost embarrassing. There's a wet spot at the front of my sweats, a dot of precum revealing that I'm likely quick on the trigger these days.

"You're so good at that," she says, followed by another breathless sigh.

I rise off my knees, press one last kiss to her thigh, and take a single step before she stops me in my tracks. "Where are you going?"

"I was just gonna grab a washcloth for you."

She perches up fully on her elbows now, gazing up at me with hooded eyes. "Just take off your shirt and use that. It's clean, right?"

"Ah." I gulp low in my throat, twisting the hemline of my shirt between two fingers. "Sure."

I suppose Harper saw me shirtless a few hours ago, but we were basking in the dim moonlight, distracted by the waves at Amber Isle. Here, in the stark brightness of my bedroom, I have to admit that I'm intimidated.

It's not that I'm not proud of my body, but it's far from perfect. I'm not lean or cut or perfectly chiseled like some of the defensive backs . . . or like the number one infielder on the baseball team. I'm a middle linebacker, which means my two-hundred-and-thirty-pound body weight is comprised of muscle covered by a thick protective layer. After all, it's a body built to tackle and defend.

I know Harper said she's attracted to me physically, but there's a part of me that knows I'm way out of my league here.

"You don't have to," she whispers, shifting until she's seated fully upright on the bed. She wraps both arms around me and slips her hands underneath the back of my shirt. Her mouth lifts in a coy smile as she adds, "I just thought it would be hot."

I shake my head, slipping the shirt off with an amused huff. Bracing her shoulders, I gently shove her back onto the bed and swipe the fabric across her bare skin, cleaning up the mess we made between her legs. There's a hamper in the far corner, where I toss the aftermath.

"Just like I thought." She pulls at my wrists, yanking until I'm bent over the top of her. Our lips meet in a fevered kiss, a quick swipe of her tongue and a little nip against my bottom lip before she pulls back. "So hot."

We shift until we're lying side by side on the bed. She curls into me, fingers stroking across my chest and down toward my stomach.

"Was that okay?" I ask, my abdominal muscles clenching beneath her touch.

"More than okay."

"Is there anything else you like?"

I realized a long time ago that neurotypical communication isn't my strong suit. In the bedroom, especially, it can be difficult to figure out someone else's body—to read their cues, learn their cries, and apply that information in order to make them feel good every time.

I spent three years learning how to please one person and one person only. I won't waste any time with Harper.

"Yes, actually." She places a chaste kiss to my neck, my jaw, my lips.

"Oh?"

"I like words, too."

My brow furrows in confusion. "Words?"

"Your words." She traces a pattern against my stomach. "Your thoughts."

"You want to know what I'm thinking while we're together like that?"

"During. Or after, even. Now?"

"I was thinking about . . ." I clear my throat, diving through the awkward lilt in my voice. I can't say I'm used to dirty talk during sex, or *after*, but I sure can try. "I was thinking about how good you felt clenching around my fingers. How sweet you tasted. I was thinking about . . . how fucking hard you make me."

Her fingers slip further down my stomach, trailing a pattern underneath the waistband of my sweats. "And now?"

"I'm thinking that I'm still hard. That I'll probably be hard for days, just replaying the sounds you make when you come."

Her hand slips another half inch down my waist. "Can I . . .?"

"Another night?" I clear my throat, doing my best to ignore the heavy throbbing inside my pants. Of course I want her to touch me, to take me into her mouth, yet there's still something holding me back.

Maybe it's because the last time someone made me feel good, they shattered me into pieces a few moments later. No remorse. No apology. Not even an opportunity to wash their scent clean first.

Or maybe, in part, it's because I feel undeserving of Harper.

Whatever the case may be, it's proving difficult to fight through this weird mental block.

It doesn't matter anyway, because Harper takes the rejection in stride. With a soft smile, her fingers tap back across my stomach toward the side of my body. One hand curls around my waist.

"So tonight is all about me, then?"

"That was just as much for me as it was for you," I say. "Probably more so."

And that's the stark truth. Harper already makes me feel good every day. It's nice that I can make her feel good, too, at least in this way.

She hugs me tight, pulling back to meet my eyes. "You're really *good*, you know?"

"What do you mean?"

"You're just so . . ."

"So?" I prompt, a crinkle in my brow.

She beams, her smile filled with unknown secrets. "Yeah," she finally says, giving me absolutely no insight.

"Okay, Harper." I kiss the crown of her head. "Do you want . . . would you stay the night? I know you have class in the morning, and I have practice, but it's late."

"Is that the reason?" she teases. "Because it's late?"

"Because I want you to."

"Yeah, I'll stay."

We snuggle under the covers together, our linked hands resting on my bare stomach. I shift a little—forward, back, then onto my side facing her, tucking up my left leg until I'm at least semi-comfortable.

I won't admit it to Harper, but there's an unavoidable ache inside my knee now. It's painful but not unbearable. I'll need to ice it the moment she leaves in the morning, but I knew the consequences of my actions before I started this.

"Harper?"

"Yeah?" she murmurs, her voice already filled with sleep.

"You're good, too," I say. "So good."

Chapter Twenty-Three

"Do you have a bikini that 'Lani can borrow?" Stella asks as she crosses into my bedroom. She rifles through my dresser drawers before I can even formulate a response, sifting through layers of lacy underwear and boy shorts.

Lai'Lani is more my size than Stella's, meaning she has tiny boobs that would never fill out her girlfriend's bikini tops. I consider it both a gift and a curse. While we can get away with wearing no bra and backless tops, any attempt at cleavage is a concerted effort.

"Top left." I chew on the end of my pen, flipping through my ergonomics textbook. "What are you guys doing today?"

"Hot tub party at Saachi's apartment." She pulls out a lime-green triangle suit, holding it up for my approval. "This one fine?"

"Yeah, of course. And are we talking about your ex, Saachi?"

"Who else?"

Stella met Saachi last October. She came into the Surfbreak with her three roommates, and they hit it off right away, dating for almost half the school year. Sadly, that's about four months longer than any romantic relationship I've ever had.

"'Lani doesn't care?"

She tilts her head, smile filled with amusement. "We're all friends."

"Very enlightened of you."

She steps closer, tapping me on the nose. "Just because my little Blue Fairy doesn't have any exes to be friends with doesn't mean it's not possible."

I cross my arms, feigning a pout. "I have exes."

"I mean actual exes. People you talked to for more than a few weeks before you started crushing on someone else."

I rack my brain for a response, coming up with a singular name from the last three years of my college life. "Rory from freshman year."

She gives me a sympathetic smile. "Honey, Rory was dating about half of Coastal at the time."

"It was an open relationship."

Stella's not necessarily wrong. I've casually dated a lot of different people since coming to Coastal. My crushes may fade quickly, but that doesn't mean the feelings weren't real at the time.

"It was a situation-ship at best. Speaking of, how are things going with Reynolds?"

"See, now that's definitely not a *situation-ship*."

"Oh, so you're in a full-fledged relationship now?" Her lips purse into a teasing smile. "He's your boyfriend, then?"

He's not exactly my boyfriend, as we haven't had that conversation yet, but I'd like to hope we're moving in that direction. Our relationship may have started as a lie—an attempt at quid pro quo —but now Luca has officially wormed his way into my heart.

"We're dating."

"I'm happy for you two, really. And for Reynolds' sake, I hope he can keep you interested."

"Stella," I whine. "I really do like him."

"I know you do. I can tell. And you've been talking to him

for a while, but you know that your super-crush on Nate just exited the picture, so . . ."

"That was nothing."

She lifts one perfectly sculpted brow. "And Luca's something?"

"He is."

"Good." She moves toward the doorway. With one final pat against the frame, she asks, "So, hot tub party? You can invite him if you want."

"Luca in a hot tub with a bunch of half-naked girls? Sounds like a place he'd be super comfortable in."

We share a laugh. "So I'll take that as a rain check?"

"I have to study anyway, but thank you. You and 'Lani have fun, okay?"

"We will."

TODAY IS one of my last shifts at Amber Isle. The late-October air is crisp and cool, but there's a residual heat to the ocean. It's been a nice morning so far, especially since I've spent most of it staring over at Luca. I mean, I've been watching the beach for any potential drownings, of course, but I've also been making googly eyes at the guy I'm dating.

He's so handsome. I can hardly see him from this vantage point, but I can picture the exact expression he's wearing. His pinched brows. His half scowl. His floppy, dark hair falling partway into his eyes.

As if he can feel the heat of my gaze, his body shifts, head lifting in my direction. A warm smile stretches my cheeks, and we exchange waves—mine is overly exaggerated and enthusiastic, while his appears to be half-cocked.

I brace myself to hop off the lifeguard stand, but he's already headed in my direction.

As he approaches, I cross and uncross my legs, flip my ponytail back behind my shoulders, twirl the front strands that frame my face. It's been nearly a week since we've spent any time together. More accurately, it's been six whole days since our first date ended in an impromptu sleepover.

We've been texting here and there, but we've both been overly busy.

"Hey." He extends an arm in my direction, offering a helping hand. "Want to hop down for a minute?"

I tap my chin. "What's in it for me?"

"Anything you want."

"A kiss?"

His cheeks flush, lips forming a shy smile. "That could be arranged."

I slide into place, legs dangling from the podium. Luca lifts both arms to meet my waist. His strong hands grip me on either side as I shift forward, landing feet-first in the sand. With a tiny smirk, I tilt my head up so he can kiss me. His lips are soft and warm, and I instantly melt against him, taking comfort in the way he holds me.

"You smell good," he murmurs against my lips. "Peaches."

I pull back, nudging our noses together. "It's my shampoo."

"I know."

I beam, appreciating the soft flutter of butterflies in my stomach. "You came to say hi."

"I noticed you staring at me all morning."

My mouth drops open, cheeks warming. "I wasn't staring . . ."

"Sure."

I playfully kick at the sand. "I wasn't."

"Okay." He trails one hand up and down my exposed back. "If you weren't staring at me, then I haven't been thinking about you all week."

"Fine, I admit it." I duck my chin, hiding a smile. "But it's only because it's hard to see you from here. I had to squint to make out your features, and that takes time."

His hand moves from my back to my shoulder before brushing across my collarbone. "Valid excuse."

"So you've been thinking about me, huh?"

"Only a lot."

"I've been thinking about you, too."

And I have been, every day we've spent apart. When I first wake up, I think about the sound of his voice. When I step out into the morning light, I think about his smile. And when I go to bed at night, I think about the way his body feels, arms wrapped around me tightly.

It's an endless cycle, a dream I wish was reality.

He hooks a finger under the thin strap of my one-piece uniform, tugging me closer. "Can you come over tonight?"

"Don't you have a game?"

"It's a home game. Come after? Not to help me recuperate or anything," he rushes to clarify. "I just want to spend time with you."

"I could come to the game, too. If you wanted?"

"Yeah, I want that." He smooths his hands down the sides of my hips, gaze dragging across my frame. "Do you . . . I mean, I have a jersey you could wear."

A giddy smile lights up my face. "Okay."

"I can drop it off on my way to the field, then."

"Perfect."

He leans down, pressing one last kiss to the top of my hair.

With a few small steps backward, he grins as he says, "I should get back to the pier, but I'll see you tonight."

It's nearing ten o'clock by the time I make it over to Luca's place. The game finished up a few hours ago, but he needed time to field interviews, debrief with the team, and take a quick shower. I'm feeling antsy after all this waiting, especially since I spent the night wearing his name across my back.

When he finally pulls open the door, I'm bouncing on the balls of my feet. "You were so amazing tonight."

The Ospreys wiped the field with the Penn Valley Pirates. Luca led his team for the second game in a row with nine tackles, including two for a loss. I don't know much about football, honestly, but I had Fletcher run me the stats after the game. According to him, Luca played like a champ.

"Thank you," he says, sweeping me through the front door. His hands come to rest against my hips as he gives me a quick once-over. "You should wear this all the time."

I tug at the sleeves of his oversized jersey. "You like?"

"Love," he says gruffly.

I twirl in place, the excess fabric billowing around my thighs. "It's just a little bit big on me, no?"

"I think it's a perfect fit."

My smile widens. "Did you see me rooting for you in the student section?"

"Sadly, I couldn't make you out in the crowd. It's pretty hard to focus up there once the game gets going, but at least I knew you were there."

"I'm gonna need to step up my game, then. Wear some face paint and bring a sign."

"That's definitely not overkill."

"It's not." I swat at his bicep. "I loved watching you play, by the way. You must be so exhausted."

"Yeah, I'm fucking beat."

I thread our hands together, dragging him down the hallway behind me. "I could give you a massage tonight, check on your knee, and then maybe you can sleep in tomorrow?"

He sighs as we shuffle into his bedroom. "I have a double shift starting at 6:00 a.m."

"Seriously?"

"Yeah, I can't afford to skip out on a Sunday." He slumps down onto the edge of his bed, pulling me into the space beside him. "Now, more than ever, I need the extra money."

My hand reaches up to cup his face. "I could help out if you wanted?"

"What do you mean?"

"I mean, my parents cover my tuition and board, so I just use lifeguarding as extra spending money. I've actually saved most of it from the summer, so I could help you out with whatever you need to give your parents."

"Wait a minute, hold on." He removes my hand from his cheek, bringing it back down to the mattress. "You're offering to give me money?"

My brow crinkles. "I just thought—"

"Yeah, that's not happening."

"It's not a big deal, really," I plead, pressing one palm against his thigh in reassurance. "I promise."

His hand covers mine. "Stop."

My smile falls. "Luca—"

"Just stop, okay? You must see me as some big charity case." He gulps low in his throat and turns away. "First the injury, now this."

"Not at all." I shake my head. "Look, I'm sorry I offered, but I—"

He stands abruptly, head turning toward the open doorway. "It's getting pretty late, actually. I can take you home."

"I just got here, Luca," I huff, allowing the heated emotion to cloud my voice. "And I drove myself."

"Right," he says on a heavy sigh. There's a stilted silence that follows, punctuated only by the heavy rise and fall of his chest.

It takes me a few moments to gather myself. My first inclination is to apologize and wrap my arms around him, but I'm not so sure I have anything to be sorry for. He can't immediately shut me out and make me leave like he did before. We agreed on transparency since then. I may have touched on a hot subject, but this reaction is unfair.

"I just see how much pressure you put on yourself, and I wanted to help," I say softly.

"No, I know." He reclaims his seat beside me, rubbing his temples. "I shouldn't shut you down like that, but we come from two very different worlds, Harper. And you should know that I'll never take money from you. I don't like owing a debt to anyone."

"I'd never think of it like that."

"It doesn't really matter, but thank you for offering. I really do appreciate you being there for me."

"Of course." I tug at a strand of hair, self-conscious and hyperaware of the space I'm occupying in his bed now. "Do you still want me to leave?"

"No." He swallows, giving me an apologetic smile. "No, I want you to stay. Will you?"

"Yeah."

"Come here, then." He shifts on the bed, pulling me into

the open space between his legs. Both arms wrap around my chest as I lean back against him. "Stay the night?"

"Only if I can sleep in your jersey."

He chuckles, low and deep, as he murmurs against my hair, "How'd you know just what I wanted?"

Chapter Twenty-Four

"You have a bye week, right?"

Harper's lying stomach down on her bed, kicking her feet into the air while she doodles the circulatory system. Much to our mutual annoyance, we've spent all of our free time together this week studying. It's a delicate balance between football practice, two sets of classes, my chaotic work schedule, and her internship.

"Yes, thankfully," I say from my spot at her desk. There's a physics journal sitting in front of me, but I can't be bothered to open it. "I could use the break."

She shuts her notebook, perching herself into a seated position. "Did you want to do something for Halloween? The baseball guys invited me and the girls to a party on Saturday." She clears her throat, attempting a casual smile. "Nate specifically told me to bring you."

A hot spike of jealousy pangs in my gut. "Nate?"

She hasn't so much as mentioned his name for weeks, but I know she's still working with the baseball team. That can't be avoided. Besides, I'm fairly certain this thing between us is exclusive.

Shit. It *is* exclusive, right?

"He's trying to be nice, I think. Make up for being—"

"A complete dipshit?"

"You could call it that, but he has been really nice the last couple of weeks. Not that we talk often, just when we're on the field or in the gym," she rambles on, eyes wide. "So, what do you think?"

"Ah, I might be busy."

Her smile fades, and it makes me want to slap myself.

"I know it's not really your thing, but it could be a good chance for us all to hang out. You've met my friends, but we haven't spent much time together as a group."

"I was actually hoping to go home this weekend and see my family."

That piques her interest. "Oh?"

"Yeah, I wanted to invite you along." I brace myself for rejection. "But if you have plans . . ."

"No, I'll definitely go with you." She pushes off the bed, settling herself onto my lap and wrapping both arms over my shoulders. "I don't have a costume yet, anyway."

"Okay, yeah." I press a quick kiss to her forehead, fighting a grin. "We'll go on Saturday afternoon, then. We can eat dinner with my parents and hang out with the kids for a while."

She bounces on my lap, eagerly pressing her nose into the crook of my neck. "That sounds great."

I hold her in my arms for a few minutes, running my hands through the ends of her golden-brown waves. I curl one thick strand around my index finger and lightly tug. "Harper, are you sure you don't want to go out with your friends?"

She nudges me playfully, shaking her head. "There's nowhere I'd rather be."

ONE GOOD THING about visiting home is that we live less than twenty miles from Boyer. It's a quick trip, one I could easily pull off on a random weeknight. Yet I haven't been back here in months. As we merge onto the exit, I let my shoulders drop, guilt swirling in the pit of my stomach.

"My parents are a little overbearing, but they mean well." I anxiously tap my fingers against the center console, one hand braced on the steering wheel. "They'll probably hound you with questions about me."

Her hand covers mine, instantly settling my nerves. "And what should I tell them?"

"Whatever you want." I flip my palm to intertwine our fingers. "Just don't mention my injury, obviously. They'd go postal."

My parents have six offspring, so they're familiar with all sorts of aches and tears and sprains. I wouldn't call them protective, necessarily, but my mom thinks I'm too hard on myself already. She projects that energy onto my dad, who then forces Taylor to look after me.

I'm already an adult man living with his older sister. There's no part of me that requires three separate parental figures, especially when it comes to problems I can solve myself.

"Easy enough."

"My brother, Elio, is likely gonna be in a bad mood. I promise it doesn't have anything to do with you."

Elio's pretty much always in a sour mood these days. At least, he is whenever I'm around. He seems angry at the world in general, for reasons I can't even begin to understand. It's not like he has anything concrete to complain about. Our parents are practically saints, and our younger siblings are perfect.

"Noted," she says with a soft smile.

"The twins, Mia and Vivia, they'll probably just be doing their own thing all night. They like to hide out in their room to play video games or whatever. My mom usually makes them something special for dinner and brings it to them. It's ridiculous."

"How old are they?"

"They're turning fourteen in a few months. I didn't realize how scary middle schoolers could be until last year."

"Hey!" She pins me with a harsh look. Or her best attempt at one anyway. "Those hormone fluctuations can be really tough on a young girl."

I stifle a laugh at her expression. "I believe you."

We round the corner, slowly pulling into my parents' driveway. A prickle of irritation dots up my spine as I take note of Elio's missing car. He won't pick up my calls, and now he's missing from our family dinner? The kid clearly doesn't give a shit about me.

"And your youngest sister?"

I turn my attention back to Harper. "Giorgie's non-speaking, so she uses her iPad as a communication device. She'll probably warm up to you pretty fast, though."

"Sounds good." She squeezes my hand, gesturing toward the front entrance. "I think I'm ready to go in now."

A wave of discomfort washes over me. "Okay."

"Are *you* ready?

"Yes," I say unsteadily, the nerves still racketing around my brain. I've never intentionally introduced a girl to my family before. With Sofia, the two of us were friends long before we were romantically involved. It was a natural, slow progression from acquaintances to friends to dating, and my family was involved from the get-go.

"You don't need to be nervous, Luca." Her tone is sweet, reassuring, and it serves to ease a tiny fraction of my anxiety. "I swear I'll make a good impression. I *have* met people before, you know."

"I'm not worried about that." I awkwardly rub at the back of my neck. "I, uh, I want you to like them."

"I'm sure I'll love them."

She releases my right hand to lean over the center console, pulling me in for a kiss as her fingers caress my jawline. When she leans back, her eyes shine with a mixture of cool gray and ocean blue. It's a familiar, calming sight.

"Let's go, then."

When we enter the house, hands linked, my mom immediately wraps us into a group hug. She sways back and forth on her heels, pulling back with a smile that stretches from ear to ear.

"We are so happy you're home, *caro*. Harper, it's so nice to finally meet you."

"You too, Mrs. Reynolds," Harper says cheerfully, her wide smile lighting up the entryway. "Thank you for letting me tag along tonight."

"Please, call me Gia. My husband, Greg, is in the kitchen chopping garlic." She ushers us both inside, nudging us toward the hallway. "Why don't you two go say hi to the girls and then head into the dining room?"

I clear my throat, prepping myself for an answer I'm not going to like. "Where's Elio?"

"He's not home quite yet." My mom's tone may be carefree, but her expression is weary.

"Shocking," I mutter.

"Give your brother some grace, *per piacere*."

With a tight-lipped smile, I nod and drop the subject. If I continue to hound her about my brother, she'll only grow more defensive. It's difficult for her to acknowledge that the two of us don't get along. And while Elio's rebellion is a sore topic for me, my parents seem to close their eyes to his indiscretions.

Sighing, I guide Harper down the hallway and over toward the twins' bedroom. The girls are lounging on a pair of beanbags with their door wide open. They're hyperfocused on a tiny television screen, tightly gripping their PS4 controllers as they battle it out on some racing game.

I loudly clear my throat. "Mia, Vivia, this is Harper. She's having dinner here tonight."

"Hi, guys, nice to meet you," Harper says, her chipper voice carrying across the room.

The girls greet us one a time with a simple "hey," barely sparing a glance in our direction.

"Where's our sister?" I ask.

Mia shrugs, sharing a look of pure annoyance with her twin. "We're not her keeper."

"Okay, guys." I let out an amused snort. "Thanks for that. I assume you won't be joining us for dinner, either?"

"Ew, no." Vivia finally glances over, pretending to gag. "Mamma made that stew with, like, scallops and stuff."

"You used to love cioppino," I say with a raised brow.

Mia rolls her eyes, button smashing her controller as she says, "Yeah, well, now we think it's gross."

I rub at my temples, shaking my head. "Okay, come on, Harps. Let's go find the sister that actually likes me."

"We like you!"

Harper and I laugh at their indignant response, trailing down the hallway hand-in-hand. I eagerly peer into Giorgie's room, only to find it empty. With furrowed brows, I guide Harper toward the living room and cup both hands around my mouth.

"Geeg, I have someone here who wants to meet you!"

Two seconds later, Giorgie bounds into the room at full speed, tablet in hand. One tiny arm wraps around my legs in a makeshift hug. When she pulls back, she taps through a few pages on her language app until she settles on a four-leaf clover.

"Lucky," the device reads back. Giorgie stares up at me with brown doe eyes and a wide-set smile. The sight instantly melts my heart.

"Where were you?" I ask, playfully nudging her shoulder. "We were looking all over the house."

She taps back to the first page, clicking on a few icons until she presses the read button. "I go bathroom."

"Ah, I see." I press my palm against Harper's back. "Geeg, this is my friend Harper. I'm sure Mamma told you I'd be bringing a guest."

Giorgie happily nods, dancing back and forth on her feet.

"Hey, Giorgie." Harper braces both palms on her knees, bending until she's at my sister's level. "It's good to meet you. I've heard a lot about you from your brother."

Giorgie selects a picture of a thumbs-up, which reads out the word "good." She taps over to a page filled with photos of our family members, selecting Elio's icon followed by a question mark.

"No, unfortunately," Harper says, sharing a laugh with my sister. "I haven't met that one yet."

"Good," Giorgie repeats, dissolving into a series of high-pitched giggles. There's nothing quite as joy-provoking as the sound of her unbridled laughter.

"Are you having cioppino with us tonight?" I ask, knowing full well the answer to my question. Giorgie hates the slimy texture of seafood, along with pretty much anything that's not prepackaged.

My sister's response comes in the form of a thumbs-down icon followed by a puke emoji.

"Alright then. I guess I'm the only Reynolds sibling who'll

be eating Mom's cooking tonight." I turn my focus back to Harper. "Please tell me you like seafood?"

"Love it," she says happily. "And I'd eat it even if I didn't."

"Of course you would." I chuckle. "Okay, Giorgie, we're gonna go help set the table."

She waves us both off, bouncing away toward her bedroom. There's a notable pep in her step now, meaning she probably enjoyed meeting Harper tonight. Giorgie generally takes well to new people, so long as her needs are met and she has access to a communication device.

In the dining room, Harper and I end up setting the table for five, including Elio, even though he's nowhere to be found. My mom steps out to bring the girls their separate plates of mac and cheese. At least she attempts to blend some carrots into the mix, but anything green is an absolute no go.

Throughout the entirety of our meal, my parents proceed to bombard Harper with small talk. It's an endless stream of questions about me, football, Coastal, and classes. Before I can successfully interject, it quickly evolves into a full-out inquisition about Harper—including her job, her major, her hobbies, and everything under the sun.

It's like a never-ending interview, but Harper takes it like a champ.

By the time dinner is finished, she's already standing, offering to clear the table and wash the dishes. Of course, my parents politely decline and instead urge us to make ourselves comfortable in the living room.

As the two of us settle onto the couch together, my body finally relaxes. I wrap one arm around Harper, but she nearly jumps out of her seat when the front door slams shut. It's not long before my brother tears into the room, a twisted smile marring his features.

"Elio, hey," I cautiously greet him, attempting to keep my frustration at bay. "This is Harper."

He awkwardly stretches both arms into the air, placing them behind his head. "Wow, she's even hotter than Sofia. Don't know how you do it, bro."

I stand from the couch, leveling him with a hard stare. "What the hell, E?"

"What?" His laughter is obnoxious. "Have you met you? I honestly don't understand how you keep pulling girls like that." He steps closer, gaze raking across the couch. "What is it about my brother, Harper? He must have a huge d—"

"Outside." I raise one flat palm, shoving him backward to cut him off. "Now."

He holds both hands up in surrender, snickering to himself as we head outside.

"What the fuck is wrong with you?" I ask, arms crossed for his safety.

He scoffs. "What do you want me to say?"

"I don't know, I figured you'd be a normal person for once!" I inhale a deep breath, steadying my voice. Despite the circumstances, I still don't want Harper to overhear me losing my temper. "First you miss our dinner. Then you act like a complete dick to my girl . . . the girl I'm dating."

"Ahh, you couldn't actually lock it down, huh?" He gives me a nasty look. "Makes sense. She's way out of your league."

"Man, I should've known you'd act like this. I actually thought you might be happy to see me tonight."

"Why? You finally decide to grace us with your presence, so you want me to drop everything just to smile at your new toy."

My fingers twitch as I tighten my grip, forcing my arms to stay folded. "Shut your mouth."

He pretends to zip his lips, dramatically dragging one hand across his face. With little to no warning, he folds over at his waist and breaks out into a ridiculous cackle.

"Seriously, is there something wrong with—" I pause in my tracks, pinpricks of ice chilling my veins. Elio is generally unpleasant, sure, but he's never acted this unhinged before. "Wait, are you high right now?"

He squares his shoulders, instantly sobering up. "What? No."

"You are, aren't you?" I drop my head into my hands, a mixture of panic and disappointment swelling inside of me. "This is rich."

"I'm not fucking high." It's his turn to shove me back this time. He moves toward the front steps, erratically fumbling with the doorknob. "Just leave me alone."

"E, stop."

He turns back, a wild, pleading look in his eyes. "Please don't tell Mom and Dad. It was a onetime thing, okay?"

I gulp. "Was it?"

"Yes." He chews on the end of his thumbnail, nervously staring at the ground between us. "I fucking swear to you. Jackson stole a little baggy of coke from his brother, and we tried it tonight. I was stressed about you coming home, and I thought it would take the edge off. I didn't even like it."

There's an unsteadiness brewing inside of me, a shaking in my bones. "That's fucked-up, Elio."

He wipes at his eyes, nodding, a few tears spilling free. "I know."

"I'll keep this to myself, but you have to promise me you won't do it again."

"I promise."

I take a couple of deep breaths before I pull open the door, whispering, "Get back in there and apologize to Harper, then go straight to bed. Next time I see you, I'm bringing a drug test."

"Could you please not mention this to Taylor, either?" he asks me, voice hushed and frantic. "I know she'd be disappointed."

"Fine," I manage to grit out.

"I'm sorry."

Well, fuck, so am I.

Chapter Twenty-Five

"I think that went pretty well, don't you?" I ask, toying with the hemline of my sundress. It's nearing nine o'clock on Saturday night, and we're finally headed back toward Coastal.

"Yeah, sure," Luca says in a noncommittal tone. His grip on the steering is tight, gaze trained on the road ahead of us.

"I mean, your parents were great. I didn't see too much of your sisters, but everyone seemed to like me well enough." I anxiously nibble on a cuticle. If he's worried about my reaction to Elio, he shouldn't be. "Um, there was some weirdness with your brother, but he apologized and everything."

"Uh-huh," he says, silently merging onto the freeway.

I place a firm hand on his bicep. "Luca?"

He shakes his head, glancing at me from his peripherals. "Sorry, you're right. My parents loved you."

"And?"

"And Elio was fucking high on coke tonight, so that's great," he mutters, despondent.

My shoulders drop. "Oh no, really?"

"Yep, my own brother felt like he needed to take drugs just to be around me. How much of a piece of shit does that make me?"

I hear the anguish in his voice, and it nearly breaks my heart. He's always putting so much pressure on himself, but I can't let him take the blame for this.

"Not at all," I say. "This isn't your fault."

"He told me he wanted to take the edge off because he was worried about me coming home." He takes a frustrated breath. "How is that not my fault?"

"Elio makes his own choices. The only thing you can do now is be there for him."

His lips form a lifeless smile. "I guess."

"What did you tell him when you figured it out?"

"I said I'd keep it from our parents but that I'm drug testing him next time I'm around. I'll just . . . I don't know, I guess I have to visit home more often."

With the way his schedule is running at the moment, that seems like an impossible feat. Luca barely has time to even breathe these days. If he doesn't allow himself to decompress, I'm worried the pressure will build and build until it all implodes.

"That might be good if you can swing it."

His sigh is so deep and heavy that it hollows out a cavity in my chest. "It's a lot to juggle, but I feel like I need to."

"Is there anything I can do to help?"

"No, just . . . just be with me." He lets one hand drop from the steering wheel, molding his fingers around my thigh. "That's all I need."

"I can do that."

We allow a comfortable silence to blanket the space around us. The freeway is quiet and mostly empty at this time of night, so all we can hear is the steady sounds of our mingled breath and the dull white noise of the car's engine.

I rack my mind for the best way to comfort him. I don't want to keep debating the topic tonight, especially since he's already entered a cycle of self-doubt. He could do with a distraction instead, a means to get his mind off the situation until he's ready to deal with the fallout.

And I might have the perfect solution.

Scrambling for my phone, it only takes me a few minutes to pull up the surf cams for Cape Casserat. As suspected, the beach in my hometown is experiencing a red tide, one that's persisted for nearly a month.

"Hey, do you think you could pull over on the next exit?" I ask, tucking my phone back into my purse.

"Uh, sure?" He cocks one brow. "We're still a few miles short of Boyer, though."

"I know, but I want you to switch with me."

He taps his thumb against the outside of my thigh. "You want to drive?"

"Mhm," I say cheerfully. "You don't start work until noon tomorrow, right?"

"Yeah, why?"

"You showed me your home; now I want to show you mine. I'm taking us to Cape Casserat tonight."

"What?" He shoots a bewildered glance in my direction. "We won't make it there until nearly midnight."

"That's perfect."

"You're confusing me."

"There's been a red tide there for weeks." I'm bouncing in my seat, heels tapping in the footwell. "It's probably the last chance we'll get this season to see the blue wave."

"Are you talking about bioluminescence?"

"Yes," I say excitedly. "So, will you go with me? I'll drive us back, and you can get some sleep before your shift."

"Fuck it," he says with a shake of his head, eyes bright with amusement. "Let's go."

We pull off onto the nearest exit and quickly swap places. Luca yanks at the bar below the passenger seat, adjusting the pitch for optimal legroom. I do the opposite, pulling myself forward a good six inches or so. Once we're all settled, I shift into gear and merge back onto the freeway, headed for my old home.

It only takes an hour for Luca to pass out beside me. He looks so peaceful when he sleeps, finally free from the ceaseless tension, so I dim the music and let him rest.

The remainder of our drive is familiar. I run this same route about three times a year now, visiting my dad whenever he can slip away from work. He's a senior account executive at a telecom company, so he's generally busier than either of us would like. He travels often, but he keeps his condo near the cape in case I ever need a safe place to land.

Despite the offer, I've never stayed the night without him here before.

It's approaching midnight when we finally pull up to the beachfront. I place a hand on Luca's shoulder, gently shaking him as I whisper, "We're here."

"Hm?" he murmurs, slowly blinking himself awake. He stretches both arms over his head, yawning and rubbing at his eyes.

"We made it here," I say softly.

"Shit, I'm sorry." He glances at his watch, clearing the sleep from his voice. "How long was I out for?"

"Just over an hour, but it's okay. I wanted you to get your rest."

Scrubbing a hand over his forehead, he asks, "Should we go check it out, then?"

"Yeah, but it's a race."

"Wait, what?" he asks, but I've already yanked the driver's-side door wide open. I'm halfway down the beach by the time he catches up with me. Both of his arms circle around my waist, hoisting me over his shoulder as he runs toward the shoreline.

"Put me down," I yell through my laughter, playfully swatting at his back.

He abruptly stops in his tracks. "Holy shit."

"What, what is it?" I squirm in his arms, flailing until he sets me down in the sand.

"I've never seen it quite like this before."

I follow his gaze, watching as an electric-blue wave crests and breaks against the shore, a brilliant smile stretching across my cheeks. I didn't know if we would still be able to catch the summer glow, but now I'm so happy we made the long drive.

"This must be the very tail end of it," I say, entranced by the glimmering water. "I saw it for the first time the summer I turned sixteen. I come back every year to watch, but the red tide was so late this year."

"Yeah, we almost never get it like this at home."

"That's probably a good thing . . . not as much pollution there. But isn't it still so beautiful?"

"It's incredible." He grins, looping an arm around my shoulders and tucking me against his side. "It also definitely smells like rotten eggs."

"Ah, that sweet sulfury smell," I say with a laugh. "Didn't you know, with beauty comes pain?"

"I tell myself that every day."

I roll my eyes, playfully bumping him with my hip. "So I was thinking about something on the drive over here."

"Oh yeah?"

"My dad has a condo just a few miles from here. He's out on a work trip right now, so we could stay there tonight, and I could drive us home first thing in the morning," I ramble, nervously twirling a strand of hair between my fingers. "If we leave by eight thirty, then we should have plenty of time for you to make your shift. Only if you want to, of course."

He squeezes my shoulder. "I'd like that."

"Oh, good, then."

"Wait, isn't tomorrow supposed to be your last shift of the season?"

"I switched with one of the girls already, so I'm on in the afternoon. You'll have to share the beach with me one last time."

"I guess I'm okay with that," he says, his soft smile melting into a smirk.

I take his hand as we wander the shoreline together, long enough to make the trip worthwhile. By the time we make it back to the car, I feel a mixture of exhaustion and happiness that's bordering on delirium.

"You want me to drive back to your dad's place?" Luca asks, opening the passenger door.

"Yes, please." I carefully slip inside as he bends down, popping a kiss onto my forehead before closing me in.

I ramble off directions as we pull out of the parking lot and onto the county roads. He turns up the stereo, humming under his breath and murmuring the words to some Wild Rivers song. He looks lighter, happier than I've ever seen him, as if a heavy weight has been lifted off his shoulders tonight.

It's not long before we're pulling into a parking spot in front of my dad's four-story condo. I watch as Luca scans the perimeter of the building, his eyes going wide before he schools his expression.

"Nice place," he says.

"It's pretty ostentatious, I know."

"Your dad lives here alone?"

"Actually, he's barely ever here. He has an apartment in the city, and then he lives out of a hotel room the rest of the time." I wring my hands together in my lap, a guilty sense of entitlement washing over me. "He keeps the condo for me, mostly."

He gives me a comforting smile. "I'm glad we could use it tonight."

"Me too," I say. "You ready to go in?"

He sighs, leaning over the center console and touching his forehead to mine. "I want to say thank you first."

"For what?"

"For this, for tonight, for everything." He kisses me then, just once, right on the lips. "Don't think I don't know what you've been doing."

"What do you mean?" I whisper, my heart swelling inside my chest.

"You've been trying to distract me from everything that's been going on."

"Is it working?"

He stares at me for a long moment, an unreadable expression on his face. I tense in my seat, hopeful that my efforts have paid off tonight, that driving us here on a whim was a good decision after all.

"You know, I've always known what it was like to be needed by someone, from my parents to my siblings to my one hundred and eighteen fucking teammates. Being needed feels endless. Until I met you, I never knew what it was like to be the one in need," he says, the corners of his lips hinting at a smile. "And I do need you, so fucking badly."

My heart is hammering, blood boiling inside my veins. "You do?"

"Fuck yes, I do." He swallows, throat bobbing as his eyes rake over me. "Harper?"

"Yeah?"

"I need you, and I want you. Tonight." He clears his throat, a flush of heat crawling up his neck. "Right now."

My mind spins, my thoughts and feelings teetering on the edge of a cliff as I decipher his meaning.

"You mean . . . like in bed?"

He chuckles, one arm snaking around my neck as he pulls me in for another long, heated kiss. Leaning back, he says, "Yes, Harper, in bed."

Chapter Twenty-Six

LUCA

"Do you really want this?" I ask, lips pressed against the hollow spot near Harper's collarbone.

We've made our way into the back bedroom of the condo, brushing lips and touching hands along the way. There's a queen-sized bed covered in throw pillows and about a dozen photographs of Harper lining the walls. Fake sunflowers sit in a hand-painted vase on top of the dresser.

My heartbeat jumps into my throat.

"Of course I do. Do you?" There's a hint of insecurity in her voice now. It makes my stomach clench to hear it, knowing I've put doubts in her head about how much I want her.

I swallow hard, forcing my eyes to lock onto hers. "There's nothing I want more right now than to be inside of you."

Her eyes widen. One hand wraps around my neck as she pulls me in for another kiss, lips so fucking soft. When I feel her smile against my mouth, I can't help but form one of my own.

I pull back, dipping my fingers underneath the tiny straps of her sundress. Slowly, I drag the material across the curve of her shoulders, watching as it slides off her body. Her feet shuffle in closer. She's blushing now—peachy and perfect—so I brush my hand across her cheek to feel the warmth.

"Luca?"

"Yeah?"

"I really like you."

I grab her hand and bring it to my mouth, pressing a soft kiss against her knuckles. "I like you, too. A whole fucking lot."

"Is it my turn to take your clothes off now?"

"All yours."

Her hands slide underneath my shirt, the muscles in my stomach clenching at her featherlight touch. She takes note of my stiff posture, pausing as she says, "Sorry, I forgot. Firm hands."

I lift my arms, pulling my shirt off the rest of the way. Her hands reach around my body and smooth over my lower back, moving toward the front of my jeans. With trembling fingers, she carefully pops the button open.

My brow furrows. "You're shaking."

"I know." She laughs, standing there in her underwear, clumsily yanking at my zipper. "I'm trying not to. I guess I'm just nervous for some reason. I'm acting like this is my first time or something, when I've actually done this loads of times. I mean, not *loads*. God, I mean like a normal, healthy amount."

"Hey." I grip her hand, sliding her palm up and over my heart. "Feel that?"

She nods as she stares up at me. My chest heaves with each calculated breath, heart drumming chaotically beneath her fingertips.

"You're nervous, too?" she asks, eyes shining.

"I just want to make you feel good."

She squares her shoulders and shakes her head, lips lifting in a self-assured smile. "Then take your pants off and get in the bed."

With a chuckle, I tug my zipper down and slide out of my jeans. My hands grip Harper's waist, signaling for her to wrap both legs around me. Once her thighs are securely tucked against my hips, I walk us both toward the bed, dipping forward until her back hits the mattress.

Her perfect body is spread out before me now, fully flushed with desire. I take a long, drawn-out moment to soak in her appearance. She's wearing a thin, strapless bralette that matches her panties—periwinkle blue, my new favorite color. And it's mostly transparent, so the flimsy lace pattern reveals a hint of her rosy nipples.

She lifts her arms, pulling the scrap of fabric up over her head. I shift into place and prop myself on one elbow beside her, before I duck down, my lips meeting the swell of her breast as I kiss the tender skin.

"Did you wear that for me?"

"I wore it for myself." Her eyes stray, gaze focused on my plain, black boxer briefs. "Why? Did you wear *those* for me?"

"Clearly."

With a soft giggle, her fingers trail down my chest, across my abdomen, and dip barely underneath my waistband. "Very hot."

"And you—" My teeth graze over her nipple, sucking it between my lips. "—are so fucking beautiful."

A tiny shiver racks her body at the contact. Her fingers curl, still barely tucked inside my boxers, mere centimeters from my growing erection. I'm aching to sink inside of her, but I want to savor this moment for a while longer. After all, we only get one shot at a first time together.

My hand slips from the curve of her breast, brushes across the side of her body, and lands on the swell of her hip. I grip her there, hooking my thumb underneath the elastic string waistband of her panties. "Can I take these off, too?"

"Mhm." She lifts her hips, helping me remove the last shred of fabric.

Goddamn. If I wasn't already painfully hard, my cock would be tripling in size at the sight of her fully naked beside me. Harper's body—from her glowing, freckled skin to the sweet curve of her hips to that perfect, blinding smile—is the stuff that wet dreams are made of.

I draw in a harsh breath. "Harper, can I . . ."

"What?"

"I want to feel you come on my tongue again."

She smiles, teeth sinking into her bottom lip. "Me first."

Her hands slip out from my boxers. With both palms pressed flat, she pushes at my chest until I shift onto my back, perched halfway up against the headboard.

"Take those off for me," she demands, nodding below my waist.

With one last hard swallow, I do what she asks. My dick is alarmingly erect at this point, throbbing for attention, and I have to resist the urge to cover myself as she openly gawks.

"It's so pretty," she murmurs, moving to caress me with her open palm.

"Jesus, Harper." I hiss at the contact. "Pretty?"

"Handsome?"

A groan accompanies the roll of my eyes. "Sure."

She strokes me up and down, two gentle passes that already have me gripping at the sheets. Her grasp is tentative, slow at first. Then she squeezes at the base, dips her head, and wraps her pouty lips around me.

"*Fuck,* that feels good."

My head tilts back, and my fingers thread through her hair. I struggle to keep my eyes open, enraptured by the sight of her head bobbing up and down on my cock but completely overwhelmed by the feeling. The pressure's already building low inside my gut, the threat of release forcing me to tap out early.

"Harper, *baby*," I mumble on a groan. "You have to stop."

She lifts off my dick, mouth parted, eyes glistening as my hands tangle in her hair. With her left thumb, she quickly swipes at her puffy bottom lip—it's a mental picture I plan on keeping for the rest of my life.

"What's wrong?" she asks, concern welling behind her eyes.

"I just don't want to come yet."

"Oh."

She shifts again, my arms falling to either side as she moves to straddle me on the bed. Her slick, wet folds press against my lower abdomen, and I nearly come on the spot.

"But I haven't . . . I mean, are you—"

"I'm ready," she says, cutting me off. "I'm so wet for you, Luca. And I need to feel you inside me."

Another low groan forces its way up my throat. "Protection?"

"Oh!" Her eyes widen, a spark of guilt settling in. "Oh, I nearly forgot. Let me grab something from my purse really quick."

In the next breath, she slides off me and bounces over to retrieve a condom. I will my heartbeat to steady as I watch her bend at the waist, her perfect ass on full display.

That's when I rifle through a series of horrible events inside my head—Jaquan tackling me during our preseason game, the feeling of my knee bending in on itself, the sharp popping sound that rang inside my eardrums—but none of it can subdue the excitement coursing through my veins. *God fucking dammit*, I'd sure like to last longer than five seconds tonight.

By the time Harper returns, my palms are full-on sweating. She parts her thighs on top of me, rips the condom package open, and slowly, painstakingly rolls it over my throbbing erection.

As she sinks herself down on top of me, I lift my hips to meet her halfway. There's a moment of brief clarity where I can feel everything—from the tight, warm suction to the low, steady pulsing of her inner walls—before it all fades away into an overwhelming cascade of sensation.

She lifts up and sinks down in a steady rhythm, grinding and slapping against me. Her palms press flat against my chest, so I grip her waist with both hands. My gaze shifts to all my favorite spots—her breasts, her hips, her eyes, her lips, that tiny divot beneath her rib cage—ultimately locking on where we're joined.

I watch, groaning deep in my throat as she rides me.

"You're so fucking perfect," I rasp, squeezing her hips until she's lifted a good few inches above my waist. As her head tilts back, I fuck into her from below, pounding harder as those little whimpers fade into heavy moans.

With a breathy pant, she begs, "More."

I grind into her, steadily pumping my hips off the bed. My grip tightens, easily holding her in place while I use my other hand to find her clit.

"Is that what you needed?" I ask.

She scratches at my chest, one hand moving up to tangle into my hair as she pulls me in for a kiss.

Fuck, fuck, fuck.

My hips snap up to meet hers, deep and frantic. I rub tight little circles into her clit and feel so fucking proud of myself when I hear the sound she makes. It's a low, deep moan that nearly has her collapsing on top of me.

"Luca, I'm gonna come."

"Come for me, baby," I say, the words barely scraping out of my throat. I force myself to take a breath, refocusing on Harper's pleasure. The last time I made her come, she told me she wanted to hear my thoughts while we're together like this. "You're doing so well," I say. "Feels so fucking perfect."

She whimpers and tightens around me then, moaning my name one last time before she falls apart.

"That's it, Harps. Let me feel you squeeze around my cock."

Her walls flutter and tighten once more before I'm met with a sweet gush of liquid heat. At the same time, I tip over my own edge, releasing into the condom in heavy spurts.

It takes a few long heartbeats for her to slide into the spot beside me. We're both breathless now, panting as we come down from our mutual high.

"Wow," she murmurs, shifting so her head's resting on my heaving chest. We're both damp with sweat, hot to the touch, faces flushed. She stares up at me, asks, "Can we do that again?"

"As many fucking times as you want," I chuckle, wrapping one arm around her shoulder. "Just give me a little time to recover."

"Five minutes, then?"

I choke on my own saliva. "You really want to kill me, don't you?"

"No, I want to fuck you," she says with a cheeky smile. "And then I want to kill you."

Chapter Twenty-Seven

WAKING up wrapped in Luca's arms has officially become my favorite pastime. He's so big and warm and cuddly, and his sturdy hands have found a home around my hips. Sighing, I snuggle in closer, nuzzling against him until our bodies are locked tight.

His breath whispers against the shell of my ear. He rasps my name and says, "Morning, gorgeous."

I stir, turning in his arms until we're face-to-face. Raising one hand, I trace the contours of his jawline with the flat of my palm.

"You know," I say in a soft voice, barely waiting for the morning fog to clear from his eyes. "Before we started this whole thing, you told me that everyone has a type."

He blinks, brow quirking. "I did."

"Well, I'm dying to know what you think your type is."

He pulls back a fraction of an inch. "Let me try to figure out the best way to put this."

"What do you mean? Is it something I'm not gonna like?"

"It's not that." He presses a palm to my cheek. "It's just, I like being alone."

My eyes widen, confusion settling in. "Okay?"

"What I mean is—" He placates me with a soft smile. "—when I spend a lot of time alone, I don't experience the same type of loneliness that some people do. Actually, I just feel like

I can finally be myself for once. I don't have to worry about what other people think of me or if the things I'm saying and doing are coming off a certain way. I can just *be*."

I give him a nod of encouragement. "Yeah, that makes sense."

"Even when I'm around my family, who I fucking love, there's always some sort of expectation there. I have to be the older brother, the strong one, the supportive one who keeps his shit together. Then, when I'm at home around Taylor, there are still things I have to keep to myself. Things I can't talk to her about for one reason or another, like with my injury, money issues, and now this fucking bullshit with our brother."

I rub the side of his bicep, squeezing once for reassurance. "You're right, that's a lot to juggle."

"So when I think about my type, I think about someone that I can be myself around. Completely." He swallows thickly. There's an uncomfortable tension in his gaze now, as if he's plagued by his own vulnerability. "Someone who doesn't expect me to think or act or behave a certain way . . . because they're content with the person that I already am."

"You want to feel the way you do when you're alone but with somebody else?"

"Exactly." He gives me a grateful smile, relaxing into the comfort of my understanding.

I blurt, "So, am I your type?"

Apprehension swirls in my belly while he thinks over a response. I self-consciously duck my head, fighting a shy smile as he tucks a tendril of hair behind my ear.

"I'll admit, when I'm around you, I do get nervous," he confesses. "You make me want to be the best version of myself. But that doesn't mean that I don't also feel so fucking content when we're together. I love being around you, Harper."

He pulls me closer, a bubble of happiness expanding in my chest. "I love being around you, too."

"Good, then."

"Man," I say with a laugh. "I was expecting you to say something like . . . hot blondes in bikinis."

He gives me a nonplussed look. "Were you really?"

"No, I guess not." I laugh again, nudging his nose. "Usually, though, I'd expect someone to give me a list of physical traits."

"I can do that, too."

"Oh yeah? Then go for it."

"Hair—" He toys with a loose strand, pulling at a tiny curl that frames my face. "—this pretty golden brown. Skin—" He runs his fingers across my cheeks and down over the column of my throat. "—soft, sweet, and full of freckles. Body—" He shifts on top of me, caging me against the bed. "—un-fucking-believable."

Warmth spreads across my chest. "Hm, how can we find you someone like that?"

"I'm pretty sure I had my head between her legs, oh, about four hours ago."

I tap a finger on his lips, blinking back shock at his dirty words. "Wow, it sounds like it's time for her to return the favor."

"Wasn't a favor."

I drag him in for a kiss, laughter spilling onto his lips. My free hand dips below his waistband. As soon as I feel him nod against me, I reach into his boxers and grip his erection, stroking him with a firm hand. He groans, low and deep from the back of his throat, his head dropping into the crook of my neck.

He holds himself over the top of me, careful to place pressure on his right knee with his elbows perched on either side of my body. I glance between us, watching, captivated by the sight of his stomach muscles tensing and rippling with each gentle tug.

"Oh . . . *shit*," he mumbles against my neck.

"We have at least twenty minutes before we have to head back to campus." I gently scratch the back of his neck, running my fingers through his hair. "Plenty of time for another quick round."

"I don't know, what if we jinx it?" He pauses, his cock twitching against my other palm. "Fuck," he groans again, "that last time really was my favorite."

"You've said that every time."

He kisses my neck, sucking at my collarbone. "Because it just keeps getting better."

Okay, so we may have given each other several more orgasms throughout the night. It was tough to fall asleep after that initial adrenaline rush. I'm not, like . . . a sex fiend or anything, but I wanted to try out a few more adapted positions after our first time. Surprisingly, there are a number of ways to intertwine our bodies without adding pressure to Luca's injury.

Despite what he deludes himself into telling me, I know that he's still healing. And I'm not going to contribute to his pain in the name of our mutual pleasure.

"Exactly my point," I say.

Lifting my hips, I grind against him, desire and heat pooling low in my core. We work together to shimmy his boxers halfway down his thighs, but my breath catches in my throat as the front door slams shut.

"Harper, honey?" My dad's concerned voice carries down the hall, barreling through the bedroom door. "Is that you?"

"One second, Dad!" We both fumble our way out of bed,

panic striking Luca's eyes as we frantically tuck ourselves back into our clothes

"I'm sorry." I shoot him an apologetic glance. "I really did *not* think he'd be here this weekend."

"Goddammit," he grumbles. "Please don't tell me I'm about to meet your father for the first time"—he gestures wildly to the obvious bulge in his jeans—"like this."

Dad calls my name for the second time, the sound of his heavy footsteps trailing closer. "Whose Outback is that out there?"

"It's my friend's," I shout back, watching Luca tense up out of the corner of my eye. "Give us a second, and we'll be right out." Dropping my voice to a whisper, I murmur, "Just think about, like, your grandma or something, and it'll go away."

"Jesus, Harper." He smacks a hand to his forehead. "I think hearing your dad walk down the hallway just put the fear of God in me, anyway. My dick's basically crawled back up inside my body."

"Then let's go." I smile, grabbing my purse off the floor and popping it over one shoulder. Taking his hand, I lead us down the hall. My dad is waiting for us at the end, foot tapping, both arms crossed over his chest. He lifts an unimpressed brow.

"Dad, this is Luca," I say cheerfully, gesturing to the six-foot-two man attempting to cower behind me. "Luca, this is my dad, Christopher."

Dad might appear to be intimidating from the outside, but I know he's putting on a show for Luca's sake. He's met many of my friends before, as well as my dates, and even the occasional hookup. I know he doesn't mind that we used the condo this weekend. In fact, I'd bet he's delighted that I finally made the trip.

"Nice to meet you, sir." Luca clears his throat, tentatively stepping forward to shake Dad's hand. "I'm sorry for barging in on your place this weekend. We sort of drove up on here on a whim and—"

"No worries, kid," Dad cuts in. "I know how my Harper can be. Free-spirited, always going where the wind takes her."

Luca tugs at the collar of his shirt, poorly attempting to conceal his nerves. "Right, yeah. Of course."

Dad gestures between the two of us. "So, this is new?"

I lean against Luca's shoulder. "Oh, we've been dating for a couple of months now."

"What happened to that girl you were with?" Dad asks, giving me a questioning look.

My brow crinkles in confusion. "What girl?"

"The blonde? The one I helped you move in with back in August."

"Oh my God, Dad." I drop my head back with a groan. "Stella and I are just friends. Best friends. I've known her for three years now. You know this."

"Then why are you living with her?"

"I don't know, to have a roommate?" I scoff, bewildered by his accusation. "To split living expenses with . . . and *stuff*."

He sniffs an amused laugh, staring at me as though he has no clue what I'm talking about. "You know you don't need to worry about that."

I chance a sideways glance at Luca, taking note of his stiff posture. This whole conversation is making him uncomfortable, that much is clear.

"Dad," I mutter, a hint of embarrassment creeping up my spine.

"What?" he asks, clueless as ever. I stare at him blankly, nodding toward my guest. "Oh, sorry. Why don't I take you both out to breakfast this morning, how does that sound? We could go to that place on the water that you like, Harper Jo. The one with the crab benedict."

"We don't really have time today," I say, offering an apologetic shrug. "We both have to work back near campus."

"Are you still working down at the beach?" Dad fishes his Tom Ford wallet out from the back pocket of his trousers. "I told you I'd up your allowance if that's the issue. Or your mother can do it. She certainly could spare the spousal support."

"No, I don't need that." I wince as he pulls out a thick wad of cash. "And it's my last shift today anyway."

He shrugs as if to say, *suit yourself*. Stuffing the money back into his wallet, he turns his attention to Luca. "You a lifeguard, too?"

"Uh, no, sir." Luca wrings both hands together, rubbing his thumb against the outside of his wrist. "I work down at the pier."

Dad gives him a tight smile. "Ah, I see."

"Luca's also the defensive captain for our school's football team," I chime in, happy to brag about my guy.

I'm so proud of how hard Luca works in all aspects of his life. If he won't boast about his accomplishments, then I'm more than willing to take matters into my own hands. Plus, my dad is a big football fan himself. It might give the two of them something to bond over in the future.

Dad visibly perks up, his attention piqued. "Is that so?"

"Yes, sir." Luca gives him a polite nod, but his expression remains guarded.

"What position do you play?"

"Middle linebacker," Luca says. "I'll be declaring for the draft this year."

It's bothering me that I can't tell what either of them is

thinking. There's still an awkward lilt to the conversation, and I'm not so sure that football helped bridge their connection after all.

"Maybe I'll have to come check out a home game with my daughter sometime," Dad offers with a smile, landing a heavy pat on Luca's shoulder. "We could all grab dinner the night before. My treat, of course."

"Sounds good, sir."

"Dad," I cut in. "We really do have to get going."

"Sure, sure, honey." Dad follows us to the front door, waving us both off. "Drive safe, you two."

Despite my offer from last night, Luca holds his hand out for the keys, approaching the driver's side of his car. An uncomfortable silence washes over us as we settle into our seats. Sighing, he puts the car in drive and slowly pulls away from the condo.

"I'm sorry about my dad coming back so unexpectedly," I say into the silent air. "And um, you know, he can be a little out of touch sometimes."

"Yeah, look . . . can I ask you something?" His grip tightens around the steering wheel, shoulders pulling back. "Just a hypothetical?"

"What's up?"

"Would you be embarrassed of me if I didn't play football?" His voice is soft, unsteady as he continues. "If I wasn't hoping to get drafted come April?"

"What?" I fumble with a response. "No, of course not. Why would you think that?"

"I mean, if I was just the Luca that works down at the pier. The guy that has to scrape together two pennies just to pay for his tuition, unsure of his future prospects."

"I like you for you." My heart sinks like a stone, carelessly tied up and tossed into the river. "If you changed your mind tomorrow and completely dropped football, it wouldn't matter to me. I just want you to do whatever it is that makes you the happiest."

The silent gears tick away inside his mind. Finally, after what feels like a period of a thousand years, he gives me a half-grin and says, "Okay."

"Yeah?"

"Yeah." He nods one final time, seemingly reassured by my adamant denial. "I believe you. I just had to ask."

Chapter Twenty-Eight

LUCA

THIS WEEK HAS BEEN FUCKING terrible, mainly because I haven't been able to spare a moment to see Harper. It's been tough since we came back from Cape Casserat last weekend. I wanted to, believe me, but our schedules wouldn't align no matter how hard we tried.

As if that wasn't shitty enough, I've been blessed with bad luck in more ways than one.

"Fletcher, come here," I call, my voice echoing across the athletic training room.

I hate to break up his flirting session with Eden, but it turns out the two of them are here for an actual reason. I mean, other than to rekindle their disaster of a relationship, that is.

I wait for a beat, rubbing some tension out of my neck as he jogs over to meet me. "Whatcha need, big guy?"

"I went a little rough during practice, so Coach wants me to KT tape my rotator cuff before I head home. Can you help?"

My knee may be on the mend now, but my shoulder's been giving me trouble over the last few days. It could be due to that overcompensation shit Harper mentioned. Or, in the more likely scenario, it's because I've been leading the team in tackles for the last three games.

"You got it, boss." Fletcher looks me over for a quick moment. When he leaves to grab a roll of Kinesio tape, I shift into a comfortable position on the bench.

"So." Fletcher clears his throat, stretching out a long strip of tape and placing it across the length of my deltoid. "How are things going with you and Little Miss Sunshine?"

I tense underneath his painful touch. "Just fine."

"Fine?" He snorts, pressing another strip of tape down across my bicep. "What a glowing review."

My response comes in the form of an evasive grunt.

"What? You don't want to swap stories about our girls?" His laughter grates on my nerves. "You know, we used to be pretty good friends when I was going out with Eden last year. Me and your girlfriend."

"Ah, we're not . . . I mean, she isn't—"

"Oh shit, Harper's not actually your girlfriend yet." He places a third and final strip, smoothing it into place with his palm. His face twists into a sympathetic grimace. "Is she?"

"We're dating," I say between gritted teeth.

"I knew something was off when I first heard. Sunshine's never really been the commitment type, you know?"

I resist the urge to scoff. "Okay."

What is with the audacity of this fucking guy?

"I mean, like I said, I used to know her pretty well," he continues, clueless, rambling on about shit he really shouldn't. "She kinda goes through these cycles of liking different people. It's almost like she just gets bored easily or something. I remember she was obsessed with her TA for months last year, then they finally hooked up, and it was like . . . poof. Never mind, not interested."

"You done?"

"What?" he asks, raising a bewildered brow.

"I said, are you done?" I shift up from the bench, standing tall in front of him. "I called you over here to help with the KT tape, not to shoot the shit. So if you're done, I think we're good."

He takes a wide step back, rolling his eyes. "Whatever you say, Ötzi."

"It's Reynolds."

"Reynolds, sure." He waves me off with another annoying grin. "See you later, man."

I straighten, muttering an insult under my breath as he walks away. When I go to pack up my shit, I check for a text from Harper first. The only thing she's sent me today is a series of smiley face emojis sent early this morning, yet the irritation still seems to melt away at the mere sight of her name.

AFTER LEAVING PRACTICE, I snuck into a physics study group to finish up a weekend's worth of assignments. I won't have any time to work on homework for the next few days, not if I want a shot at spending a few uninterrupted minutes with Harper.

Unfortunately, that means it's already past ten o'clock by the time I make it home.

"Taylor, what's going on?" I ask, stepping into the whirlwind of chaos that now occupies our home.

There are piles of clean laundry strewn around the living room, pants with out-turned pockets, and couch cushions knocked out of their rightful places. My sister, usually calm, cool, and collected, looks completely strung out as she sifts through a jar of change on the floor.

"Nothing, it's fine," she says frantically. "I'm figuring it out."

I glance around the living room again, confusion etching my brow. There's a notable absence here, considering my slobbering welcome committee is nowhere to be found.

"Where's Bentley?"

"He cut his paw on a rock outside earlier." She moves off

the floor to rearrange the couch, so I step in to offer a hand. "I had to take him to the emergency vet, and now he's sitting in his crate in my room. I just don't want him running around the house and hurting himself even more."

Concern washes over me. "Is he okay?"

"Yeah, he seems completely fine now." She sighs, gathering up a wad of clothing and tucking it into her laundry bin. "He's actually completely passed out in there. Unfortunately, it cost me nearly six hundred dollars just to wrap his paw and get some fucking antibiotics."

"Oh, Tay. I'm sorry." My stomach dips. "Do you . . . do you need some help paying for it?"

"I normally wouldn't ask, you know that." She shoves the last bit of discarded clothing away, our living room returning to its once-neutral state. As she shifts closer to me, I can see the tightness around her eyes and know that she's holding back tears. "But it's just . . . I've been saving up for my lab fees for next school year, and I had to lend some cash to Elio a few weeks back, so—"

My blood pressure drops. "What do you mean? What did you lend him money for?"

"Don't give me that look." There's a defensive curve to her posture now, arms folded across her chest. "He just needed some money for those classes at the junior college, okay?"

"Bullshit," I say, my jaw twitching.

"Luca."

"No, seriously, Taylor." *Fuck.* I run a shaky hand through my hair. "Our parents already cut down on Georgie's sensory gym to help him pay for that."

She lifts a shoulder, then drops it. "Well, it's expensive, and I just want to help. I'm . . . worried about him."

"Worried about what?"

"Okay, listen, I promised I wouldn't say anything, so . . . just don't go flying off the handle."

My pulse is pounding in my throat. "What is it?"

"Last month, when I went home to visit, I noticed Elio was acting strange. He looked pretty strung out, too. Bloodshot eyes. Erratic behavior. I don't know, he was—"

"Being more of a dick than usual?" I ask, cutting her off, shell-shocked by her admission.

"Exactly." She purses her lips together, guilt clouding her expression. "When I confronted him about it, he told me he had just been up all night studying. But when I pressed further, he admitted that he took some Adderall. I think it was just a onetime thing, though. At least, he promised me it would be."

I'm stunned. Absolutely fucking stunned. "You've got to be kidding me."

"No, Luc. I think he's really worried about passing his classes, especially with the financial stress it's putting on the family."

I scrub a hand over my forehead, sighing long and deep before I say, "He's playing us, Taylor."

She blinks back her disbelief. "What do you mean?"

"He was high when I went home last weekend. Did some coke with his buddy to 'take the edge off.' Like a complete dipshit, I believed him when he told me it was a mistake. I promised not to rat him out, either."

"Oh my God." She gapes at me. "What are we gonna do?"

"I don't know, host a fucking intervention," I nearly shout, leveling my tone when I notice her flinch back. "We need to talk to our parents first, though. In the meantime, don't give him any more fucking money."

"I won't." Her shoulders fall, face pinched with concern.

"But, um, Luc . . . I still don't know how I'm gonna pay for all of Bentley's vet bill."

"Right." I clench my hands into tight fists, willing my heartbeat to settle. "Look, don't worry, I can cover half of it. Okay? Just give me until next paycheck, and I'll have the money."

I'm lying through my teeth now because there's no fucking way I'll have enough money by then . . . not unless I can invent a way to be two places at once. Or if I cut out a week's worth of meals during this next pay period. After all, there are ways to make food stretch, as long I'm still loosely following the team's meal plan.

I guess I'll just have to make it work.

"Thank you." She wraps one arm over my shoulder, squeezing me into a quick hug. "I owe you one."

"No, you don't. Bentley's just as good as mine."

"Okay . . ." She trails off, taking a deep breath to pull herself together. "I have to get to work, but I love you. Bentley should be out for the rest of the night. We'll figure out what to do about E at some point this weekend."

"Sounds good. Have a nice night." I muster up my best attempt at a smile, but I'm frozen in place as she ties her serving apron across her waist. When the front door shuts behind her, I let my head drop into my hands.

I'm practically shaking by the time I pull out my phone.

Luca: Can you come over? I need to see you.

Harper: Now?

Luca: Yes

Harper: I can leave my place in 15. Should I bring an overnight bag?

Luca: Please

I'M on the porch waiting for Harper when she shows up, no more than a half hour after I texted. She's already wearing her pajamas, hair tossed up into a loose bun. Even after everything, the sight of her fuzzy pink slippers padding up to my doorstep brings a genuine smile to my face.

"What's wrong?" she asks, pulling me into her arms.

I duck my head into the crook of her neck, breathing in her comforting scent. There it is—my sweet peach, sunscreen, and the hint of salt water that always seems to linger on her skin.

"Can we talk about it tomorrow?" I mumble against her neck. "I just . . . tonight I just want to hold you and forget about everything else."

"Yeah, okay." She takes my hand, gripping tight, guiding me inside and down the hallway. "Let's get in bed."

Without another word between us, I strip down to my boxers. We fall back onto the mattress together and duck under the covers. My body relaxes ever so slightly as she tucks herself against my side.

I'm frustrated, I'm exhausted, and I'm so goddamn stressed. Right now is not the time to be doing this, but I don't think there's anything I can do to stop myself. The question's going to tumble out of me whether I like it or not, and I suppose I have that fucking asshole Fletcher to thank for this.

One last deep breath, then, "Harper?"

"Yeah?"

I tighten my grip, pulling her even closer to me. With my pulse thrumming behind my ears, I let the question run free: "Do you think I could call you my girlfriend now?"

Her breath catches, and she goes silent for a long moment. There are about a million regrets flashing through my mind by the time she finally responds.

"Is that what you want?" She bites her lip, the corner of her eyes crinkling. "For me to be your girlfriend?"

My entire body vibrates with nerves. "Yes."

She giggles, actually fucking giggles, and I choke out a sharp breath.

"Then yeah," she says. "You should probably call me that."

"Okay." *Finally.* Fucking finally, there's something good here. I slip my fingers into her hair, nuzzle against her neck, nip her earlobe between my lips. "Thank God."

Chapter Twenty-Nine

IT's BEEN near radio silence since I slept over at Luca's house last weekend. He woke up early on Saturday morning, then headed out of town for an away game. On Sunday, he worked another long shift at the pier. All week long, I've been texting and calling him when I can. He does respond, but it's short, sweet, and to the point.

I know he's busy, overwhelmingly so. I just miss him.

We still haven't talked about what went wrong when he called me over that night. Now, I'm worried he may be spiraling. I can only hope he finds the space and time to confide in me soon. Hopefully, I've set the stage well enough for that to happen tonight.

I already sent Stella away, and I've prepared something special to help him relax. If he's not ready to talk yet, then I guess that's okay, too. I can help him in other ways.

When I hear his knuckles rap against the front door, I shoot up from my spot on the couch, practically running to greet him.

"Hi," I say, suddenly nervous as I take in his slumped posture. "You okay?"

"I'm alright." Luca lifts a hand to my face, cupping the side of my cheek. "It's good to see you."

I lean into his touch. "I missed you."

"I missed you, too." He follows me inside, softly closing the door behind us. "I know we haven't talked much this week, but you've been on my mind a lot."

That perks me up. "Really?"

He takes a step closer, placing both hands on my shoulders. "Of course," he says, surprise flickering behind his eyes. "I think about you all the time. Don't you know that?"

I drop my gaze, staring at a spot somewhere in the middle of his chest. "You've been pulling back a little bit this week, so I wasn't sure."

"I just have a lot going on." He shakes his head, tightening his grip in a firm squeeze. "It's nothing to do with you, or us, or anything like that."

"I know, but I want you to know that I'm here for you. If you need to vent or if you need a distraction . . . even if you just want to spend the night together and avoid all of our problems. I can do any of it."

"I do know that," he says, allowing emotion to grip his voice. "I'm sorry for being MIA, Harper. I just get wrapped up in my own head sometimes, and everything else seems to fall to the wayside, but I don't want to do that with you. I told you I needed you, and I really do. Right now, you're pretty much the only good, consistent thing in my life."

My nerves instantly dissipate, his earnest expression wrapping a blanket of confidence around me.

"I'm glad I can be that for you. Does that mean you finally want to talk about what's been bothering you?"

"I do, yeah." He releases his grasp on my shoulders, bending down to remove his shoes. He places them in a neat little pile near the door before training his gaze back in my direction. "I could use a minute to decompress first, though. It's been a hell of a day."

"Okay, well, if you wanted to relax . . . I, um, I ran a bath for you."

He stops in his tracks, brows lifting. "Wait, what?"

"Yeah, I got the bath going right before you got here. I bought some bubbles and this, like, manly soap. And a candle— peach scented because I know you like that."

"*Harper.*"

"Luca," I echo his stunned tone. "I'm forcing you to relax tonight whether you want to or not. It's not a big deal."

"It *is* a big deal." He flashes me a rare, heart-stopping smile. "Baby, you are so fucking perfect that it makes my head spin."

A furious blush heats my cheeks. *Baby.* I'm fairly certain the only other time he's called me that was when he was inside of me. At the time, I was too distracted to realize just how much I liked it. I've never been someone's baby before, never dated anyone long enough to have a real pet name.

It's a harmless four-letter word that millions of couples use, but when it comes from Luca, *my God*, it is so damn cute.

"Oh," I hum. "Thank you. I think you're pretty perfect, too. Now, come with me."

I take his hand, guiding him down the hallway and into the dark bathroom. There are a few candles lining the shelves, but I haven't lit them yet. The bathwater is still steaming hot, condensation fogging up the mirror and swirling in the humid air. Bubbles overflow from the tub.

"This looks like exactly what I needed," Luca says, voice dropped to barely above a whisper.

"I'm glad." I open the bathroom cupboard and pull out a lighter for the candles. Once they're lit, the sweet smell of peaches filling the room, I turn back to Luca. "You should take your clothes off now."

He chuckles. "You're always trying to get me out of my clothes."

"I happen to like you out of your clothes."

His smile widens, instantly melting me into a puddle on the floor. "I like you out of your clothes, too."

I step forward, fingers tracing the hemline of his T-shirt. Together, we slowly tug the material up and off his body. Once he's fully stripped down to his boxer briefs, I run my hands over the thick layers of muscle that line his abdomen.

"You're so warm," I murmur, dipping my thumbs into his waistband.

"Go ahead, then."

With his permission, I push the thin cotton the rest of the way down his hips. He steps back, his underwear lying in a pile in the middle of our feet. Before I can help myself, my gaze drifts down, down, down, settling on the prized possession between his legs. By the looks of it, he's half-hard already.

"Quit staring at it," he chides, soft laughter echoing around the tiny room.

My eyes shoot up, and I give him a guilty shrug. "Woops."

"You're really gonna make me stand here completely naked while you still have all your clothes on?"

"If you'd just get in the bath already, then you wouldn't have this problem."

He holds both hands up in defense. "I'm getting."

I shamelessly watch as he strides over to the tub. When he turns, the muscles in his back flex and bulge as he hoists himself into the bubbly water, the soft glow from the candles reflecting on his tanned skin.

"It's too bad there's not room in there for two," I say.

He groans, stretching his arms high above his head as he

shifts into a comfortable position. "I bet you we could make it work."

"Luca, you barely fit inside there on your own."

"Yeah, and you're pretty damn tiny in comparison. Look." He bends his knees until they're peeking halfway out of the water. "There's a spot right here between my legs."

"This is supposed to be for *you* so you can decompress like you wanted."

"And this is how I'm choosing to relax." He beckons me over with one hand. "With you pressed up against me in this bathtub."

"Fine." I shimmy out of my clothes, tidying them into a stack on the countertop. "But no funny business. This whole thing is about relaxing, okay?"

"Got it." His brows are stern, but there's an unmistakable smirk on his lips. "Absolutely no funny business."

I lift one leg and dip into the center of the steaming water, carefully lowering myself into the bubbles. Luca loops one arm around my waist. It takes some cautious maneuvering, but we manage to fit in here nicely together.

Sighing, I snuggle in firmly between his outstretched legs. His dick presses into me from behind, causing my mind to shift course. "Okay, maybe a *tiny* bit of funny business."

He laughs, tugging at a strand of my hair. "*Harper*."

"What?" I tilt my head back against his chin. "You're the one with an erection right now."

"Oh my God," he groans. "I'm in the bathtub with my girl-friend, completely naked, and her ass is pressed up against me. If I wasn't hard, I feel like that'd almost be an insult."

"You're right." I place both hands on his thighs, shaking off the thought. "Okay, let's change the subject. Um, we can talk about our parents?"

"What about our parents?"

"My dad called me the other day. He's gonna be here some-time next week to have a little pre-Thanksgiving dinner together. He invited you to join us if you have the time."

He presses a kiss against my shoulder. "I'll make the time."

"Okay, I wasn't so sure with how busy things have been lately."

"I can make it work." He runs one hand through my hair, absentmindedly twirling a strand between his thumb and fore-finger. "Besides, it'd be nice for me to redeem myself. You know, since he walked in on us while my pants were down around my ankles."

I lightly slap the top of his thigh, water splashing against the side of the tub. "You're so dramatic. He did not *walk in on us*."

"Might as well have," he grumbles.

"He really doesn't care about that. In fact, he hasn't even brought it up once since that day."

"Really?" He tenses against my back. "Your dad is defi-nitely not what I expected."

"What were you expecting?"

"Just, I don't know, maybe a little bit of protectiveness for his one and only daughter."

"No, my parents aren't like that at all. I don't think they really expect too much of me in the first place."

He hugs both arms around me. "What do you mean?"

"I love my parents, I really do. And I'm not saying that they're bad parents or that I really have anything to complain about. They've always provided for me and supported my deci-sions in the end, but they just don't really take me seriously."

"How so?"

"They think certain things I do are a waste of time, I guess?

Like they think I'm living in some la-la land with my head up in the clouds. And they just don't understand what I'm doing with school and my internship."

I move my hands from his thighs, twisting them together in my lap as I ramble. "My mom's forty-four years old, and she's already 'retired,' living off family inheritance and spousal support. And my dad . . . he thinks sports medicine is a 'low-paying field.' I don't know, it's like they just expect me to marry rich or live off their money forever or something."

He sighs, pressing a kiss to my crown. "At least it's nice that you'll always have a fail-safe, though."

"Yeah, I suppose. I just wish they didn't act like I'm somehow destined to fall into their safety net."

"Well, most of us don't even have the choice." His tone is soft and nonaccusatory, but it still serves to fracture my conviction.

"Yeah." I let my shoulders slump, embarrassment washing over me. With everything Luca has going on right now, I should've never even brought this up. "Yeah, you're totally right. I shouldn't be complaining."

"Harper, no." He swallows, voice thick and heavy with regret. Swiping my hair onto one shoulder, he presses his nose to my neck and murmurs against my skin, "I'm sorry, you have every right to complain. And I'm sorry you don't feel like your parents support your ambitions. They should be so proud of you and everything you've accomplished."

His words are like a balm to the uneasy feeling in my stomach. "They *are* proud of me, I think. But I'm just not sure it's for the right reasons."

"You know *I'm* proud of you, right?" He kisses me again, three soft pecks against my shoulder, my neck, the side of my cheek. "For every reason. And for what it's worth, I think you're going to make an incredible sports therapist in a few years."

"Yeah?"

"How could I not?" I can feel his smile against my skin. "You've already saved my ass on more than one occasion."

"Thank you for saying that."

"You're welcome." He releases his hold on me, sliding his palms from my knees up to the top of my thighs. "Now, come on, it's my turn to make you feel better."

I close my eyes and tilt my head back, letting the warmth of the water and the rough pads of his fingertips bring me comfort. When he finally slides them inside of me, pressing against all my favorite spots, everything but Luca disappears from my mind.

Chapter Thirty

LUCA

My nerves are shot.

I'm meeting Harper and her dad for dinner tonight. He's chosen some upscale restaurant near the water, one of those places where they don't bother to list their prices. *His treat*, Harper reassured me. While I'm not entirely comfortable with the idea of him paying, there's not a shot in hell I'd be able to afford it myself.

Money's tight, as always. I managed to scrape up the funds for Bentley, but I've been living off bags of rice and dried beans ever since.

I'm also worried about making a good first impression tonight. It takes me quite a bit of time to warm up to people and for them to warm up to me in return. I know we've already done our initial introductions, but I was flustered beyond belief then. Now, I have no reasonable excuse for being my usual clueless self.

It doesn't help that I've been on the verge of panic for the last few weeks.

My concern for my little brother is growing by the day. Harper's been helping me stay calm since we talked things over, sending me daily affirmations and working hard to distract me. It all helps, but the tension won't resolve until I confront the issue head-on.

Luckily, Taylor and I have already concocted a foolproof action plan. We're going to wait until Elio's trapped at home during Thanksgiving break. It gives us the opportunity to host a mini-intervention after dinner, especially since he's not likely to miss out on his favorite meal of the year.

Until then, I'm attempting to clear all thoughts of the situation from my mind. It's a problem for another day. Right now, my brain needs to fully focus on my girlfriend, her father, and how to discreetly find the cheapest meal on an unmarked menu.

Blowing out a breath, I take one last look in the mirror before ducking out of the house. I dressed in the same dorky button-up and trousers that Taylor picked out months ago. I may not feel like myself, but at least I look somewhat presentable, I guess.

Honestly, I never usually think about what I'm wearing or how it might look on me, but what I do know is that Harper called me handsome the last time I wore this. That's reason enough to throw it on a second time.

By the time I pull up to the restaurant, Harper has sent me a text saying they've already been seated. Thankfully, I'm not technically late, but it did take me a few extra minutes to avoid the valet out front.

While a hostess leads me to their table, I stuff my hands into my pockets and tap one thumb against my thigh. Three beats on, three beats off—it's a rhythmic trick to get me to calm the fuck down.

It doesn't work.

"Hey!" Harper's chipper voice greets me as I sidle up to the pair of them.

She stands, pulling me in for a hug, placing a chaste kiss to my cheek. I free my hands from my pockets—eyes quickly trailing over her gorgeous frame—before turning to shake her dad's hand across the table.

"Mr. St. James—"

"Christopher," he says with a smile, cutting me off.

"Christopher, sir, thank you for inviting me to join you."

"Sure thing." He nods, taking a long sip from his glass. It appears to be whiskey served in a thick Glencairn, neat, and there's no doubt in my mind that it's top-shelf. "My little girl speaks highly of you."

"I consider myself very lucky to have her."

"You know, it's been a while since I've met a boyfriend of my daughter's." He nudges Harper, tipping his glass toward me in a faux toast. "Honestly, I thought she was into girls."

Out of my peripheral vision, Harper's eyes go wide.

"Ah." I clear my throat, attempting to keep the bitterness from my voice. "I hear you can like both."

"Yeah, Dad, come on." Harper's voice is pleading, but it still carries the same light, airy tone as usual. She's not irritated with him for his comment, even though she probably should be. "We've been over this a million times."

"Oh, I know." He laughs, taking another drawn-out sip. "I just thought you preferred them, that's all. You change your mind with the seasons, anyway. Well, actually, a little more frequently than that, right?"

Harper's smile slowly fades, one corner of her mouth tipping into a frown. "Not really."

"Oh, sorry, honey." There's a casual wave of one hand, immediately dismissing her. "You know I'm just messing around. Your mother and I always liked that about you—your ability to flit from one thing to the next."

"I mean, I've had the same career aspirations since Uncle Allan took me to that Carolina baseball game. I was only, like, sixteen at the time." She looks straight at me while she explains, like the prospect of convincing her dad is already a lost cause. "I watched Darnell Williams get wheeled out on a stretcher, and I've been gunning for sports medicine ever since."

"Of course, sweetie." He smiles, wide and unassuming. "And you have plenty of time to change your mind if you like. You're only twenty-one, after all."

She closes her eyes for what must only be a few quick seconds. Still, I swear I can almost see her float outside of herself. When she comes back, she gives her dad a soft smile and says, "I probably won't, though," in the smallest voice I've ever heard from her.

"With all due respect, sir, Harper's one of the most dedicated students I know."

"Right." He laughs again. This time, it grates on my fucking patience. "And when I was her age, I was dedicated to many things that have nothing to do with my career. Namely, partying and girls."

I clench my fists, suddenly sick of biting my tongue. "Sorry, but—"

"Dad, let's just change the subject." Harper cuts me off before I can make an actual mess of everything. "Shall we?"

She places a warm, comforting palm against my thigh, and I pat the top of her hand under the table. It barely takes the edge off. My girlfriend may be good at letting things go, but it's certainly not my specialty.

We spend the rest of the night drinking, eating, and carefully avoiding controversial topics. There are plenty of good moments, sure, but her dad continues to make little digs no matter the subject—poking fun at her dating history, her chosen career field, and even her personality as a whole.

Near the tail end of our meal, while waiting for the check, my frustration hits an all-time high.

Harper has just finished recounting a funny anecdote from her childhood, the joy and the laughter bouncing off her in waves. Despite my irritation at the third member of our party, it even generates a chuckle or two from me.

"Harper, honey," her dad quietly chastises her, his tight smile filled with condescension. "Everyone's staring at ya."

"Oh, sorry." Her laughter dims as she glances around the room, ensuring that she hasn't caused an actual disruption. There are a few guests looking at our table, of course, but it's nothing to be concerned about. In fact, they're probably only looking because she's fucking beautiful and happy, and they wish they could be sitting with her instead of their boring-ass partners. "I didn't realize I was being so loud."

"You weren't, baby. You're fine," I say, staring pointedly at her dad.

"You're right. You're right." He immediately plays it off, taking note of the pissed-off look on my face. "No big deal."

Goddammit.

I understand exactly where Harper was coming from now that I've seen it firsthand. A hundredfold. From my vantage point, it almost seems like she's a joke to her father. And sadly, I don't think she's able to see the true extent of the situation.

She loves him too much to assume the worst.

THIRTY MINUTES LATER, Harper and I find ourselves walking down the street toward my car. I parked a few blocks away from the restaurant, while Harper's dad picked her up from her apartment. It didn't take much convincing for him to let me drive her home after dinner. In fact, he already had plans to head back to the city tonight.

I'm sure cutting off the detour saved him a few precious minutes.

As we settle into our seats, there's an eerie silence that washes over us. I can tell she feels uncomfortable, but I'm not sure how to tactfully broach the subject.

"Harper, look—"

She shakes her head, plastering a flimsy paper smile on her face. "You don't have to say it."

"Are you sure?" I sigh, long and heavy. "Because I feel like I have to say it."

"I mean, you can if you really want to."

"Your dad's a jerk." I reach an arm over the center console, shaping my fingers around her thigh. "You're fucking perfect, okay?"

"I know I told you he doesn't take me seriously, but he's not usually that bad. I promise." She laces the tips of her fingers through the gaps in mine. "Something was just off with him tonight. I think maybe he was trying to act cool around you for whatever reason."

"Why on earth would he want to do that?" I scoff. "Actually, better question, why would he ever think treating you like shit would impress me?"

"He wasn't treating me like shit. He was just being clueless."

"If that's what you want to believe."

She blinks over at me, wide eyes shining with forgiveness. "I choose to give him the benefit of the doubt. I know my dad loves me. Sometimes the things we say come out the wrong way ... despite our intentions."

Again, Harper proves herself to be too damn good for this

messed-up world. She's the most nonjudgmental person I've ever met. To be honest, it seems to bring her a helluva lot more joy and happiness than the rest of us.

"I suppose you're right."

She turns her phony smile up a few notches, cheeks tightening as it fades into something genuine. "I'm fine, really."

"Okay . . ."

She traces an X over her chest and says, "Cross my heart."

I drop the subject, mentally searching for some way to change the night's course. Harper—my confident, sweet, and carefree girl—deserves something to take her mind off the disappointment.

"You know, I think I have a few bucks in my cup holder." I move my hand from her thigh, rifling through the change until I come up with enough for a large cone. "I could swing by that place you like? Pick up some chocolate ice cream with gummy bears."

A soft pink stains her cheeks. "You remembered."

"Of course I did. Who could forget something so disgusting?"

Her jaw drops in a playful scoff, arms crossed over her chest. "You're just mad that you're boring."

I pocket my change and return my hand to its rightful place atop her thigh. "Sure am."

On our drive over to the Golden Cone, Harper sifts through my glove compartment in search of a pen. She pulls my hand onto her lap, doodling some flower pattern on the back of my wrist. When we coast up to a stop sign, she flips my hand and scribbles her first initial on my upturned palm. There—right at the base of my thumb—is a capital *H* with a loopy little heart above the center.

It's silly, inconsequential really, but for some reason, it still makes my pulse hum heavy in my chest.

Moments later, while we wait at the drive-through window, I grab her hand and scribble a tiny cursive *L* in the same place. There's a weight in the pit of my stomach now, a desperate, aching need to make her just as absurdly happy as she makes me.

It may be an impossible feat, but I'm sure as hell going to try my fucking best.

Chapter Thirty-One

EDEN AND FLETCHER are fighting again.

I've been running damage control all morning, but there's little I can do to help remedy the situation at this point. Apparently, Eden overheard him flirting with some other girl after the football game last night. When she confronted him about it, he came back with the worst possible excuse: "We're not technically dating anymore, so what does it matter to you?"

I'm surprised Eden was able to withhold herself from slapping him in the face. She said she wanted to, badly, but there were too many witnesses to risk it. My girl's not prone to easily forgive and forget, so the fact that she opened herself up for a second chance is a big deal. Now, I doubt she'll ever give Fletcher the time of day again.

Unfortunately, there's still nearly a month left in the semester, so the two of them are stuck interning together until winter break hits. I'd ask Luca to help run defense, but I highly doubt he'd involve himself in some petty drama like this. Well . . . he might if *I* asked him to, but he's already got more than enough on his plate to deal with.

He's running himself ragged trying to balance everything, yet he still manages to make me feel like a priority. It's honestly remarkable. We have plans to meet after his shift at Amber Isle this afternoon, but for now, I'm posted up in Eden's apartment, watching her shovel french toast down her throat.

"He's just such an ass," she says through another massive, syrup-soaked bite. "Princess this, princess that, what a load of shit."

"I just don't understand his motive," I say, dipping some more french bread into the eggy concoction beside me. "He acted like he really wanted to work things out."

"That's just it. It was all an act."

"I'm sorry, sweetie." I toss the bread into the pan and listen for a sizzle, flipping it once it's perfectly seared on one side. "I can only imagine how awful you're feeling."

"You've never had your heart broken, have you?"

"Well, not really." I pile up the last of the toast onto her plate. Untying the apron around my waist, I join her at the kitchen island. "I've never been in love."

She gives me a sideways glance. "Not even with Luca?"

"Oh, I, um . . . maybe?"

Am I in *love* with Luca? I honestly hadn't put much thought into the idea yet. It's true, there are a lot of things I love about him—the way he makes me feel, the way he looks at me, the way he tries so fucking hard in all aspects of his life—but does that mean I'm actually in love?

If it does, then I guess I've fallen headfirst without even realizing it.

Luca's mine, and I'm his. Truthfully, I can't imagine my life here at Coastal without him now. So yeah, I guess that does mean I'm in love with him. It's a scary thing to admit to myself, even scarier to think about admitting it to him.

It's just . . . I know the whole *love* thing hasn't worked out so well for him in the past.

"You just figured it out, didn't you?" Eden asks with a knowing smile, popping the last piece of french toast into her mouth.

A welcome heat climbs my neck. "I guess I did."

"The girls and I have known for ages."

"Sure you have." My arms cross over my chest with a dramatic huff. "You guys know everything."

"Thank you. We're very smart." She stacks our dishes together, giving them a quick rinse before loading them in the dishwasher. "They're coming to relieve you in about an hour, by the way."

"Oh my gosh, I don't need relieving." I frown. "I like being here with you."

"Don't worry, I know you have plans with Luca today. I'm not bothered." She clicks her tongue, waving me off. "At least one of us should be living out our romantic fantasies."

"You know I would stay here if you wanted me to, right?"

"I know you would, which is exactly why I want you to go. I love you too much to subject you to this—me crying about Grant all damn day." She plops back down onto the barstool beside me, dropping her head onto my shoulder. "Lord knows he's not worth it."

"He really isn't." I stroke the top of her hair, "Not if he can let someone as incredible as you slip right through his fingers."

"That's it." She closes her eyes, a watery smile lifting her cheeks. "Go on, say more nice things about me."

I twirl a thick, dark strand between my fingers, admiring how soft and shiny it is. "Has anyone ever told you that you have amazing hair?"

LATER THAT NIGHT, Luca and I cuddle up on a blanket together at the beach. We're watching the sunset at my favorite spot, about thirty yards shy of the shoreline, the chilly November air sending a tiny shiver up my spine.

"You cold?" he asks, tucking me against his side. "I think I still have a sweatshirt in my car for you."

"I'm okay." I gesture toward the open water. "Actually, I was just wishing it was warm enough for us to go swimming right now."

"Yeah, that's not happening." He chuckles, running his hands over the goose bumps lining my arms. "We'd definitely freeze our asses off."

I give him a playful shrug. "Might be worth it. Seems like a good time for screaming underwater."

"What do you mean?"

"Have you never done that?"

His brow quirks. "Can't say I've ever had the inclination."

"It's a great stress reliever. I always find myself swimming out there during spring finals." I can hear the wistful smile in my voice. "I just duck my head under the water and yell. It feels so good."

"Maybe when the weather warms up again, we can try it together."

I nudge him with an elbow, excitement buzzing around in my stomach. "Better yet, we could do it tonight in the bath."

"Sounds romantic," he deadpans.

"Oh, shush." Laughter bubbles out of me. "Like you're the authority on what's romantic or not."

He scratches at the back of his ear, his sudden nervousness apparent. "I think I've done a pretty okay job lately, haven't I?"

"Yes, you have." My eyes drop to his mouth. "Speaking of, you should probably be rewarded for it."

He breathes in, slowly, eyes heavy-lidded. "What did you have in mind?"

I tilt my chin, and we both lean in for a kiss. His lips are warm and soft, a shudder running through me when our tongues touch. I roll my body closer, and then his hands are everywhere—my hips, my waist, the back of my neck, up and into my hair. I reach my own hand between us, fingers frantically searching for the zipper on his jeans.

"So that's what you had in mind, huh?" He rasps the question, his answering smile pressed against my lips.

I manage to pop his button open with one hand. "I really want to."

He slides his hands out of my hair, gaze anxiously darting around us. "Out here, though?"

"It's dark, and the beach is cleared out. I bet no one's around for miles."

"Yeah." Another slow breath in. "You're probably right."

"So you're okay with it?" I shift myself on top of him, straddling his outstretched thighs. *God,* I want to touch him everywhere. He leans back, one hand propping himself up while the other finds its home around my hip. "You want this?"

"I want *you.*"

"Then have me," I whisper as he drags me in for another earth-shattering kiss.

He's quick to bury his tongue in my mouth, his hand squeezing and kneading against my hip. I sink down further, grinding into his rapidly growing erection, desire pooling low in my belly. I swear we both stop breathing.

I'm desperate to feel him slide inside of me right now, but there's something else I want to do first.

My fingers make quick work of his zipper, tugging it down and shucking his pants off. I reach into his boxers and wrap one tight fist around him, pumping a few times as a soft groan rumbles from his throat.

His head drops back, the corded muscles of his neck flexing as he swallows. "*Shit,* that feels so fucking good."

"Tell me what you want," I say, one hand sliding underneath his T-shirt.

I push up against the fabric, hinting for him to help me remove it. When he does, I kiss a trail from his neck across his pecs and down to his waistband. His hand covers mine, squeezing it tighter against him.

"Yeah, *yeah.*" The affirmation tumbles out of him, followed by a combination of ungodly sounds that make my panties even wetter. "Just like that."

"Is that good for you, baby?"

"So fucking perfect," he says, pushing a thick thigh between the junction of my legs.

I rub myself against him, my sundress riding up and exposing my damp panties. I'm sure he can feel the wetness dripping against his bare leg, but I can't bring myself to care at the moment. My hips swirl and grind as I work him over, desperation growing with every tiny twitch of his cock against my palm.

"What else?" I ask in a breathless pant.

"I want your mouth. *Fuck*, I want you to wrap those perfect, pouty lips around my cock."

I nearly choke. "What?"

He stiffens beneath me, wide-eyed with apprehension. "Sorry, was that too much?"

"Not at all." I blink up at him. "I'm just surprised."

"I've, uh, I've been thinking about what to say while we're together like this . . . what words you might like."

I practically come on the spot, my head, my heart, and my fucking vagina simultaneously combusting at the thought. "You have?"

"I just want it to be good for you," he says softly.

My smile grows. He is so absurdly sexy, and he doesn't even know it.

"Well, keep it up, champ, because *that* was everything."

He snorts out a laugh. "You're ridiculous."

"And *you* are so hot."

I shift myself off his thigh, shimmying until I'm perched between his legs. He works his boxers the rest of the way down as I move into the perfect position, his erection growing underneath my appreciative gaze. It doesn't take much encouragement for my tongue to flick out, tasting him, running along the thick purply vein that curves around his length.

My lips encircle his thick tip, and I suck him partway into my mouth, softly at first, until I get the hang of it. I continue to lick and suck, spurred on by the sweet praises floating out of him. *So perfect. So hot. I can't wait to fuck you.* At the sound of his rough, uncontrolled groan, I tilt my head, pushing down until I'm nearly choking.

"Come here, baby." He loops one finger through the strap of my sundress, tugging me up and off his dick. "Let me fuck you before I come down your throat."

With two gentle hands, he pushes me onto my back and climbs on top of me. His fingers dip down as he yanks my panties to the side, swiping his knuckles against my slit and rolling his thumb over my tight bundle of nerves.

"So wet," he says, "Do you want me to fuck you with my fingers?"

"Too impatient for that."

I pull my dress over my head as he leans to the side, fishing in his jeans pocket for a condom. It takes him a few moments to roll it on, so I mentally prepare myself to be fucked into the sand. Luca says his knee is *"practically one hundred percent now,"* thank goodness, which means I'm expecting full functionality tonight.

He moves over me, lining himself up at my entrance, pressing his full weight against me as he whispers into my ear, "You ready?"

"Please."

He pushes into me slowly, canting his hips until his cock hits the perfect angle. As he roughly thrusts into me—hands pressed down on either side of my head—his lips meet my neck and leave a trail of wet kisses along my collarbone.

"Do you like how that feels?"

"It's so good," I murmur, a ragged moan ripping from my throat.

"Do you want more?"

My fingers thread through his hair as I attempt to control my breathing. Panting, I finally manage to say, "Any more and I might just . . . *oh shit,* I might just pass out."

He chuckles, slowing his tempo but continuing to pound me into the blanket. There's a sort of recklessness behind his movements now, as if fucking in public has suddenly opened up a new door for him, for us, for the shameless side of him begging to be unleashed.

"God, you take my cock so well. A perfect. Fucking. Fit," he says, each word punctuated by a thrust.

I cry out, arching my back as my hips lift to meet him. I've almost reached the point of oblivion, but there's one more thing I need to tip me over the edge.

"Harper, I'm gonna come," he rasps against my throat. "Are you close?"

"I'm so close. I just, I need . . ."

He smooths a hand over my sweaty mass of hair, tucking it behind my ears. "Tell me what you need, baby. You can do it."

"Can you suck on my tits?"

With a cheeky smirk, he dips his head and pops a nipple into his mouth. He rolls his tongue over it, lapping and sucking before he nips the sensitive bud with his teeth. It only takes about ten torturous seconds before I completely fall apart, writhing beneath him. With one last powerful thrust, he joins me there.

We catch our breath, silently slipping back into our underwear as he tucks the used condom away. Out of the corner of my eye, I watch Luca take a deep exhale and glance down the beach, ensuring that no random straggler has caught the show of a lifetime. As soon as he discovers the coast is clear, he pulls me on top of him and runs his hands along my sides.

"I love watching you come," he murmurs.

"Damn, you're getting really good at that." I tap one finger on the end of his nose. "The talking thing."

"It's pretty fucking easy when I've got you underneath me. For some reason, I just want to spew out whatever shit comes to my mind. Plus, your reactions make it so much better."

I'm practically glowing at his praise. "Yeah?"

"Yeah, being with you is the best I've ever had." He kisses me again, slow and deep. "Every. Single. Time."

"It is for me, too."

"Good." He gathers up the rest of his clothes and slips them on, passing my dress over as he rearranges the blanket beneath us. Sand is fucking everywhere, so there's no doubt in my mind we're going to need that bath later tonight.

"So," he starts again, an awkward note behind his voice now, "I've been meaning to ask you about something."

My nose wrinkles. "What's up?"

"There's a game this Saturday after Thanksgiving. It's part of rivalry week, so our team's playing against Dayton. Danny's gonna be around, obviously, and he wants us to get together for another double date." His shoulders tense. "What do you think? I know last time was fucking awkward, so you can say no."

"Of course I'll go, but I honestly don't know why you still talk to him."

He gives me an exaggerated eye roll. "Okay, Miss Forgiveness."

"Hey, I'm not totally infallible." I laugh, shoving at his chest. "At least *some* things have to be irredeemable."

He shrugs. "He's still my best friend."

"I thought I was your best friend."

"Okay, well, he's my longest friend."

"Fine, fair enough."

He perks up, swinging an arm around me. "So we're going, then?"

"Yeah, we'll go."

"Thank you," he says softly, pressing a kiss to my forehead.

"I'd do anything for you. You know that, right?"

His cheeks flush, lips quirking into a smile. "I do now."

"Tell me something. If you could do anything . . . if money wasn't an issue and you had all the time in the world, what would you do?"

"I guess I would travel."

"Where?"

"My mom's family is originally from a small town in southern Italy, so maybe there. We don't have many ties to the place these days, but I think it would be kind of cool to go check it out someday." His fingers brush the stray hairs across my forehead. "What about you? I'm sure you've traveled all over."

"I did do a lot of international travel growing up. There are still some places I'd wanna visit, but one thing I've always really wanted to do is go camping."

He cocks his head to the side. "You've never been camping?"

"Nope, never." I give him a tired sigh. "My parents aren't really the camping type, if you know what I mean."

He rears back, eyes glinting with mischief. "I'll take you camping."

"You will?"

"Of course."

Anticipation thrums through my body at the idea. "Okay, maybe we could plan a trip somewhere in the spring after you get drafted."

"And if I don't get drafted?"

I give him a stern look, confidence seeping from my voice as I say, "You will."

He nods, his smile piercing me as he laces our fingers together. "Then I guess it's a done deal."

Chapter Thirty-Two

LUCA

It's chaos inside my head, and there's little I can do about it.

Taylor and I had plans to host an intervention with Elio tonight. At the last minute, she was invited to meet her new partner's family in the next state over, so I'm stuck carrying the load on my own. They've only been dating for about five weeks now, but she says she's never felt this way about anyone before.

I'm happy for her, truly. She deserves this.

Besides, who am I to ask her to stay? I know she feels terrible about it, even though I'm fairly certain I can handle this on my own. Elio's not someone I should be afraid of. I'm the older brother, the responsible one, and I can lay down the gauntlet all by myself.

I just might need a little extra mental prep beforehand.

Right now, the plan is to wait until our parents and siblings head to bed, hopefully after a family holiday well spent. Post turkey and stuffing, of course, since it's my intention to catch him in the best mood possible.

Harper warned me to go easy on him before I left today. She said he's *"just a kid"* and that we all make mistakes when we're that age. While that may be true, I'm almost positive he lied straight to my fucking face. Not only that, but he took money from Taylor's pocket and, indirectly, from mine. It pisses me off, especially when he knows how strapped for cash we all are.

Not to mention, our little sister, Giorgie, really fucking needs the money he's been skimming off our parents.

Being the kind person she is, Harper offered to go home with me for moral support, but this is a family matter in the end. I can do this alone like I've always done. Plus, I wanted her to spend time with her roommates for Friendsgiving. It's their tradition, apparently, and I've been eating up enough of her free time as it is.

It's nearing six o'clock by the time I realize my plan is officially fucked. The table's nicely set, the turkey is well rested, and my little siblings are already loading up on mashed potatoes. That's one of Giorgie's preferred foods, thankfully, so she feels comfortable enough to join us for the meal.

Unsurprisingly, though, my little brother is nowhere to be found.

With a tired, frustrated sigh, I ask, "Mamma, where's Elio?"

She waves a flippant hand, pretending to tidy the napkins on our perfectly prepared table. "Oh, your brother's at a friend's house. You know Jackson?"

Yeah, I definitely know Jackson, the same fucking kid Elio got drugs from a few weeks ago. If he's off doing that again— rather than spending a nice family holiday together—then I might actually lose my mind.

"Are you kidding me, Ma?" The reality of the situation weighs heavy in my chest. "He's seriously missing Thanksgiving dinner with us?"

Her hands move to fuss with Vivia's hair, patting down the flyaways as my little sister swats at her. "Luca, *non è importante.*"

"Yeah, it's a big deal," I argue, lifting a brow in disbelief. "He's being a complete jerk."

"*Eh basta!*" She gestures to the empty chair at the end of the table. "I don't see your sister here, either."

I blink at her, incredulous. "Taylor actually had somewhere important to be tonight. I can guarantee you E's just trying to avoid spending time with me."

"You'll see him later, Luc," my dad cuts in, gaze narrowing in my direction. He carefully carves up the turkey, one thick piece at a time, loading up a plate to serve his wife first. "Give your mother a break."

"Yeah, I *will* see him later." I rub at the back of my neck, blowing out a heated breath. "Tonight, because you're going to give me Jackson's address."

My mother tsks. "After dinner, *caro.*"

"Sure," I relent, taking a plate from my dad's outstretched hand, "after dinner."

In an attempt to enjoy the rest of our meal, I push the frustration to the back of my mind. It's no easy feat, considering I'm now flaming with anger, but I'd rather not stress my mom out any more than I already have. Besides, my little sisters seem to be enjoying themselves well enough. It's a rare occurrence for all three of them to stay seated at the family table.

And I don't want to ruin the fun with a sour attitude, so I sit myself down, shut myself up, and enjoy my damn food in peace.

After helping my parents clear the table, I take some time to tuck Giorgie in for bed. There's this book she's obsessed with about a little witch called Hazel, so naturally, she picks that one for me to read, forcing me to switch voices for each new character. It's goofy, sure, but even I'll admit I make a pretty awesome Toad.

Besides, spending half an hour laughing with Geeg is exactly what I needed to clear my mind.

. . .

WHEN I ARRIVE at Jackson's place an hour later, it's pretty fucking clear there's a party going on. Loud music is booming from the house, the front lawn is scattered with drunk teenagers, and the distinct smell of marijuana is wafting through the windows of my car.

It sure seems like kids these days don't give a shit about being caught.

Sadly, in order to find a vacant spot, I'm forced to park a few blocks away from the house. There are a lot of cars here tonight, which serves to irritate me even more. It's fucking Thanksgiving, for God's sake. These kids should be spending the holiday with their families. At least, Elio should since he has no good reason to actively hate us.

As I walk up to the front door, I pause for a long moment, attempting to ground myself first. I don't want to go in there guns blazing, completely and totally pissed off at my brother from the get-go. I need to be rational for a moment. Approach this with caution. It's the only way I might be able to get through to him.

After my third and final knock, a tall kid in a letterman's jacket opens the door for me. His gaze flits up and down my frame, two quick passes before he opens his mouth and says, "Dude, aren't you a little too old for this?"

"I'm looking for my brother," I mutter, forcing back an eye roll. "Elio Reynolds."

"By all means." He swings the door open, gesturing behind him and into the packed house.

With a shake of my head, I power on through, parting the crowd until I reach the kitchen. Surprisingly, I spot the little shit almost instantly. He's pouring himself a drink into a classic red Solo cup. It's a disgusting-looking mixture of juice and Everclear, exactly what I'd expect my little brother to be drinking right now.

He doesn't even bother to look up when I enter the room—completely oblivious to my presence—so I take a shot and ask, "What the hell are you doing here, E?"

His head darts up at the sound of my voice, eyes wide with a panic that quickly fades into anger.

"The fuck, Luc?" he spits out. "Seriously?"

"Yeah, *seriously*. You're really gonna skip out on tonight of all nights to go to a fucking party?"

He glances around us, scanning the perimeter of the room before taking a step closer. He clearly doesn't want any of his little friends to hear me berate him. "Mom and Dad didn't give a shit, so why does it matter to you?"

"It matters because I know you're a fucking liar," I say, unable to keep my volume down. I truly don't care if every person at this goddamn party hears us arguing. "I know you've taken money from Taylor and our parents. You say you're paying for classes at the community college, but I bet you're not even taking them, are you?"

His nostrils flare, body tense and eyes wild at the accusation. He drops his voice to a low murmur and asks, "Can we do this outside?"

"Sure." I toss a hand up. "Outside, it is."

He runs his fingers through his hair, tugging at the roots, lips flattened into a tight line. He's actually angry with *me* right now? Truthfully, it wasn't my intention to embarrass him tonight. I'd rather not drag him by the ear out of his friend's party, but at this point, he's given me no other choice.

"Lead the way," he says, gesturing wildly toward the crowd.

I head back to the front door, pushing through the

entryway until we're both out in the open air. He stands in front of me on the lawn now, arms crossed, eyes downcast. Normally, I wouldn't force the eye contact, but I need to see if he's hiding something from me.

"Look at me," I demand.

He lifts his chin and stares me straight in the face—eyes bloodshot, cheeks flushed—and it's pretty damn evident that he's high again. My heart fractures a tiny bit at the sight of the confirmation.

"So the classes *are* fucking fake, aren't they?"

"I was doing them, I swear," he says on a long exhale. "But I failed a test, and then I couldn't catch myself back up. It's not my fault."

"And the money you borrowed from Taylor?" My eyes narrow. "You wasted that on a class you were already failing?"

He stares at his feet, a muscle in his jaw tensing. "No."

"The drugs, then? Is that what you're spending money on?" I snap, acid burning in my throat. "Pills, coke, what else?"

"Nothing, man." He shakes his head, a pitiful curve to his shoulders. "I'm not."

I scoff, raising my voice as I shout, "Don't lie!"

"Don't fucking yell at me! You're not my father."

"No, but I am your brother, and you're being so careless right now. You realize you're taking money out of our baby sister's pocket, right?" At this point, my temper is untamable. "You're fucking everything up, E."

"Just shut up!" he screams, head in his hands. "You're being so goddamn dramatic."

"You want to see me be dramatic?" I throw my hands up, fire pouring out of me. "Because I can get dramatic."

"Oh, fuck this." He spins on his heel. "I'm out of here."

Fuck, this is not going how I wanted it to go. How I needed it to go. I was supposed to enter into this conversation all calm, cool, and collected, not rip his fucking head off in the process. Taylor would *not* be proud of how I'm handling this right now, nor would my girlfriend.

"Wait," I call, reaching out with one hand to stop him.

My fingertips barely graze the back of his T-shirt when he whips around and shoves me with all his strength, instantly toppling me to the ground. I land—knee-first, unable to catch my balance—on the rough pavement of the driveway.

The harsh, disturbing sound of my popping kneecap rings through the now-silent air. Mind-numbing, spine-tingling pain reverberates throughout my entire body, and I have to bite down on my tongue to keep the tears at bay.

"Shit, shit." My brother's panicking now, frantically scrambling toward me. "Luc, I-I'm so—"

"Don't say another fucking word," I manage to grit out between clenched teeth, my breath leaving me in a series of harsh pants.

My mind is reeling, spiraling out of control, creating every worst-case scenario possible. If my knee is actually broken, I might as well consider this my early fucking retirement. I pinch my eyes closed, attempting to clear my head as I reach for my phone.

"What are you doing?" Elio steps back before he can help me up, arms hanging limply by his sides. "Are you calling the cops?"

I clutch my phone to my chest. "No, E, I'm not calling the *fucking—*"

"Shit!" a nearby voice calls out. "Did someone say cops?"

From there, everything quickly descends into chaos. "Cops! Cops! Cops!" is repeatedly shouted around the lawn, traveling like a high-speed game of telephone throughout the remainder of the party. About thirty seconds pass before everyone starts to run, funneling out of the house in droves.

"Elio, man, what are you doing?" I glance up, watching as my brother's friend tugs on his sleeve. "Come on!"

"Yeah, I'm-uh, I'm coming," Elio says, sparing me one last guilt-stricken glance before darting off with the rest of them.

Now I'm stuck, lying here alone in the driveway of some kid's house, my fucking kneecap completely popped out of place. No matter how hard I try, I can't push myself up off the ground.

I think I might be sick. I roll onto my side, clutch my knee to my chest, and vomit out the entirety of my Thanksgiving dinner.

In an instant, my shot at the draft slips through my fingers like sand.

Chapter Thirty-Three

I'm on my second helping of Stella's homemade pumpkin pie when I feel my phone vibrate in my pocket. I pull it out, the sight of Luca's name instantly filling my body with warmth.

"Hey, babe!" I chirp, dashing into the other room for privacy. "I'm so glad you called. How was—"

"Harper?" Luca's ragged voice cuts me off. "I really need your help."

My stomach drops, an acute sense of dread washing over me. "What's wrong?"

"I'm hurt," he croaks out. "I can't get myself up off the ground in order to make it back to my car. I know you're with your friends, but I don't want to involve my parents in this, and Taylor's out of town." He's silent for a few long minutes, voice dropping to a tortured whisper, "I didn't know who else to call."

"No, I'm so glad you called me." I reach for my coat, frantically slipping it over my shoulders. "What happened? Where are you?"

"I fell and hit my knee. I'm outside of some kid's house, a friend of Elio's." His breathing is shallow, carefully measured. I can almost visualize him crumpled on the ground—alone and hurting—and it makes me want to burst into tears. "I can text you the address."

I slip my shoes on, hopping on one foot as I gather up my purse. "Okay, um, you said your car is there?"

"Yeah, I parked a few blocks away."

"Should I bring Stell?" I swallow, fear clenching in my gut. It's an uneasy, ugly sort of feeling. A worry so deep it resonates in my bones. "She can drive my car so we don't have to worry about coming back for yours later."

"Oh, shit. Er, is there anyone bigger you can bring?"

"Bigger?"

"Like a guy, maybe. Someone who could help me walk." The pain in his voice grates inside my head. "I don't know if you girls will be able to get me into a car."

"Oh, I could try and give Fletcher a call?" *Shit, shit, shit.* I highly doubt Fletcher would do me any favors right now, but I'm kind of running short on male friendships these days. "I don't know that he'd actually come, considering he and Eden are on the outs right now."

"No, not Fletcher." He groans, a frustrated sigh slipping out. "And please don't involve Eden, either. I don't want this to get back to Coach."

I rack my brain for a solution. "What about some of the guys on the baseball team?"

"No, sorry." He swears under his breath, mumbling something I can't quite understand. "I don't trust those guys. I guess, just—"

"I have access to the DME trailer," I say, suddenly hopeful. "I could grab some crutches for you, but it's gonna take some extra time to get there."

"Okay, that's perfect."

With my fingers anxiously tapping against my phone, I walk back out to the kitchen. Stella and Lai'Lani are sitting at the table together, blissfully unaware, chatting and kissing in between bites of pumpkin pie. Muting the call, I give them a quick rundown of the situation.

Unfortunately, it's going to take us at least fifteen minutes to run to campus for the crutches, then another thirty to make it over to Luca.

In one last-ditch effort, I unmute the call and ask, "Are you sure you don't want me to call an ambulance?"

"That'll probably take just as long," he says, exhaustion filtering through his words. "It's also way too fucking expensive."

"I could pay for—"

He huffs, cutting me off. "Please don't start that right now."

"Okay, okay." I grab my keys off the entryway table, tossing them to Stella. "We're on our way, alright? Just hang tight."

WHEN WE ARRIVE on the scene, Luca's sitting by himself on the pavement. He's perched up with both arms behind him, legs stretched out. There's a pile of vomit to his right and a wide rip in the knee of his jeans. At least there doesn't seem to be a lot of blood, but I brought a first aid kit just in case.

As soon as Stella cuts the engine, I dart out of my passenger seat, crouching down beside him.

"Oh my God," I murmur, quickly scanning his body from head to toe. "Why are you out here all alone? How'd this even happen?"

"I got into it with my brother." He glances behind me, cheeks flushing, tensing as he takes note of Stella's presence. "I think it was partially an accident on his part, but then he left me here to rot."

"Oh, Luca." I lean down, pressing a soft kiss to his forehead. "I'm so sorry."

"I'll be fine." He closes his eyes, pinches the bridge of his nose, shakes his head. "I just need to get off this cold ground."

I wave Stella over to bring us the crutches. As a ragtag team, we carefully hoist Luca up off the ground, one of us tucked underneath either side of him. It's difficult due to his size, but we manage to make it work.

Once the crutches are in place, he's able to hold himself up well enough to slide into my car. I hop in the back seat, while Stella drives us the few blocks over to his Outback.

As I help him maneuver back out, he tosses a bashful "thank you" over his shoulder to my roommate.

"I'm gonna take him to the ER," I tell her quietly, one hand poised on the small of Luca's back. "I'll see you at the apartment tomorrow."

"I hope everything goes okay," she says, her smile filled with sympathy.

"Me too," I murmur. "Thanks for your help."

Luca's car is a bit smaller than mine, so it takes some extra finagling to get him situated. He adjusts the passenger seat as far back as it'll go, attempting to stretch his leg out while I switch the car into drive.

As we pull out of the neighborhood, there's a tense, awkward silence that fills the air. I don't want to be the first to break it because I'm not so sure Luca can even hear himself think.

"I'm sorry, Harper," he eventually says, pure anguish marring his handsome face.

"Don't be sorry. You have nothing to be sorry for."

He drops his head into his hands. "I ruined your night with your friends."

"You didn't ruin anything, okay?" I reach for him, one hand clutched tightly on the steering wheel. "There's nowhere I'd rather be. We're gonna take you to the doctor to get checked out, and everything's gonna be okay."

"Okay," he whispers back.

A sorrow-filled expression sits on his face for two more long hours, the total length of time we sit together in the ER waiting room. When the nurse finally calls him back, I breathe a sweet sigh of relief.

I couldn't take another second of his silent, heavy wallowing.

It's not that I'm bothered by him being upset, but the inability to offer any tangible support is making my skin crawl. At least, after his visit with the doctor, we'll be able to come up with a solid plan moving forward. That will make us both feel better, I'm sure of it.

When Luca wobbles out on his crutches thirty minutes later, he holds up his discharge papers with a tight near smile.

"Good news is that there's no break or fracture," he says, slipping into step beside me.

"Dislocation?"

"Yep, with a minor ligament tear. Same place as before." He hands me the papers as we head back out to the car. I quickly scan them over, relief flooding me when I confirm the results for myself—no break, no fracture, just a patellar dislocation. Adjusted, corrected, and on its way to healing. "The doctor relocated it, but it's gonna take anywhere from three to six weeks to heal up."

"Oh, that's such good news."

"Could be worse, I guess." He shrugs, puffing out a heavy breath. "He says I need to completely immobilize it for at least a week. I don't know what the fuck I'm gonna do about Saturday's game."

"You need to talk to your coach about it first, right?" I wrinkle my nose. "Come up with a plan for healing."

"Oh, fuck no." He scoffs, patting the side of his crutches. "He's not gonna know anything about this."

I stop in my tracks, one hand softly grazing his shoulder. "Luca, this is really serious."

"I've done this before, remember? I just need to come up with a valid excuse to stay off the field for the next couple of games, and I'll be fine."

"That's really not a good idea. I think you need to—"

"Can we please talk about this later?" He all but snaps the question, face pinched with frustration. "I just want to go home, ice my knee, and try to forget this night ever happened."

"Okay, yeah, of course." I drop my gaze to his chest. "I'll drive us back to your place."

THE NEXT MORNING, it's nearing ten o'clock by the time Luca starts to stir. Thankfully, it's still Thanksgiving break, so we don't have classes or practice to think about right now. And he already texted his parents last night, telling them not to worry. I'm not sure exactly what excuse he gave them, but I know he's not quite ready to open up to them yet.

It's for the best, anyway. He needs to tackle this one problem at a time, otherwise, he's going to burn himself out too quickly.

"Good morning, sleepyhead," I quietly murmur, running my fingers through his rumpled hair. "Can I get you anything?"

"Would you grab the crutches for me?" he rasps, stretching his arms above his head and turning onto his side. "I just want to get up, get this day started, and figure out a plan of action."

"Of course." I press a kiss to his shoulder before hopping out of bed, his T-shirt dangling halfway down my body. "Do you want to talk over how you're gonna tell your coach?"

He presses both palms to his temples, groaning. "Like I said last night, I'm not telling him anything about the injury."

"This isn't like last time, Luca." I tuck his crutches against the side of his bed frame, helping him maneuver into a standing position. "You're just now recovered from your previous injury, and now you've re-torn the same ligament. That's another six long weeks of healing."

"*Three weeks*, Harper," he bites out. "The doctor said I can heal in as little as three weeks, which means I can still play in a bowl game. It also leaves me open for postseason all-stars."

"You're putting your health and safety in jeopardy if you do that." I furrow my brows, anxiously scratching at my forearm. "I don't understand the harm in speaking with your coach about this. If you're truly healed in time, then he'll let you play anyway."

"You know our athletic trainers always err on the side of caution." He shakes his head, expression slipping into a blank slate. "I can't risk that happening here."

"I'm normally always on your side, but I honestly don't think I can condone this."

"That's fine." He cocks his head to one side, tone flat. "I don't need your permission."

"Luca, come on," I plead, emotion clogging my throat.

His nostrils flare as he attempts to turn away from me, breaking any last semblance of eye contact. "I think I'm finished with this conversation now."

"Please?" I give him one last chance. "If you won't talk to your coach about this, then I'm gonna have to contact Jaqui Nerrie myself."

"Like hell you are."

"I'm trying to look out for you here," I say softly, carefully, willing him to understand how serious this truly is. "You have so much going on right now, I'm worried you're not thinking clearly."

"I'm thinking perfectly clearly." He takes a deep, shuddery breath. "And I know that if you contact anyone on my team, you and I are done."

I reel back, stomach dropping like a lead weight. "What?"

"If you go to the team's athletic trainer behind my back, then I don't see how this relationship can continue."

My heart beats faster and faster, pounding in my eardrums now. I bite the inside of my cheek, forcing myself to be patient with him. He's hurting and he's panicking, that's all.

Everyone says things they don't mean when they're in a bad mental state.

"You don't really mean that," I say, my shaky voice betraying my doubts.

"I don't need you interfering in my life, Harper." His tone is eerily calm—patronizing almost—as if he's talking to a child. "I've done just fine on my own for twenty-two years, okay? Stay out of this, I'm begging you."

"I don't think I can do that." I keep my gaze on his face, worrying at my lower lip. "We can figure this out together, and everything will be okay, I promise."

"You just don't get it, do you?" His cool, careless façade finally cracks. "You've spent your whole life living in some sunshiny alternate reality, pretending everything is just peachy. Because for you, it always has been. Meanwhile, I'm stuck down here in reality with the rest of the world. You know, that place where people have real fucking problems to deal with."

"Oh." His words sting. Like a hand on a hot stove, they burn me without warning. "Silly me, I thought you said I was perfect."

"Harper . . ."

"Is that really what you think of me?" I let the hurt wash over me, pull me under, drown me so completely. "That I couldn't possibly understand you?"

"Sometimes it seems that way."

"I see," I croak, caught off guard by his admission. I had no clue he felt this way about me. In fact, before today, I was pretty damn certain he felt the opposite. "I suppose it's nice to know how you really feel. Do you even care that I love y—"

"Harper, *don't*." He pins me with a harsh gaze, cracking me into a hundred tiny pieces. "Don't say something you don't mean."

"Why on earth would you think I don't mean it?"

"Because you fall in love like it's a goddamn hobby. And I really, really can't handle hearing something that's not real, not right now."

Shame and embarrassment cloud my vision, shaking me out of the numb sort of daze I put myself under. "You don't take me seriously at all, do you?"

"I-I'm sorry." He scrubs a hand over his face, propping a fist under his chin. "I'm not trying to hurt you. I think, right now, I just need space."

Space, space, space. The word ricochets inside my head, sending me into full-blown meltdown mode.

"What does that mean?"

"It means that I need some time to figure things out on my own, without you around."

Tears well up in the corners of my eyes. "So, to be clear, you're breaking up with me right now?"

He stares at the floor, voice dropped to a volume that's barely audible, yet somehow, it still pierces my ears. "Yeah, yeah, I guess I am."

"Wow." A single tear slips free, trailing down the bridge of my nose and silently dripping onto the floor between us. "I really don't know to make you believe that I'm in love with you. And I'm certainly not going to beg you to love me back. You want to deal with things your own way, *alone*, then be my guest."

I gather up my clothes, my shoes, and my purse, slipping my pants on under his T-shirt. Reaching for the door to his bedroom, I spare him one last glance. "I really hope everything works out for you in the end."

Without another word, I turn on my heel and slip out of the room, the silent tears streaming down my face. As I scramble down the hallway, poised to leave, the sound of Luca calling out my name rings heavy in the stale air.

But no matter how much I might want to, I can't bring myself to turn around and face him again. There's nothing left inside of me for him to break. So instead, I continue on, walking myself right on out of Luca's life.

Just like he fucking asked me to.

Chapter Thirty-Four
LUCA

SINCE ENTERING HIGH SCHOOL, I can count the number of times I've cried on one hand.

The first time, I was fourteen years old, a freshman who had barely made it onto the varsity football team. I was trying to be impressive in the weight room, but I ended up dropping an eighty-five-pound dumbbell on my foot. I think three whole tears leaked out.

The second time was the spring of my senior year. I had just been accepted at Dayton University, but then I lost out on a full-ride scholarship. I tried so fucking hard, but in the end, I couldn't come up with enough money for the deposit in time. Back then, I let one solid tear roll all the way down my cheek.

The third and final time was this morning, about thirty seconds after I made the biggest fucking mistake of my life.

Watching Harper walk away obliterated me. The only thing that made it worse is that I pushed her to do it myself. It's my own fucking fault for getting so wrapped up inside my head, for treating her like garbage, and for telling her I needed space.

Space. God, I fucking hate that word.

I should've never said the things I said, spoken to her the way I did. It hit me like a freight train the second after she left. I called for her, but she didn't turn back. She kept on walking straight out of my house, out of my life, and I can't blame her for that.

I panicked, and I fucked up. Majorly.

It's not a valid excuse, but in that moment, the only thing I could think about was my future blowing up in my face. The detonation of everything I've worked for my entire life. What I should've kept in mind is that Harper could've been my future, too. Now, I'm not so sure I have enough words to earn her forgiveness.

Since then—after six hours of wallowing in my own pit of despair—I've managed to inject my brain with a sense of rationality. Harper's tears were like a brutal wake-up call for me. It's near torture, but I've been replaying her words on a never-ending loop inside my head. And the conclusion I've finally come to is that she was right about everything.

Of course she fucking was.

I don't know what I was thinking trying to hide this at the end of our season. It's become more than evident that I need to speak to my coach and figure out a plan moving forward—sooner rather than later.

But first, I need to try and beg for my girlfriend's forgiveness. Even if she never takes me back, I won't be able to get my head on straight until I apologize.

If I ever have to relive the pain of breaking her heart—of shattering her spirit into pieces like that—I might as well never play football again. Nothing could hurt me worse, which is why I had Taylor drop me off in front of her apartment just now.

I can't let myself go another minute without trying to make amends.

Leaning on my crutches for support, I raise one weary hand to knock on her front door. After railing on me for ten straight minutes, Taylor made me practice what I planned to say on the ride over. Now, I'm afraid I'm too fucking nervous to remember a single word of it.

When Stella opens the door and first catches sight of me, her expression slips into a nasty frown, arms folded tightly across her chest. She taps one foot, impatient as she asks, "What do you want?"

I choke back the lump in my throat. "Is Harper home?"

"She's here," Stella murmurs, fire in her eyes. "But I'm not so sure she's gonna want to see you. You know I had to pick her up outside of your house earlier, right?"

"Fuck, I know. I just want to tell her how fucking sorry I am." I stare past her, blowing out a shaky breath as I hope for a glimpse of my girl. "That's all."

"Let me go check with her first." She jabs a finger right in the center of my chest, lips pressed into a flat line. "Do not step inside this apartment until I come back, okay?"

I nod, a spark of hope blooming inside of me. "Okay, you got it."

By the time Harper finally walks toward me, it feels like I've been waiting in this open doorway for hours. She looks so fucking beautiful, even with her eyes all puffy and red-rimmed from crying. The sight of her like this, heartbroken because of my actions, has me regretting the day I was born.

As she steps closer, her expression is guarded, both hands shoved into the pockets of her hoodie. Stella doesn't bother to return with her, but I can see that she's left the door cracked open just down the hallway.

"Did you need something?" Harper asks, blinking up at me.

"Other than you, no." I fight to keep my voice from cracking. "God, Harper, I'm so fucking sorry for all the careless shit I said to you earlier. I didn't mean it. Not a fucking word."

She wrinkles her cute little nose, sniffling just once. "Sorry, but it's pretty hard for me to believe you right now."

"I was hurting, and I took it out on you, the one person who really didn't deserve it." I grip my crutches to keep myself from stepping toward her, fingers blanching. "If I could take it back, I would in an instant."

She angles her head. "Which part?"

"All of it. Everything."

Her eyes pinch closed, and she gives me a sad, watery smile, one that immediately sends a pang of discomfort through my body. "So you changed your mind, then?"

"There was nothing to change my mind about." I'm pleading with her now, willing her to believe me despite my earlier cruelty. "All that shit I said was so far from how I really feel about you, about us. I swear."

"That's not what I mean." She blows out an impatient breath. "I mean, you changed your mind about talking to your coach. And what, now you feel bad that you broke up with me over it?"

"I did change my mind." I balance on my right crutch, running a ragged hand through my hair. "I realized you were right all along, but it's not just that. I never should've asked you for space when you were just trying to help."

"Okay."

My throat constricts. "Okay?"

"I get that you regret it, but I still don't think you under-stand the extent of how your words affected me. You wouldn't even let me tell you that I love you, Luca. You said that I fall in love like it's a *hobby*, like my feelings and emotions aren't just as fucking real as yours are?"

She steps back, gaze locked on mine, and I can feel the full magnitude of her sorrow. "And maybe I haven't gone through what you've gone through, but that doesn't mean I don't face real problems, too."

"I know that." I wince, a bone-deep ache settling in my chest. "I wasn't lying when I told you I think you're perfect. Everything else I said today was a lie. And I do, I do believe that you . . . love me." My voice drops to a tortured whisper. "Or that you did before I fucked everything up. I just wasn't ready to hear it at the time."

She frowns. "So what are you saying exactly?"

"I'm saying that I want you back." My next inhale burns right through me, scorching me from the inside out. "And that I'm sorry. And that I was wrong, about all of it. If I ever have the privilege of hearing you say those words to me again, I'd never fucking take them for granted."

I watch, heart bottoming out as a range of emotions flicker behind her eyes—anger, frustration, helplessness, finally settling on an overwhelming sense of disappointment.

"I don't know, Luca. You really, really hurt me." A single tear stains her flushed cheeks. "I thought I could trust you. I thought I could count on you, but you broke my heart."

"I know, baby. I know." I balance on my crutches, shoulders drooping. "I panicked, and I let you down. I understand if you can't find it in yourself to forgive me for that."

"Maybe you were right, anyway." Something soft and broken washes over her expression. "Maybe we're just too different."

"No, I wasn't right about anything." My heart squeezes. "And I love our differences."

"I thought I did, too. I think . . . I think I just need *more* time to think. Why don't you take care of yourself first, figure out your future, and then maybe we can revisit us?"

Raw, unfiltered emotion croaks out of me as I say, "And what if I want *you* to be my future?"

"Then I guess you shouldn't have spoken to me the way you did this morning. How about you take that space you asked for, and I'll do the same? At least for now."

While I'm proud of her for standing her ground—for not allowing anyone to mistreat her and get away with it—my stomach curls at the thought of spending the rest of my life without her.

"I'll give you your space." I swallow back the pain and regret. "I'll give you anything you ask for, but just know that's not what I really want. It never was."

"Okay, well, it's all I have to offer right now."

"I understand." I release a defeated sigh, yearning to reach out and touch her. Just one more time. "But Harper, I-I'll miss you. So fucking much."

"I'll miss you, too." She perches a hand on the doorframe, signaling for me to leave. "But you should really go."

I manage a nod, holding back the three words I so badly want to say to her. It's not the right fucking time. Of course it isn't, because I fucked it all away. But God, I wish she knew just how deeply I care for her.

Instead, I respect her wishes, hobbling away without so much as another word. At the sound of the door closing behind me, shutting me out once and for all, I have to physically restrain myself to keep from dropping to my knees.

By the time I make it back down to the car, I'm fairly certain Taylor's gone through LÉON's entire debut album. She gives me a hopeful look and a thumbs-up through the front window, but I shake my head, letting my shoulders drop. Once I'm awkwardly tucked back inside the passenger seat, she pats me on the arm.

"Sorry, buddy," she says. "I was really rooting for you and Happy."

I lean my head against the side window, puffing out a regretful sigh. "Me too."

She shifts the car into drive, glancing at me out of her peripherals, gaze filled with sympathy. "You still want me to take you over to the athletic training center?"

I scrub a hand across my forehead. "Yes, unfortunately. I have an appointment with Coach in a little less than an hour."

"And what are you gonna tell him?"

She slowly pulls out of the parking lot and onto the main road, headed toward campus. As I watch Harper's apartment building fade into the background, I pinch my eyes shut, drowning out all sense of desperate longing. If I want to have any hope of making it through the rest of this day, this week, this year, I can't be solely focused on what I've lost.

The only way to move forward is to move through.

"For once," I say, "I'm gonna tell him the fucking truth."

Chapter Thirty-Five

THE MOST CHALLENGING part about maintaining my boundaries is that I have no clue how Luca's doing right now. I think it's making me itch. I know that it's only been a little over a week since we've spoken, but it feels like we're already worlds apart, separated like the highs and lows of a king tide.

I'm so tempted to ask Eden how he's faring with the team. But I won't because I'm not so sure I can bear to hear about his suffering, no matter how angry and disappointed I might be with him.

I hate the idea of Luca feeling hurt and alone, physically or emotionally. That still doesn't mean I'm willing to forgive, forget, and move forward just yet.

His words sliced into me, pierced something deep inside my soul. Knowing he could lash out at me like that again—say things he says he doesn't mean—has scarred me. It's bred an insecurity that goes even deeper than the one my parents instilled.

A small part of me worries now that I'm too much for him . . . or for anyone, for that matter. That, inevitably, the people I love will start to believe that I'm a girl made of fluff, living in a dream world that doesn't exist.

But I suppose I can't live in fear of the unknown. Luca could hurt me again—of course he could, just as I could hurt him back.

It's a calculated risk, one I have to ensure is worth taking before I dive back in.

For now, I'm throwing my concentration into finishing up the fall term, acing my finals, and putting my best foot forward in this internship. There are only two more weeks left until winter break hits, and all things considered, I've had such an incredible experience with the baseball team so far.

The guys have been welcoming and responsive to all my ideas, plus I've learned so much from my supervisor, Minh, in such a short time. He's coming in as a close third to both Professor Gill and Jaqui Nerrie on my list of sports med idols.

I may have started this internship for the wrong reasons—chasing a boy I have no real interest in—but I can't bring myself to regret how everything panned out. Nate and I have rebuilt our bridges now, anyway. It's more of a casual acquaintance-ship, which I'm more than fine with, although he does still invite me to every baseball party at his house.

All of us are out on the field again today, one of the last outdoor preseason practices before the weather turns. After finishing up a round of footwork drills, Nate comes to rest on the bench beside me, kicking both his feet up.

"I heard your boy's out for the rest of the season," he says, casually tipping his chin in my direction.

"What?" I reel back, scrunching up my nose. "Where'd you hear that?"

"It's going around everywhere." He furrows his brow, brushing some dirt off the knee of his pants. "'Ötzi Reynolds got into a fight and tore his MCL.' Did you . . . not know about it? I figured you two were still together."

"His name's Luca," I say pointedly. "And no, I knew about the injury. I just . . . I didn't know what the end result was."

"Yeah, I mean, it makes sense." He shrugs, head dropping

back as he stretches out his pitching arm. "That kind of tear is pretty fucking nasty."

I sigh and shake my head, murmuring out a distracted "Mhm, yeah."

He searches my face. "So, if you didn't know . . . does this mean you two aren't together anymore?"

I manage to suppress an eye roll, my curiosity wilting. "Not currently, no."

He perks up. "So you're available, then? Would you—"

"No, sorry." I wince, attempting to let him down easy. Considering everything that's happened this term, I'm not sure why he would even try. "I'm not really available or, um, interested."

"Yeah, no worries."

He pats the bench, gives me a tight smile, and stands to leave. As he's walking away, I cover my face with my hands, aching to reach into my bag for my phone.

In the grand scheme of things, what harm could one little text do? I could quickly check in with Luca, ensure that he's not spiraling out of control, and then go back to taking my space.

I blow out a breath, working to distract myself from the thought—nibble on a cuticle, tap my fingers against the bench, scratch at my forearm. Fiddle around with the Surfbreak poker chip in my pocket. In the end, I choose not to even tempt myself, keeping my phone tucked safely away inside my bag.

It wouldn't be fair to either of us to break my rules now, not when I still need more time to think.

TWO MORE PAINFUL weeks of silence pass before I spot Luca at the pier. I've successfully avoided Amber Isle for the most part, on the off chance that he might still be working. But today happens to be a balmy Sunday, finals are over, Stella's working, and I'm a girl in need of the best burger on the beach.

From my spot at the counter, I can see that he's seated on a bench, rifling through a box of fishing equipment. His head is turned toward the ground, and he hasn't spotted me yet. By the time I finish up with my meal, I decide that I might as well approach him.

Standing a few paces away, I clear my throat and toss out a pitiful little "Hey, Luca."

His head darts up, eyes widening in surprise. He clears his throat, wipes his hands down the front of his jeans, and carefully pushes himself into a standing position.

With warmth flooding his cheeks, he says, "Hey, Harper."

I bite my lower lip, gaze trailing across his tall frame. Despite his obvious exhaustion—tilted posture, dark circles, pale complexion—he looks good. Just as ruggedly handsome as always.

"Can I join you for a minute?" I ask, gesturing to the slatted wooden bench behind him.

He carefully nods, reclaiming his seat as I move in next to him. It's quiet—peaceful for a moment—only the whooshing of the waves breaking the silence between us.

"So, how's that space treating you?" he finally asks, voice soft and low.

I shrug, murmuring, "Just peachy."

He slumps down. "Really?"

"No, no, I wish." I let out a self-deprecating laugh, a nervous smile playing along the edges of my lips. "Told you I'm a horrible liar."

His gaze softens. "So you have been missing me, then?"

"Of course I have." I shift to face him, studying his guarded expression. "Do you miss me?"

He smooths a hand over his face, shaking his head. "I miss every-fucking-thing about you."

I arch a brow. "Oh yeah, like what?"

"I miss your eyes, your lips, your hair, your smile. The sound of your voice when you're happy. The way you blush when I say something you weren't expecting. The smell of your skin after a day at the beach . . . Touching you for touching's sake. Kissing you just because I can." He takes a deep breath, swallows low in his throat. "God, there's no fucking question that I miss you, Harper."

"Oh." I'm fairly certain he just stole the air from my lungs. "I guess that's a pretty good answer."

He reaches for my hand, pinches his eyes shut, retreats without touching me. "Do you think you could find it in your heart to forgive me?"

"I forgive you." I slowly breathe in through my nose, out through my mouth—one long, deep exhale. "I-I'm just not a hundred percent sure where to go from here."

"Okay." He awkwardly scratches at the back of his neck, rigid in his seat. "Well, um, I think you should know that I've been seeing someone."

I work to keep my bottom lip from trembling, shock and confusion coursing through me. "What?"

His brows shoot up. "God, *fuck*, I mean . . . not like that. I mean I've been talking to a therapist. Coach set me up with someone, says I need to work on my mental fortitude just as much as I need to build myself back up physically."

He wrings his hands together, tension pouring out of him. "So I'm out of hands-on practice for the rest of the regular season, but now I've got PT twice a week, plus my meetings with a mental health counselor. I've only been going for a couple of weeks so far, obviously, but I think it's been really good for me."

A profound sense of pride courses through me, enveloping every negative thought and emotion I've had over the last three torturous weeks. If losing me is what it took to kick Luca's ass into gear, then I'm so fucking happy to know it was all worth it in the end.

"Wow, I'm really glad to hear that."

"And, uh, I talked to my parents about everything that's been going on. The injury, the money, my brother . . . They're getting him the help he needs. And they've also worked out a payment plan for Giorgie's gym. My therapist helped me realize that I've been taking on way too much this term." He reaches for me again. This time, we both let him pull my hand into his lap, tangling our fingers together. "I-I know you've told me that from the beginning. I really should've fucking listened to you."

I squeeze his hand. "I'm so happy for you, Luca."

"Thank you." He gives me a lopsided smile, one that warms me up like my favorite blanket. "You know, I wouldn't have ever gotten to this point without you pushing me."

"I hate to ask, but what about the draft?"

"Coach says I might still be able to play in a postseason all-star game. That is, if I keep healing the way I have been. Then I can do the Combine in February and go from there. I still have a pretty fair shot." He gives me a sheepish look. "I think, rationally, I should've realized that's how things might work out. I guess I'm not used to shit going my way, so I tend to catastrophize . . . as my therapist so kindly pointed out."

"It's fair. You've had it rough." I lean into him, pressing my cheek to his bicep. "I understand how scared you must have been. Believe me, I really do."

"Sorry, that was . . . a lot about me." He chokes out an awkward cough. "How have you been?"

"It's okay, you deserve to worry about yourself for once." I cross my legs, twist a strand of hair between my fingers. "But I've been okay. My internship ended on a great note. Finals were okay. I've actually been spending a lot of time with Eden since her breakup with Fletch. We've been having fun, but . . . I don't know, I feel like a piece of me has been missing since we ended things."

"So do I." His hand leaves mine, fingertips grazing against my cheek, caressing me. "Do you—would you maybe want to try again?"

I suck in a breath. "I do want to be with you, but . . ."

"I get it, it's okay." He pulls his hand back, squares his shoulders. "You don't have to say it."

"No, Luca. I've had my time to think, and I want us to get back together." I lean closer, pinning him with the most serious look I can muster. "But when things get rough, you can't speak to me like that or push me away ever again. From now on, we deal with all of our problems *together*. As a team."

"Together." He nods his agreement, a broad smile stretching across his face and sparking an ember in his eyes. "Always. I fucking promise."

Chapter Thirty-Six

LUCA

IN THE BEGINNING, I never could've imagined myself falling in love with Harper. I'd like to think it happened gradually, but the truth is I think I've been in love with her for a long while now. I just wasn't able to admit it to myself.

It's not a feeling that generally comes easy for me. *Love.* God knows I've been burned by it before. But loving Harper, the girl bathed in sunlight, feels as natural and effortless as breathing in my sleep.

I've learned and grown from my mistakes when it comes to her, to my family, to my health. They're mistakes I'm committed to never making again. Losing her—spending those three agonizing weeks apart—showed me how important it is to keep my head on straight.

When I'm overwhelmed now, I'm dedicated to finding a solution, one that doesn't involve me breaking my own back in the process. My new therapist is a godsend in helping me with that, among the many other issues I've been facing lately.

I'll admit it's been difficult coming to terms with ending my season early, but spending this last week with Harper has lightened my mood considerably. She's cheered me up in almost every way imaginable. And her forgiveness is something I won't take for granted.

This is our first weekend back together, and I've been racking my brain for a way to thank her. Something that's affordable but memorable. Something that might make her smile.

With a little help from Taylor, I think I've come up with a decent enough idea—it's simple, low-cost, and local. Plus, I have it on good authority that it's something she's been itching to do.

By the time she arrives at my house, I have her surprise all set up in the backyard. I greet her at the door with a soft kiss, take her hand, and guide her around to the back. It's nothing too fancy, but I've set up a few heat lamps, a fire pit, and a tent packed to the brim with thick bedding.

It's a few days before Christmas, a whopping twenty-eight degrees overnight, so it's too fucking cold for the real thing. Otherwise, I would've set this up near the beach for us.

"Luca." She tugs on my arm, practically bouncing on the balls of her feet. "You did this for me?"

"I know it's not technically real camping, but I promise to take you again in the spring," I say nervously, attempting to gauge her shocked expression. "And every year after that."

She snakes her arms around my waist, gazes up at me, lifts onto her tiptoes. Her lips press a sloppy kiss to my cheek. "And what if I have a better proposal?"

"What's that?"

"You can take me camping in the spring like you promised, but next year, *I* get to pick our trip." She taps her chin in thought, smiles wide. "I'm thinking a small town in southern Italy might be nice."

I pull her closer, leaning down to capture her lips in a bruising kiss. My heart stutters in my chest, there's an anxious sort of fluttering in my gut, and the tips of my ears are burning.

When I finally pull back, I drop my forehead to hers, whispering, "I hope you know much I love you."

Her eyes shine. "You do?"

"God yes. I'm so in love with you," I say, my voice thick with emotion. "Honestly, I think I've been a little bit in love with you ever since that first day at your apartment. You know, when you asked me to take my pants off."

She steps back and laughs, tiny lines spreading around her eyes. "Aw, I remember how shy you were back then."

"I wasn't *shy*. I was fucking intimidated."

"By me?" Her mouth hangs open. "I'm, like, the least scary person in the world."

"Well, you certainly scared me back then." A slow smirk tilts my grin. "Still do sometimes."

"Hey!" she whisper-shouts, slapping me on the shoulder.

"Kidding." I cup a hand around the back of her head, placing a kiss to her crown. "The only thing I'm scared of is losing you again."

"I don't want to lose you, either." She swallows, heavy and low, as she threads our fingers together. "You know, you never mentioned what happened that first weekend we were apart. I know you didn't play in the Rivals game, but did you ever end up meeting with Danny and Sofia?"

"No, definitely not." I shake my head, a rueful sigh slipping from my lips. "I thought about it, but in the end, the only person I wanted to spend time with was you. I think I'm gonna take a break from that friendship for a while, anyway. At least until I'm in a better place, both physically and mentally."

"That's probably a good idea." She rubs her thumb along the outside of mine. "You need something that fills your cup, not something that depletes it."

"Exactly right." I chuckle softly. "Have you been talking to my therapist?"

"No, but I probably could've told you that myself a long time ago."

"Very true." I squeeze her hand. "You're pretty good at being right."

"You know I love you, too, don't you?" Her voice is eager, passionate as she looks up at me, those blue-gray eyes sparkling with adoration. "So much."

"I know you do." I lift our clasped hands, sweeping a kiss across her knuckles. "And that makes me feel really fucking lucky."

"I feel the same way."

Following another quick kiss to the cheek, she drops my hand and steps a few paces away, carefully surveying our surroundings. Her gaze flits to the tent, then back to me, brows lifted in question.

"So, are you gonna show me what you have set up in there?"

"The tent?" I ask, tilting my head. "It's just sleeping bags and pillows. I have some stuff for s'mores in the house if that's what you're getting at."

"Mm, nope." She moves toward the tent, unzipping the entrance as she glances back at me over one shoulder. "I'd like to see where we're gonna sleep tonight . . . maybe test it out?"

"Test it out?" I scratch at my forehead, shooting her a quizzical look. With a playful waggle of her brows, she uses two fingers to beckon me forward. "Oh! Oh yeah, let's test it out."

Once we're securely tucked inside the tent, we make quick work of removing our clothing, desperate to reconnect physically. Harper runs her hands across my abs and up to my shoulders, carefully pushing me onto my back. She wastes no time climbing on top.

Before I can even form a rational thought, she rips open a

condom package and rolls it down over my hard length. I'm not even sure where the hell she got it from, but I suppose I'm glad my girl comes prepared.

"Impatient much?" I ask playfully, running my fingertips along the sweet curves of her waist.

She dips her head, capturing my lips in a heated kiss. Her body melts against mine, chests flush, tongue pushing into my mouth. A quiet moan slips free.

"Sorry, I've just really, really missed you," she says, reluctantly pulling away.

My hand curves around her neck, dragging her back against me. "God, I've missed you, too. So much."

She angles her hips, lifting up until we're perfectly aligned. One hand wraps around my erection, teasing the tip inside of her, slowly running it across her slick folds. She's so fucking wet and ready, so I tap her clit just once before finally sliding home.

As she clenches around me, grinding her hips low and slow, I let her take full control. Her fingernails dig into my chest while she rides me, seeking out her own pleasure on my cock.

"That's good, baby." I reach a hand between us, rubbing my thumb over her clit. "You're so fucking pretty like this."

She bounces faster at my praise, her tiny little whimpers taking on a mind of their own. At this point, I'm fully lost in my lust-filled daze. I'm fairly certain I almost die when her hands move to cup around her breasts. She kneads the soft flesh, rolling her nipples between her fingers, a low hum of a moan breaking free.

I know I've already said it before, maybe more than once, but this time with her is definitely my fucking favorite.

"Luca," she rasps, slowing her pace. "Can you fuck me now?"

I clasp both hands around her hips, driving into her from below, loving her harder with each passionate thrust.

"It's you and me," I murmur on a groan. "Always."

"Always," she echoes.

When we come together a few moments later—her clutching tightly to my shoulders—I swear to God a tear almost leaks out of my fucking eye. Sometimes, I still can't rationalize the fact that this girl is actually mine. And that I'm hers, for-fucking-ever.

I've spent a large part of my life believing that I'm not enough. For anyone or for anything. That all my hopes and dreams—supporting my family, playing professionally, finding real love and friendship—were far-fetched, relatively unachievable for a guy like me.

It wasn't until I met Harper that I started to believe differently. Although I've had to face some major setbacks over the past few months, I've also built a greater sense of confidence and security in myself. Truthfully, I never thought I could feel this fucking happy or complete.

Learning, loving, and then losing Harper has shown me exactly what I've been missing out on all this time. And there's not a shot in hell that I'm gonna let myself lose her twice.

It's the two of us from now on.

Together. Always.

THE END

Epilogue

HARPER

5 YEARS LATER

"Juney, come on, sweetie," I say as I attempt to wrangle my daughter out of her car seat. "We're gonna be late."

"Mama, nooo," she whines, putting up quite the fight. Her little legs kick against the back of the seat, lips turning down in an exaggerated pout. Normally, I'd be swayed by those sweet, puppy-dog eyes, but we don't have time to compromise today.

"What's wrong, baby?"

She grabs my face, pulling at my cheeks. "We go Nonna's house?"

"No, Juney." I check my phone screen, anxiously noting the time. "Your dada's playing today, remember?"

She blinks up at me. "But Geegee?"

"We'll go see Geegee another time, okay?" I laugh, tugging at a tiny curl of her dark brown hair. "Today, we have to watch Dada's game."

"Noo." Her eyes go wide, head frantically shaking back and forth.

"Yes, sweetie," I say softly. "Don't worry, we'll have fun. Uncle Elio's already inside waiting for us."

Her little frown melts into a smile, blue-gray eyes sparking with interest. She lifts her arms, finally allowing me to unbuckle her belt and pull her out of the car.

"Are you excited to see your uncle?"

"Uh-huh." She nods, slipping her hand into mine.

It's the first game of the regular season for Luca's team, the Carolina Bobcats, but we're the last people to park in the reserved section at the stadium. Of course, due to the chaos of toddlerhood, we're running late as usual.

"Okay, good." I carefully shut the door with my free hand, quickly double-checking that we have everything we need. "Today, we'll watch the football game, and then next week, we'll go to Nonna's house. Sound good?"

She gazes up at me, her smile stretching a mile wide. "Okay, Mama."

By the time we make it into the stadium, the family box is already packed to the brim. I stop along the way to chat with a few girls—some spouses and partners I've befriended over the last four seasons—before we spot Elio seated near the front. His legs are kicked out, a baseball cap pulled down over his eyes.

Elio's not interested in big crowds these days, but he's still been making an effort to come to the games. At least, ever since he reconciled with Luca, that is. Unfortunately, it took him a while to get clean and sober after that fateful night back in high school. Almost an entire year went by before he even so much as spoke to his brother again.

Eventually, their parents were able to help him get into rehab, earn his high school diploma, and accept a spot in Coastal U's electrical engineering program. After all, it only makes sense that he'd follow in his eldest sister's footsteps.

"Hey, El." I clap a heavy hand on his shoulder, smiling as he jolts out of his seat.

"Hey, you two." He wraps me into a quick hug before squatting down to June's level. "How's my little Junebug?"

"Hewo, Ewo." June giggles at her own rhyme, stretching her arms up and out toward her uncle.

Elio grins wide, lifting her without question and perching her onto the side of his body. He wraps one arm underneath her legs to hold her up, lifting a brow in my direction.

"We're great," I murmur, ruffling my daughter's hair. "Somebody was really excited to see you today."

"Is that right?" He taps his niece on the end of her nose. "Was it you, Juney?"

"Mhmm."

"I'm excited to see you, too. You're growing so much!"

She beams up at him. "Mama said I a big girl."

"You *are* a big girl. You still want to sit up on my shoulders, though, right?"

"Yes, p-ease!"

"You got it." He flips June so she's facing forward, swinging her body up and over his shoulders. His hands wrap around the front of her ankles to secure her into place.

"So, how's school going so far?" I ask, reaching into my bag for a snack pouch and passing it up to June. I'm sure she's a little peckish by now. Besides, it serves as a good distraction while we wait for the game to start.

"Fine, as usual," he mutters. "But *God*, I'm so ready to graduate already."

"I know the feeling."

"How's the team treating you?"

"Pretty good," I say earnestly. Once I earned my Master's in Applied Neuromechanics and Sports Medicine, I secured a position working with my alma mater's hockey team. This is officially my second year as their athletic trainer, and it's been a blast so far. "Our regular season doesn't start until October, so it's a pretty tame schedule for me right now."

"That's good." He taps June's ankles, earning himself another quiet giggle. "You know, I've actually got one of your guys in my calculus class." His voice drops to a whisper, protecting the innocent ears above him. "He's a total dick, though."

"Sounds about right. Who is it?"

"Holden Becker."

My brows shoot up. "Does he know you're my brother-in-law?"

"Doubt it." He scoffs, lips downturned with frustration. "The only time he looks in my direction is to roll his eyes."

A pang of disappointment shoots through me. "Hmm, I guess I'll have to whip him into shape in the weight room."

"Could you?" One corner of his mouth ticks up. "Torture him a little for me?"

"I can make it happen."

He laughs, nudging me with his elbow. "I knew there was a reason I always liked you."

"Sure you did." I shake my head, lips pursing into a playful smirk. "Speaking of, I promised Juney we'd go to your parents' house next week. Do you want to join us?"

"Is Luc coming?"

"I'm sure he'll come along." I wrinkle my nose. "Well, unless he has a last-minute conflict with the team or something."

"I'll be there, then." He gives me a sympathetic smile. "I know once the season picks up, he'll barely have enough time for you and June, let alone anyone else."

"I know, it's always tough. Can you believe this will be his fifth season with the Bobcats already?"

"Not at all." He shakes his head in disbelief. "I also can't believe June's gonna be two years old in a few months."

"I know, it's honestly so sad. I thought she'd be my baby forever, but now she just wants me to call her *big girl*," I pout, reaching for my daughter's tiny hand. "Isn't that right, Junebug?"

"I a big girl, Mama."

"I know, sweetie." I tap my fingers against her palm, glancing up to give her a watery smile. "I know."

It's been a little over an hour since the game ended—the Bobcats winning by a landslide—and June's practically passed out on Elio's shoulders. We had a nice afternoon of snacking, napping, and cheering along with the rest of the crowd. Now, the three of us are waiting patiently as the players file into the family box.

Towering over the group, June is able to spot Luca before anyone else. "Dada! Dada!" she shouts, kicking and flailing her legs against Elio's chest.

He crouches down, lifting her up and over his shoulders. As soon as her feet hit the ground, she runs full force in Luca's direction. I watch, captivated by the sight of my handsome husband as he picks her up and twirls her around, popping a big, sloppy kiss onto her forehead.

"Hi, baby girl. I missed you." Luca's grin widens as I approach. "And I missed your mama, too."

"You played so great today," I say, wrapping my fingers halfway around his upper arm.

"I did, didn't I?" He leans down, pressing a chaste kiss to my lips. "Did you see that last tackle at the six-yard line?"

"Of course I did." I squeeze his bicep. "Amazing, as always."

"Thanks, baby." Luca acknowledges his brother with a nod,

smiling faintly in his direction. "Hey, E. Thanks for coming to watch the game."

"Sure, man, of course." Elio taps his wrist, flashing us an apologetic smile. "I actually have to head out, though. I've got loads of studying to do for my calc pre-exam, but I'll see you at Mom and Dad's next week, right?"

Luca turns toward me, lifting a questioning brow. "Is that right?"

"Yeah, I promised Juney earlier. She wants to go see your mom and Giorgie."

"Of course she does." Luca shakes his brother's hand. "Guess I'll see you then, bro. Good luck with your test."

"Thanks."

We all take turns waving Elio off. Once we're finished, he tips his chin and adjusts the bill of his hat, pulling it lower over his face before heading out of the box.

"So, what do my gorgeous girls want to do when we get home tonight?" Luca asks, pressing a series of kisses all over June's cheeks. She giggles, twisting around in his arms, her little legs tucked up against his side.

"Park, park, park," she happily chants.

"You want to go to the park, Junebug?" He taps his chin in thought. "You know, it's pretty late for that tonight, but maybe we can go in the morning. We'll call Taylor and see if she wants to bring Bentley along."

"Puppy!" June shouts, her sweet laughter echoing around the box.

"Are you sure, Luca?" I ask, brows dipping with concern. "You don't want to sleep in tomorrow?"

"Nah, I'm about to crash hard tonight, so I'll be good to go bright and early." He grabs my hand, bringing it up to press a kiss against my palm—right at the base of my thumb—in our lucky spot. "Plus, I want to spend as much time with my girls as possible."

I kiss him back in the same place, pressing the pad of my thumb against the cursive *H* and the loopy, little heart I drew on this morning. Per Luca's adamant request, it's become part of our pregame tradition.

"Sounds perfect to me."

"You know, I don't think I'll ever get over seeing you both up here, wearing my jersey and cheering me on."

"It *is* pretty great, isn't it?"

He dips his chin, resting it against our daughter's head. "Definitely one of my favorite things."

"Ours, too, even though I had to bribe Juney to come into the stadium today."

"Oh, I don't blame her." He swipes some hair out of June's eyes. "I'd get bored watching me play, too."

"Well, I hope you know *I* never get bored of you."

"Of course you don't." He steps forward, looping one arm around my shoulders and nearly crushing June between us. "You love me too much."

"I do love you," I say. "So, so much."

"Just as I love *you*—both of you—always."

Acknowledgments

My baby girl, for being my light at the end of a dark tunnel.

My husband, for supporting me endlessly.

My editor, Sandra, for helping me turn this book into something I can be proud of.

And most importantly, my All Stars (Becka, Erin, and Hannah) for inspiring me to take the leap, for listening to me ramble, and for always allowing me to be unapologetically myself.

About the Author

Ki Stephens is a romance enthusiast who finds comfort in the happily-ever-after . . . with just a little bit of angst along the way. She has a special interest in works that include neurodivergent characters like herself. When she's not daydreaming about books, Ki enjoys working with kids, creating art in her backyard studio, and spending loads of time with her baby girl, her husband, and their three pets.

www.kistephens.com